WINN'S FALL

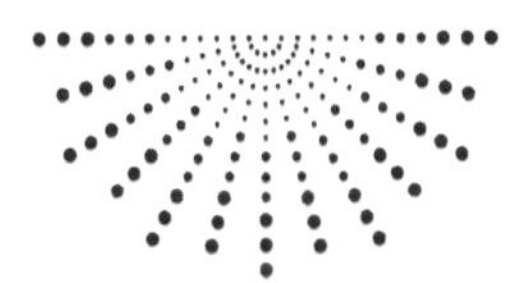

CLAIR BRETT

This is a work of fiction. Names, characters, places and incidents are products of the author's imagination or are used fictitiously and are not to be construed as real. Any resemblance to actual events, locales, organizations or persons, living or dead, is entirely coincidental.

CB publications

86 Riverside Ave.

Lisbon, NH 03585

Cover design: Victoria Miller

Author photo: BLC Photography

Copyright © 2020 Clair Brett

ISBN:

Ebook: 978-0-9983317-7-5

Mobi: 978-1-7352906-1-4

Paperback: 978-1-7352906-2-1

www.clairbrett.com

All rights reserved. No part of this book may be used or reproduced in any manner

whatsoever without written permission, except in the case of brief quotations

embodied in critical articles and reviews. For other permissions contact the author.

❀ Created with Vellum

DEDICATION

In the process of writing this book I lost my adoptive mother and my biological mother. They went two months apart. There have been many times since that I stop and think, boy would I like to talk to one of them. They were amazing women, who at my most vulnerable had my best interest in mind. As I edited, I had not realized how much Zoe missed sharing her experience with her mother, and the times when she noticed "motherly" behavior from others. I have been lucky to have some fabulous women in my life who have stepped next to me when I would have felt very alone in this world. Thank you, no words can express my gratitude.

CHAPTER ONE

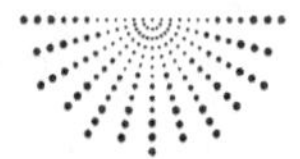

"Father, I do not wish to go. I am perfectly fine staying with you," Zoe Chase protested. Didn't her father understand she had been through enough and being shipped off back to England alone was only making it worse?

"It is not negotiable," her father said, not giving her any heed as he dove into his eggs and sausage.

"You always say everything is negotiable," she pertly reminded him. She sat with her arms crossed, her eggs, toast, and jam forgotten. Her father chuckled and gave her a sideways glance.

"Yes, I suppose I do - but in government, not the raising of daughters." He sat back in his chair and scrutinized her. She never liked him looking at her so, because he saw things no one else did. He was the only one who could read her mind. It had only been her and her parents traveling for her father's diplomatic post for the crown. Now, she would be alone. "This is not a punishment, Zoe. Zoe, look at me," he bade. She had pushed her eggs around her plate, making a mountain scene with them.

"I know Papa, it is just that-- well, we only just left mourning from Mama's death, and I have never traveled alone. I wish to stay with you for a while longer." She tried to explain without giving away her real fear.

"You will have no trouble finding an interested man to be your husband, my dear," her father comforted. It frustrated her how he could so easily get to the point of the matter when it came to her. "What I am concerned with is whether you will make a choice. You drag your feet, making decisions." He continued buttering a large piece of bread and adding a slice of ham on top.

"Whatever does that mean?" Zoe asked with mock annoyance.

"I mean, sweetling, if you choose a husband the way you choose a bonnet, you will be in your dotage before you let the poor saps know your choice."

"Papa, kidding aside. I don't even know what criteria I should judge them by. I have no experience. If mother were here--" Her voice caught in her throat, and she took a sip of cider, breathing deep to keep the tears at bay. After a year of mourning, she thought she would be over this. At first, she was sure she would never stop crying. Her mother's death such a shock to everyone, but over time she could smile and eventually didn't feel so melancholy every day. Now, however, it was the first realization that her mother would miss out on all of her life's events from this moment forward. She had passed just when Zoe would need her most. Her father leaned over and put his hand over hers, squeezing comfortingly. He, too, had tears in his eyes.

"This is the most difficult thing you and I have ever done, but the truth is your mother wanted you to be part of the upcoming season in London, and I agreed with her. We mourned her, but as wonderful as she was, we have lives to still live. Find a husband, give me grandbabies, have grand-babies of your own, know love, know hurt, all of those things not yet done. Your mother would be in a terrible rage at me if I let you stop the flow of life." His eyes held so much emotion, sadness, fondness, and love. Theirs had been a love match, she was sure of it, though neither of her parents ever spoke of their courtship. Zoe would settle for nothing less for herself, but she dearly wished her mother were here to guide her in finding such a thing.

"Papa, I do not know what to consider. How do I know when I meet him?"

"Well, my dear, with your connections, and your dowry, you will have an endless supply of suitors, I would imagine. Your Aunt Dorothy will know about their families and such, but it is the one who touches you here." He put his finger over her heart. "That is the man for you," he said with a smile.

"Was that how it was with you and mother?"

"Your mother would agree that fate also plays a role in the game of matrimony, and it isn't my story to tell, it was your mother's."

"Father, that hardly gives me any guidance in what I am to look for." She felt as exasperated as ever.

"I think you need to think about the important things in

life and find that one person who you feel will be there for you and make life not so hard. That is what I think."

"I still don't want to go." She brought them back to the original argument.

"I know," he said with warmth, but without offering another option.

"So, the ship leaves on Saturday?"

"Yes."

She sighed but argued no more. She began planning in her head how to possibly pack all of her belongings in such a short amount of time.

"I believe the donkey wasn't given enough credit. Which one really, was the ass?" Cyn asked as she sat on the chair, embroidery in hand. "And what in God's name is that smell?" she complained.

"Cynthia." Her mother spoke sharply as she fussed over Winn, who was laid out on the couch with a large piece of meat over his left eye. "It could have killed him," she snapped. At this, Winn let out a bark of laughter, and Cyn hmphed.

"Well, it would put an end to all this nonsense. I mean, isn't that what Winn is trying to do? Just kill himself on his terms?" She asked loud enough to scare the bark off a tree.

"Must you yell so like a crone, dear sister?" Winn asked, hoping to stop both women in his life from making any sound. The vibrations ripped through his head like a cannonball.

"Well, personally, death by donkey would not be what I would hope to have printed in the rags about me, but to each his own." Winn didn't have to look at her to know she added a nonchalant shrug to punctuate her point.

"You're right, I would rather have it printed that I died in the arms of a beautiful woman, with an empty plate of venison on the table and an empty bottle of cognac by my side." He responded before he remembered his mother was in the room. It brought him back to that fact when the only one on his side swatted him in the chest.

"I am thinking if you are considering the merits of loose women and drinking, you will live yet another day, and need no more fussing," his mother pointed out. Winn felt her skirts brush his arm as she moved back to her seat.

"My apologies, Mother."

"Humph," was her answer.

"It was something to see," his friend, Reid Garrick, the current Earl of Hayhurst, spoke up. "That is, until he was kicked."

"I am sure it was quite a lark, however dangerous," replied Winn's mother. The butler entered, carrying a glass of water with a small vial of powder. Winn knew it was the butler with no need to open his eyes because the man couldn't walk quietly if being hunted, not to mention a decided hitch in his stride from an injury caused as a young man.

"Peter, I know what you are offering, and I am having none of it. I do not wish to spend however many days of my life remaining in a laudanum haze. Pain means life, and I will aptly embrace it while I still can." He knew the butler wouldn't give up until his mother gave him the sign to leave, and after only thirty ticks of the clock, he heard Peter turn and walk back down the hall.

"Well, I can see that you are in the best of care, old chap. I must be off. Dinner at Lord Hudson's this evening. I'll call tomorrow. See if you are up for a ride." Reid stepped up and slapped him on the arm, which had been resting over his good eye and forehead. The jolt of the movement sent a wave of nausea through his body. All Winn could manage after that was a grunt. After the footfalls, and the door shutting, his head and stomach agreed to stop reeling. Winn wasn't sure where he had gone wrong. It all seemed so simple, but apparently, the donkey's approval had not been taken into account.

"Why is it, brother, that you have to daily put your life and our nerves in danger?"

"You know very well why," he grumbled.

"No, I do not," Cyn answered angrily. "There is no reason to put your life in danger every day just because you think you will die soon, anyway."

"But don't you see the beautiful irony?" he asked. "If I am doing things to enjoy the life I have, and I die in the process, who loses? I was enjoying life, and death claims its next victim of the family curse. I refuse to let it keep me in fear."

"So instead you tempt it, like a snake charmer?" Cyn asked, concern in her voice. "If you keep this up, you will kill yourself before the curse does it for you."

"All the better, don't you agree?" he asked with sarcasm.

"That is enough. Both of you stop talking about such things. We should not provoke that which we do not understand," their mother interjected. "And besides, we have much more pressing matters to attend to."

"What?" Winn asked, not having been home the past week to know what was going on.

"I received a letter from Zoe, two days hence. She is

coming home!" Cyn said, the happiness evident in her voice. "Her year of mourning is over, and her father wishes her to choose a husband during the season."

"Zoe?" That name was familiar. Winn tried to think back to who Zoe was, but the throbbing wouldn't allow it.

"My friend? Zoe Chase? You can't possibly have forgotten her. We were the best of friends that summer her mother visited us," Cyn reminded him.

"Zoe? Oh, was that the gangly mud-haired girl? She was all arms and legs if it is the one I'm thinking of. Just limbs with a mop of freakishly dull curls bobbing up and down. All right, I remember her now," he said, and was immediately punished for his meanness by a well-thrown pillow to the head. "Argh, if I vomit on mother's good rug, you will get the devil," he reprimanded his sister.

"For such a callous comment, I would hit you with an anvil if I had one. Zoe is still my dearest friend, and you will be kind. She will need as much support as possible to find a husband. Since being absent from the Ton for so long, she will not have it easy," Cyn snapped.

"I also received a missive this morning from Lady Lambert, Miss Chase's aunt, asking for our support. I was thinking of having a house party before the season gets started. We would need to come up with a list of potential suitors and some other young ladies, perhaps older who have a season already tied up to equal the numbers."

"Oh, mother, that would be a wondrous idea! Zoe and I could look at the field and narrow it down to only those in real contention. We wouldn't waste time at the beginning of the season weeding out those out of contention," Cyn said enthusiastically.

"Remind me to bring you, dear sister, the next time I go to a horse auction. You seem to have this good flesh, bad flesh thing tied up," Winn said dryly, not wanting a gaggle of unmarried women filling his country home. "And while you are at it, why don't you decide on one of the leftovers for yourself. After all, you're still in need of a husband, in case you had forgotten."

"That is enough, Winthrop."

"Winn, Mother," he corrected.

"Regardless, you need not be in such a dark mood. It is not your sister's fault that you cannot ride a donkey, and it kicked you in the head. Zoe was like another daughter to me. We will help her. And yes, we mean you, too," she pointed out.

Winn groaned. He needed to savor getting kicked by a donkey, because it would likely be the best feeling he would have in the foreseeable future. Why couldn't the damned curse just come and take him now? What good is a curse if unable to use it to your advantage? He tried to no avail to ignore the chatter of his mother and sister. The next time he had to be carried into the house -- and there *would* be a next time-- he would instruct them to bring him to his study and not any room where there was a female in residence.

"Mother, we simply must have a ball for Zoe. She will need a proper coming out," Cyn schemed.

"Oh, that is fabulous!" her mother exclaimed loudly, obviously forgetting the man with the head injury. "Winthrop, Winthrop! Would you suggest having the ball at the beginning of the house party, or the end? Winthrop!" his mother prodded, apparently not forgetting him at all. Winn had had all he could take of noise for the time being, and decided he

could feel his way to his rooms on his hands and knees if need be.

"Mother, I don't particularly care about a ball at any time. I can see that you and Cyn have gads of planning. Please just inform me of when I am to prance around like your trained peacock, and I shall be there." He rose slowly, as gravity seemed to slip and undulate around him. He kissed his mother on the head and sent a half-hearted wave to his sister before groping his way to the door.

"All right, dear. I'll check on you later." He heard his mother call behind him. Again, it would be splendid if the bloody curse could be more accommodating.

CHAPTER TWO

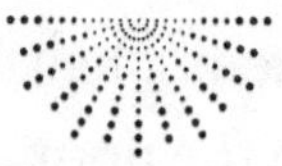

Books, Zoe decided, would be the only place pirates and ships would remain romantic. It had been two days on land, and she still felt woozy when she walked. Her aunt, who had met her at the docks with hugs and tears, brought her to the Lion's Gate Inn for a proper meal, a much-appreciated bath, and good night's sleep. The second day found her at the modiste's being measured for a whole new wardrobe, compliments of her Aunt Dorothy.

"There is entirely too much black in your wardrobe, my dear," Aunt Dorothy said after emptying every bandbox and chest she had brought home with her. Zoe didn't disagree, but being in mourning and being a diplomat's daughter required her to step up and take a more public role. She had been forced to dye most of her clothes for the occasion. "I dare say the few pieces you have are ghastly pastel. With your pale skin, I would think you to look the deceased and not the mourner," she said in disgust. "Well, there's nothing to be done but to order you a whole new wardrobe. Luckily, you are a few years from the blush of youth, so no one will think it untoward if we choose more dramatic colors to match your complexion. I should think that will also help you stand out from the young debs in the assemblies dressed as slips of rose petals."

"Aunt Dorothy, I appreciate the offer, but I do not need a whole new wardrobe. Many of these gowns were almost new when mother passed. They are still in excellent shape." Zoe didn't enjoy being a burden to anyone, even family.

"Nonsense. You will keep those for mourning. No doubt, you will go into mourning again at some point, and now you will have a full wardrobe for such an occasion. It makes perfect sense," she said with a pat of the hand. "I want to do this. Your mother was my beloved sister and would have done the same for my daughter, had she been in the position to do so. You are so like her, you know," her aunt said, with tears in her eyes and nostalgia thick in her voice.

"Thank you, I take that as a great compliment. She was an amazing woman," Zoe said, trying to busy herself by repacking the multitudes of dressing littering the chamber.

"Now, on to happier thoughts," said Aunt Dorothy, clearing her throat and sniffling a bit. "What is your favorite color? We will make sure your come-out dress is at the very least adorned with it. It gives a girl confidence when she is surrounded by things she loves," she said, helping Zoe with the cleanup.

"My favorite color is green, but not that seafoam green they are always making me buy," Zoe said, happy to admit her distaste for the subtle colors that washed her out her entire life. "I love emerald green, as deep as the Atlantic Ocean."

"Well, my dear," answered her Aunt, "nothing like churning the pot a bit. I am just glad you didn't say puce." Both women laughed.

The modiste's appointment went as planned, and her aunt arranged for the lot to be delivered to Sussex post haste. Upon learning of Zoe's arrival, her mother's dearest friend, and her daughter, who was Zoe's most beloved friend, offered to help Aunt Dorothy in sponsoring her season. There was to be an early house party which would culminate into the whole party departing for the season to London.

Zoe was not looking forward to riding for the entire day in a carriage. A Sennight in the most comfortable bed in her room at the inn was preferable, but the prospect of seeing Cynthia again made the likelihood of the long ride more appealing. Settling in and taking out the letter her aunt gave her from Cynthia on her arrival, she finally had enough energy to read her friend's plans for her come out. She read as London slipped by. Her aunt sat quietly for as long as Zoe thought she could stand it.

"So, what has Lady Cynthia to say about the upcoming events?" she asked Zoe with interest.

"Well, she is very excited to see me. She said there are two weeks before the house party."

"Good, good, that will give us time to make sure you are prepared. They say this round of debs is a fine group, so we will need to outshine them from the start." Aunt Dorothy spoke as a general would speak about his first showing in a battle. "Of course, you will be fine, my dear. Just fine, but no one ever failed from being too prepared."

"She said she and her mother are working on a list of potential suitors and will go over them more, including my criteria, when we get settled."

"Oh, splendid. Cynthia has had two seasons already. I fear she may put herself on the shelf if she doesn't act soon, but she and her mother will better know the eligible males than I would. My dear Anabelle has been happily married for three years now. She is with child, so will not be attending. Perhaps when we move to London, we will call on her."

"Oh, wonderful. I was hoping to see Anabella. We exchange correspondence from time to time. Who else will be at the house party? Not that I would know anyone there."

"Well, Lady Burton most likely will invite a few of the debs you will mix with in London. It would be a splendid idea to help ease your way and help you make some friends. She would pick only those who would also see it as an opportunity to make acquaintances and not just a chance to hunt for a husband."

"Good, I was not clear how that would work. I am sure the competition can be fierce."

"Well, it is, if you are desperate, but those who rise to the top understand good manners must still avail," her aunt commented with annoyance. "The season brings many into the circuit that do not belong. And many with, mostly to no fault of their own, bad upbringing. Why, when my Anabelle was in the throes of her season, two other girls had a brawl in the middle of a dinner party. A *brawl*," she punctuated.

"Whatever for?" asked Zoe, getting more nervous by the moment. All she needed was a husband. One, not all of them. The last thing she wanted was to do something that would shame her mother's memory.

"Whether a gentleman was on whose dance card first. Can you imagine?" Aunt Dorothy spat. "In the end, the gentleman in question had left an hour before. Served them both well, I say." She punctuated her comment with a nod that made her mop of curls bounce.

All Zoe wanted to do was get through this, making no major faux pas. She would not win any awards for being graceful, or for that matter, well-timed. She was lucky that her diplomat father had a good portion of humor in his system because she would try anyone else's nerves. Her best hope would be to find a gentleman at the house party and then not have to worry about all the nonsense of the London route.

The ship travel allowed her plenty of time to consider her criteria for a husband, so it would be easy to procure a list for Cyn upon arrival. She had spent most of her time in her cabin, as the other men made her uncomfortable. Father had hired a guard and sent along her maid as a companion and chaperone, but she was still more comfortable alone.

"I hope this is not so very tiring. I have a general list of criteria, and with Cyn's help, I am sure we can be done with this business post-haste," she confided in her Aunt.

"Yes, I am sure you would like to think that, my dear." Her Aunt replied with a good bit of condensation. "You may trust your criteria, but often fate decides that the one most suitable does not match your list at all. We will see the available lot and work from there."

Her father had mentioned she had difficulty picking a hat, and he was right. She couldn't imagine what it would be like to walk into a shop and choose a live, walking, talking *husband.*

How does one do that? A hat you only make use of for a season, perhaps two, but a husband must be kept around much longer. Zoe sighed and laid her head back on the squabs. Might as well catch a nap before their arrival. She was losing hope that the next few weeks would be restful. While she made to sleep, she considered her list once again to have it clear in her mind.

1. Must have a kind heart
2. Must be responsible
3. Must be practical in all things
4. Must have gainful employment (if a second son)
5. Must have adequate connections
6. Must be willing to slay dragons
7. Must have a sense of humor
8. Must have passable good looks (all teeth would be a plus)
9. Must be good with children
10. Must like to read and the arts
11. Must Love me (Note to self, do not share this in the original list)

She drifted off to sleep, trying to imagine the man who had all these qualities. If there was one.

"Are you sure you are healed?" Reid asked, with doubt in his voice.

"You doubt me?" Winn laughed as he circled the contraption the men had spent many days planning and building.

"Yes." His friend answered soundly.

"I am as fine today as I was a week ago," assured Winn. "What are your concerns, this time?" he asked.

"If you must ask, I am not certain you are capable of understanding. This is madness."

"You thought this a great idea two months past," Winn pointed out, tugging on the ropes to double-check the knots.

"Yes, then I sobered up."

"Oh, posh. You, Lord Hayhurst, seem to be losing your nerve," Winn said, slapping his friend on the back as he passed to double-check the balloon. "I've been meaning to discuss that with you. Perhaps it is age."

"Really? I rather think it is watching my closest friend attempt to kill themselves every waking moment. It does something to a man," he implored Winn.

"Nonsense. I refuse to take the credit for your propensity to come down with the vapors. You know you are as excited as I to see this thing fly. Admit you are not," Winn challenged. His friend stood stoic with his arms crossed, staring down Winn.

"Fine," he finally gave in with a cocky smile. "I will admit if it goes, I will be impressed. But that doesn't mean I think you should be in it."

"Fair enough, good chap. Duly noted. Yes to the ascension, no to the cursed man as captain," Winn checked the barrel straps like he was checking off a list.

Reid leaned back against the pole in the hay barn and relaxed his stance. "Were all the Earls of Burton this lackadaisical about their lives? Because if they were, I think there is no curse, just a lineage of fool-hardy men who had no respect for their own lives," he said darkly, as Winn continued his safety check of the homemade hot air balloon.

They had chosen the hay barn because they could suspend the balloon by the hay hook in the front until the fire had created enough hot air to fill it. Then Reid would cut the string, and Winn would be on his way. A solid plan. The only small hole was how Winn would get down. Oh, he knew he would get down eventually, but there were two questions: one, how high would he get; and two, which depended on the answer to number one, how fast would he fall when the fire went out? Winn chose not to dwell on such negative details. The sound of his friend clearing his throat brought Winn back to the point.

"No, in fact, my grandfather was the most docile man. He didn't even care to hunt. So when a stray arrow shot him while sitting in his garden, they thought it the great irony of the family. My great-grandfather had quite the zeal for life I am told, but in the end, he died from a fall down the front stairs. Tripped on a piece of loose carpet. I do not intend to die by carpet, or worse yet, some fool's stray arrow. No, those stories stick with a dead man, and I will not be here to dispute them. So you see, I am adamant about my demise. I want a better story than the others," Winn quipped to his friend, who knew his facade but didn't call him out on his foolishness.

"Well then, death by poorly made balloon ascension it is. Let us get underway, shall we?" Pushing off the pole and helping to grab the squid-like apparatus, they made their way out the doors to the launch area. Winn had hoped to get underway earlier in the day, but his mother had insisted that he join her and Cyn for a late breakfast to discuss the impending visit and ensuing maylay they referred to as a house party and come out. He managed, but only just, to sit through the meal and conversation. They peppered him with questions about the gentlemen on the list and their merits as potential husbands. How the bloody hell would he know anything about how a man will behave as a husband? He did point out some serious character flaws in a few on the list that would mark them as a bad seed to begin with. No need to add a wife to get the impact there. Hayhurst yelled from out on the hay hook beam that he was ready for the rope to be tossed up.

"As soon as I get this tied off, I'll be down. Don't start the fire until I am down there to help," he demanded. Winn waved him off and began to look at the makeshift basket with more reasonable eyes. If he needed to jump free, he would have difficulty getting his legs out, because of the depth and narrowness of the barrel. He decided he would need to try it out before take-off. By the time Reid made it back down to the ground, Winn was attempting to jump out of the barrel.

"That's reassuring. The operator of the craft is practicing a crash landing," he commented dryly.

"No one ever died from being over-prepared."

"Oh, is that what you are?" he joked.

"Just light this bloody thing," Winn countered, jumping into the basket and remaining. As the small fire came to life, both men watched the balloon fill and become like the schematic they had created.

"Ready?"

"Ready. Cut the rope," Winn said with a wave, as the

basket slowly rose off the ground. He tugged the balloon away from the barn and toward the open field. "Meet me over in the east pasture. I think that is where I'll end up!" he yelled with excitement to his friend, getting smaller and smaller on the ground. Winn turned to see the countryside open up to him, and he wished he could freeze this image to share it with Cyn and his mother. If they could see this, they might understand better. Live an entire lifetime in but a moment, he thought.

"How much farther?" asked Zoe as she tried to stretch her leg but couldn't get it straight enough to work out the cramp. She decided she was not as good a traveler as she had once thought. A new item to add to her list of criteria - a man who keeps his feet on home soil.

"Not so far now, dear," Aunt Dorothy assured her, taking a chance to pull back the curtain and take in the scenery. "I say, what is that?" she asked, pointing out the window across the field. Just as the words left her mouth, the driver pulled the carriage to a halt in the road. Zoe leaned out her window to see about the commotion. On the horizon, bobbing slowly across the open field, was a small balloon with a basket attached. Well, no, it wasn't a basket, it was a barrel. Zoe had attended balloon ascensions in Europe with her parents, but those were much more majestic.

Seeing this as an opportunity to get some air and walk her cramp out, she banged on the top of the carriage for the driver. He dismounted and opened the door, helping her out. Her aunt remained inside. The air was cool on her face, not stuffy like the inside of the carriage or putrid and coal filled like London. Zoe watched as the small vessel bobbed along, like a boat in the ocean. Some boys must be proud of themselves, she thought. As the craft drew closer, she could just make out a male form in the bucket. Perhaps, it was not children, but young men from a nearby academy, because the figure was not a child.

So captivated she was, watching it approach that she didn't pay any heed to the carriage driver leading the horses down the road, or the fact that the obvious man was motioning for her to move until it was too late. He would run her over, was her last thought. At the last moment, the man in question jumped from the barrel, kicking it as he did so and sending it flying to Zoe's left, just missing her. The man was not so lucky. He landed on his feet, but the momentum of his flight propelled him forward. He managed to get an arm around her, twisting so that when they hit the ground, he was on the bottom. She splayed across his body, with only the wind knocked out of her.

His body was hot and dampened with sweat, but it cushioned her like a plush pillow. Lifting her head, she was staring into eyes that used to belong to a much younger boy. Laughing eyes that sparkled when he smiled. Winthrop, the Earl of Burton. Then she realized he was not just smiling, he was laughing. She began to struggle to get out of such an inappropriate position in the middle of the main road. She could hear her aunt fussing and heading her way.

"My Lord, you need to let me up," she demanded. When she attempted to move, he held her fast with his arm. "My Lord, please," she continued.

"You know, I was wondering how hard the landing would

be, but I think given the possibilities, this was the best outcome. Don't you agree?" he asked, shaking his head, still smiling from ear to ear.

"I think, Lord Burton, that you will let me go before I box your ears for being so impertinent. If I do not get the chance, my aunt will undoubtedly make sure she does so," she spat. He still didn't move. Her manners dictated she remain formal, but she needed to bring him back to the situation. "Unless you will propose marriage here, I suggest you let me up before we have company."

At the realization of the fact that he was holding a lady and it was most inappropriate, he cleared his throat. His eyes dulled, no longer sparkling. "Of course, how rude of me. I am so sorry. I guess I just let the moment take my senses." He apologized, allowing her to roll off him. Winn bounded up, plucking her from the ground and setting her on her feet as if she weighed no more than a feather. Her face burned as her aunt, the driver, and an unknown gentleman on horseback came to meet them at once.

"My dear, my dear, are you injured?" Aunt Dorothy asked, touching her face, arms, and head as she looked for injuries.

"I'm fine. Had I gotten out of the way in time, we would not have collided. Please, let me apologize for stopping your flight," she said, turning to Burton, who was watching her like the rest. "I am fine, truly. It will take more than a slow-moving balloon to best me." She tried to make light of the event. The man on horseback dismounted and walked up to Burton, slapping him on the back, she assumed in congratulations for the successful flight. She had to admit, it looked like he was enjoying himself before she cut him off from an open path. The balloon continued to float along down the road by itself, which made Zoe giggle because, really, it looked like it was going out on a great adventure. She tried to cover her mouth and contain it, but before she knew better, it was bubbling out, making her cheeks burn, and her mouth stretched from too much disuse. She turned to find Burton staring with an odd expression, his head tipped slightly.

"Well, don't you think it a funny sight? It appears as if the balloon is headed out on a grand adventure alone," she said, still smiling and giggling a bit.

Burton's smile broke out once again, bringing the sparkle back into his eyes. "Yes, it appears so. Perhaps I have missed the best of the journey, by bailing out." Then he laughed out loud. Before they could turn and acknowledge the other onlookers, there was a loud bang that rang out, and tiny bits and pieces of the balloon material floated to the ground landing on what used to be the basket but was now a pile of wood shards.

"Oh dear!" she heard her aunt gasp from behind her. Other than that, the entire party remained silent, looking at what was left of the apparatus.

"Well, dear boy," the man who had joined them on horseback said to Burton from behind, "I see you missed your opportunity once again. Death by balloon would have been one hoot of a story. Sorry, old chap." He slapped Burton on the back again.

Zoe didn't know what to think about the exchange. It made no sense to her. Why would he say such a callous thing? Were these men friends or enemies? Only an enemy would wish a man dead. She felt the need to defend him, for she was confident a man with a brain in his head would not try to die.

"Now see here, sir, that wasn't a very sporting remark. What if he had still been in that basket. It is a lucky thing I was in his way. Why I just may have saved him from a horrible death," she said, using all her five feet two inches for intimidation effect. She hadn't realized she had been wagging her gloved finger in his direction.

"Forgive my insensitivity, my lady. I meant no disrespect. It was but a jest," the man apologized and bowed in greeting.

"Yes, well, thank you," said Zoe. She was not sure he was sincere, but she would not think poorly of someone who attempted to make amends. His comment still bothered her. She had left her father, who was still healing from the loss of his wife, and she was still trying to reconcile not having her mother. Both her father and she agreed that her mother would want them to live fully, so the idea that someone as hail and hearty as Lord Burton would try to bring death upon his family was preposterous. Besides, a man who got so worked up over a ride in a hot air balloon must genuinely love life and want to experience every bit it offered.

"Come," her aunt demanded. "We need to get you settled. I want you to rest after your ordeal, my dear. You might be in shock."

"I am no such thing, Aunt Dorothy. I have no ill effects," she assured her aunt, but then she looked up into Burton's eyes and wasn't so sure. Her heart hammered into her chest, knocking her off-kilter like she had one too many champagnes at a ball. "Perhaps, you are correct. It has been a long journey, and I am eager to get settled. My lord." She curtsied to Burton and his friend, who she still didn't know, and allowed her aunt to lead her to the carriage. If it had been tight quarters before their stop, it was insufferable now. As soon as her aunt got settled and shut the door, her view was no longer filled with Burton, but the dark, interior of the coach. The driver mounted and guided the horses back to a quick pace.

"Are you quite alright, dear?" her aunt asked with concern, seeing something in Zoe's countenance.

"As I said before, I am perfectly well," Zoe reassured her.

"Why did you not introduce yourself to Lord Burton? You must have been acquainted as children, with as much time as you and your mother spent with his?" she inquired. Zoe had noted that her aunt had chosen to not make introductions, which would have been the polite thing in that situation.

"I am not sure, to be honest," Zoe admitted. "I just didn't think it the time, I guess."

"I see. Well, that is probably a good tact. Keep Lord Burton wondering, then when he sees you and recognizes you, it will put him off balance," Dorothy said, with pride in her voice.

"Whatever would I want Burton off balance for?" Zoe asked, perplexed. She then noticed the smile on her aunt's face and the twinkle in her eyes, and she realized Dorothy thought her being manipulative would make him interested.

"Oh, dear Lord, no," Zoe said with embarrassment burning her cheeks. "I would not have even considered-- What I mean to say is that Burton and I-- Well, no." She gave up trying to put anything into the form of an explanation. "I would never toss my cap toward Burton, Aunt Dorothy. Never," she stammered.

"Why ever not?" her aunt asked, surprised. "He is well set in society, with an Earldom. Your families are close. Plus, he has more than enough money to care for you many lives over. Not to mention, he would not be a trial to greet at the breakfast table each morning."

Zoe felt her face heat even more and was sure her ears were about to catch fire. "Really, Aunt Dorothy, I am not interested in Winn. It would be too awkward. We played together as children. I would die from embarrassment. Please, let us not mention. Please," she pleaded with her aunt, who still seemed to plot.

"If you say so, dear heart. I would never want to put you in an uncomfortable position, but I think it would be a most advantageous match," she countered, but said no more and began to look out the window. "Oh, finally, we are arriving," her aunt changed the topic.

"We are?" Zoe asked in surprise, but then realized they would have had to have been close if she ran into Burton. He would be near his estate. Was it the travel that made her forgetful, or did she harm herself when they collided? The remembered impact sent a new wave of heat through her body, but with an added tingle that she didn't care to think on. Winn was her fondest friend's brother and a childhood playmate. It seemed wrong to think of him in such a lascivious way, but, the tingles didn't feel wrong at all, and since she remembered her cheek coming into full contact with his very solid, but cushioning chest when they landed, she was certain brain trauma was not an option.

The carriage came to a full halt, and she could hear men yelling and running outside. Zoe took the time it took a groom to set out the steps and help her aunt down to scold herself. Perhaps she was sweet on him when they were young, but that gave no credence to such thoughts now. She was here to find a husband with a precise list of criteria. What was the chance that Winthrop, Lord Burton, would possess any, much less *all*, the items on her list? She needed to set aside her preposterous notions this moment. It would only complicate an already monumental task.

She allowed a footman to hand her down, more like her rational self. Only men with her list of criteria could be counted to share of her time. She was sure once settled, fed, rested- in that order- she would sit with Cyn and go over the list of potential suitors, and then she would find any number of men more suited to be her husband.

"Zoe!" She looked up at her name being called and saw Cyn standing at the top of the stairs leading to the house, waving. Once having Zoe's attention, Cyn lifted her skirts and skipped down the stairs while Zoe allowed the groom to help her alight from the carriage. She then ran to Zoe, engulfing her in a tight embrace. "Oh, Zoe, I am ever so happy to see you. It has been so long," she said, then stepped back to arm's length, not letting her go, but looking Zoe up and down. "I would not have recognized you had we passed on the street. You have changed so," Cyn said, pulling her back into the embrace.

"Really?" Zoe asked with some trouble as she had very little air left in her lungs. "You would not have noticed my hair?"

"Well, true, your hair is still just as deep brown, isn't it?" she admitted, and both women laughed. "Come," she said, looping Zoe's arm inside hers, leading her up the stairs into the house. It was just as Zoe remembered it. The ceiling was high and rounded and painted with a vignette of angels in the heavens. Zoe and Cyn would lie on the floor, legs stretched out in opposite directions with their heads next to each other, and make up stories of what would happen when they got to heaven.

"Nothing has changed," Cyn said with pride. "Do you remember our heaven stories?"

"Every one of them. Perhaps we will have to make another before the house party begins." Both women laughed. She followed Cyn into the day room but would have found it herself. It felt like she was home. Her mother had brought her here as a young girl when her father got sent to a more dangerous diplomatic post. She and her mother stayed for more than a year. Father had insisted because he didn't want them in danger. She hadn't thought about it much until the past year, when a diplomat's daughter was taken by a local tribe in India and held for over two months. When she could finally escape, she had been marked horribly. Zoe knew that the incident was also one of the catalysts for her move home. Lord Chase missed them during their visits home to England and didn't want to think what this separation was doing to him. Death was so hard for those still living. She understood why her father wanted her here, but she couldn't help thinking it was leaving him alone.

"Are you quite well, dear?" She heard Cyn asking and realized her feet had stopped moving.

"Ah, sorry, just memories," she said with a deep sigh and a pinched smile. She promised herself no tears. Her mother would not want it. Life was not for crying; it was for living. If she lost her control now, she might not stop. Cyn patted her hand and gave her a gentle squeeze around the shoulders. No words were necessary.

From behind, they could hear Cyn's mother and Aunt Dorothy coming through the hallway, chatting to each other. Zoe could remember as children sneaking to the door and listening to their mothers talk and laugh as they were having tea. Her eyes burned, and she felt a pull on her heart. The younger women waited for their counterparts to amble in and choose their seats. Once the women settled, a maid entered with a tea tray, followed by another with a tray of cakes.

"I was certain you would be famished from your trip. I know I always am hungry when I travel from the city," Lady Burton explained. Zoe didn't much care for the why, but she was thankful for the food and the distraction. For fear of sickness from the rough travel, she avoided eating. Sickness wasn't an issue on the ship, but since disembarking back onto land, her sea legs wouldn't leave. She had managed to not get sick, but her stomach was growling for those cakes.

"Oh, thank you. I am quite hungry. In fact, I may make to embarrass myself if I don't take care. It looks scrumptious," Zoe said, while diving into the small glazed tea cakes which melted in her mouth. She closed her eyes, savoring the taste. The women laughed. As everyone settled in with their tea and cakes, a silence filled the room. If Zoe didn't lead them to discuss something, talk would begin about her mother. "Cyn, your letter said you and your mother had made a tentative list. Is there anyone I would remember?" She asked, getting down to the business at hand.

"Well," Cyn looked at her mother, and both women smiled, happy with their efforts. "We have come up with a list of five, but we were hoping you could give us a bit of guidance as to what your criteria are." She sat, waiting and watching Zoe. Perhaps she wasn't as odd as she had thought by making her list of criteria.

"I do," Zoe answered. "I had time on the ship to consider my purpose for the next several weeks." She reached into the pocket of her dress and pulled out a small leather notebook. She turned to the page and handed it to Cyn. The two women bent over the list, every once in a while making a clicking noise. When they finished, Lady Burton gave it to Aunt Dorothy. Cyn turned and took up a notepad that lay on the table, and both women looked it over, talking to each other in hushed tones. Cyn scratched a name off the list but added another at the bottom, then another. "Well, does that help or hurt my options?" Zoe asked, nervous that her requirements were too particular.

"Well, dear, like any bride to be, you need to know what it is you want in a husband. But to find a true match, you need to also know which things on your list are negotiable."

"Negotiable?" Zoe asked, not quite understanding.

"My dear," Aunt Dorothy took her hand and patted it, "You will not find one man that has all those qualities you wish. It is a game of odds. If you can find one man that fits most of your criteria, you need to be happy."

Zoe had not considered that idea. She was normally very pragmatic. Her mother told her never to accept less than the best from those around her. She said not to compromise on the crucial things. Isn't choosing a husband one of those important things? Zoe looked over at Cyn, who had an encouraging smile on her face, but her eyes held something Zoe felt was uncertainty.

"Oh sweeting," Lady Burton intoned, "it is not that we won't find you the perfect husband, but that doesn't mean he will have the same qualities on your list." Again, she looked at Cyn.

"It is just that your list is very-- well, particular. Most women put those things on the list that are more general, like blue eyes or a good horseman. The criteria you have may not be so easily discovered in a ballroom, or over dinner at a house party," Cyn explained, giving Zoe a kind smile. "I will say, we were able to drop one gentleman off the list immediately from what you gave us. He is known to be a bit nervous and well, cowardly."

"Well, perhaps you could give me some suggestions for those things I should have included." Zoe tried not to let her frustrations show. If the goal was to spend the rest of her life with this person, she should not settle, should she? Politics were important, and her husband must be interested in talking about it. He needed to challenge her intellect, as well. She also wanted to have a husband that would slay her dragons if she asked it of him.

"Oh, don't look so forlorn. We have only begun," Cyn said, offering Zoe another cake and giving her a dazzling smile that helped to set Zoe's mind more at ease. "We have a lot of work to do before we expect you to put your cap toward anyone," she reassured her. Zoe took the cue and settled back into filling her stomach with tea and cakes. It would be hours yet until dinner, and she needed to make sure she would make it.

"I will admit, I was a bit surprised when we received the letter from your father asking for our assistance. I would have assumed your mother had secured your hand to a prince or other well-connected lord on the continent," Lady Burton said, casually enough, but it didn't stop the stab of pain which always hit Zoe unawares. Her throat felt small, and her attempt to force words through it failed. She looked at the dainty lace napkin in her lap and toyed with the edging.

Finally, Zoe gained her control once more and continued, "Mother was persistent that I have a true English come out and season. She was also hoping father would retire from traveling abroad sooner, and she wanted me to be close to her in England." She wished her voice could be stronger, but the restriction would only allow a faint ghost of her true voice. "Father is busy, and he didn't feel he would do such a bang-up job as a matchmaker. He assured me that a group of English women would do the job justice," she managed this with a hint of humor.

"Well, he was correct," Aunt Dorothy said with confidence. "I have not met a man that could choose a mate for himself if Venus herself floated down from Olympus, much less finding a husband for a proper young lady." The other women laughed and nodded their agreement. Zoe was thankful that none of them reacted to her reaction when they mentioned her mother. She was so tired of those pity looks she would have to withstand when accompanying her father to dinners and salons.

"Would you like us to call for more tea?" Lady Burton asked, bringing Zoe back to the present. She hadn't realized she had eaten more than her share.

"Thank you, but no. They were wonderful, however." She answered suddenly, feeling very weary. Everywhere she looked, she saw her mother. She hadn't thought it would be that way. She sat quietly, uncomfortable with the center of attention she had become, and would not end until they finished this business.

"My dear, you look perfectly travel-worn. Let me call for a bath, and you can rest until dinner. I would assume some time alone is just what you need to adjust." She pulled the bell, and within seconds the butler entered the room. Lady Burton spoke in hushed tones as the butler nodded his understanding, bowed, and left to do the Ladyship's bidding.

"Cynthia, why don't you show Zoe to the south corner suite." Zoe couldn't help but notice a silent exchange between mother and daughter, but whatever it was, it was brief.

"Of course," Cyn answered and rose with Zoe. The women looped arms and made their way out of the room. Zoe would have liked to settle in a quiet place and giggle while discussing the local boys, or some other fun event, but she was bone tired and wanted nothing more than to sink into a hot bath and find a well-sprung mattress to sink into for hours, or days. "You, my dear friend, are carrying a lot on your shoulders," Cyn commented as they took the stairs to the family rooms.

"I'm fine, just tired from so much travel," Zoe assured her, even though she knew her childhood friend could see through her brittle smile.

"You are home, you know that, right?" Cyn asked with firmness in her voice. "You are always welcome here. It is a place where you don't have to smile if you do not care to. You can even curse, and I will simply hide my giggle," she said, making both women laugh.

"You would not, you would probably curse right along with me, for laughing out loud."

"True, I love to curse. Winn says I am most accomplished at it as well, more so than any other woman in his knowledge." Zoe smiled and could feel the color flood her cheeks, remembering her earlier encounter with the daring lord.

"What?" Cyn quizzed her sudden blush.

"What, what?" Zoe asked, looking straight down the hall.

"Oh no, you don't. There is a what, and I will not relent until you tell me," Cyn demanded.

"It's nothing. He and I ran into each other today, is all," Zoe answered. Why she didn't want to share her misadventure with Lord Burton, she didn't know. "He didn't recognize me, and we only spoke for a moment, so I didn't have time to remind him."

"How rude of him." She shook her head.

"Oh no, truly, it was not a situation where he would expect to see me, please don't even mention it. Please." Zoe knew her voice sounded more desperate than it should. Cyn stopped, turned, and examined Zoe. Not wanting anyone to consider her too carefully, Zoe turned and began her way down the hall again.

"Very well. Why you would want to give my brother one bit of allowance, is beyond me. You always had a soft heart for his wickedness," Cyn pointed out, making Zoe's cheeks burn anew.

"I did no such thing. I would point out that most times, you and I were closely connected to Win-- Lord Burton's wild adventures so had I born him out as the culprit we would have been held accountable as well," Zoe defended her actions as a young girl.

"Very true," Cyn admitted, "but we had fun." Both women

laughed in agreement. Cyn stopped in front of a door deep in the family wing of the house. "Here we are."

"Isn't that your room?" Zoe asked, looking around her and trying to get her bearings. She had assumed they would put her in the guest wing as she was when she lived here with her mother.

"Well, mother knew you would want some privacy once the other guests arrive, I would imagine. So what better place than deep within the family wing," Cyn assured her. She opened the door and walked into the large spacious private parlor, which gave way to a dressing area and bedchamber beyond that. She noted a door to the left of the bedchamber.

"Where does that go?" Zoe asked, pointing to the door.

"Oh, five years ago, Winn did some major updating to the manor and had a private water closet put in each room in the family wing. I will be honest and say that I did not see the need for such a luxury at the time and thought him rather loose with his money, but now I wouldn't know what to do without it. I dearly dislike leaving to go to house parties, because I know I will not have it," Cyn admitted. Zoe had stayed in a few posting inns on the continent while traveling with her parents that had such luxuries.

Next to the fireplace to the left of the four-poster bed was a large copper tub being filled with steaming buckets of water by a steady stream of footmen. A maid had laid out linen with several soaps. They had put lavender in the bath, and the steaming vapors pulled the scent up and out into the room, calling her.

CHAPTER THREE

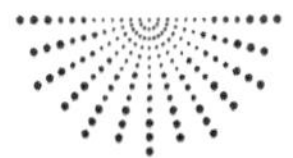

"Are you planning on staying here until your guests go to London for the season?" Reid asked as he entered the small hunting lodge Winn had remodeled a few years ago.

"If that were an option, yes," Winn answered as he finished dressing the fat pheasant he snared earlier. As a boy, his mother could not keep him from following the head groomsman and the gamekeeper like a pathetic puppy. At the time, it was just for male companionship, but the skills he picked up from them both have served him well. Not that he would ever need to as an Earl, but if the predicament ever availed itself to him, he would not starve, freeze, or for that matter, get rained on. He would do very well caring for himself.

"What on Earth?" Hayhurst asked as he crossed the room and peered at the feathers piled on the table.

"Dinner, dear boy." He stood holding his catch by the legs,

letting the naked, cleaned bird dangle from his fist, "and there is also a nice plump rabbit roasting in the pan."

"Now that, I smelled down the lane." His friend moved to the open fireplace and inhaled the fumes of sizzling rabbit with fresh herbs. "You know you are bordering on hedonism? No self-respecting Earl catches and cooks his own dinner." Satisfied, he found a chair at the well-worn worktable, careful not to get too close to the pile on the table.

"I am certain my secret is safe with you, as you never seem to miss a meal that I have prepared in the field," Winn fired back.

"True, true. I suppose it is to my benefit that you remain hidden from your guests as long as possible then."

Winn put the bird to stew, with the field vegetables he had also harvested from the wild garden behind the cabin, then picked up the table. "What guests? We don't have any guests for another two weeks," Winn assured his friend.

"Sorry, chum, but you are mistaken. The carriage carrying your young, beautiful victim from earlier continued to the house. When I crossed the lawn to go check on my stables, I saw it being unloaded of numerous chests and bandboxes."

"What? That makes no sense. I am certain mother told me no one was to arrive, well, except for--" Winn's words froze. It couldn't be. It was not even possible.

"Yes?" Reid prodded

"It can't be."

"What?"

"Mother told me the only people coming so early would be Zoe and her aunt, but that--that woman was not Zoe Chase."

"Are you certain? Didn't you say you haven't seen her since you were children?"

"Yes, but you don't understand. Zoe, well, Zoe is a good seed, but no one would venture to call her pretty. Handsome perhaps, but that might even be a stretch." Winn poked at the rabbit, moving it around to brown all sides.

"Girls do that, you know," Reid commented dryly, pouring wine out of the pitcher on the table, pushing back on the chair legs.

"Do what?" Winn asked, with a bit of annoyance in his voice.

"Grow up," his friend said dryly, "It is dastardly inconvenient of them, but one moment they most resemble a pickerel flopping with no grace on the shore, and the next they damn well take your breath away. Most unfortunate for our calm, consistent, mental state, but there you have it." He continued taking a fortifying drink of his wine.

Winn, hmphed. He couldn't disagree, but this was Zoe. The poor thing had so far to come. It was difficult to fathom her, making the leap. He did, however, need to know. If it was Zoe, he may just need to remain at the hunting cabin until she left, because he was sure she would not have replaced her quick wit and fast humor for looks. Putting those characteristics together with the warm, lush, curvy creature he rolled on the ground with today could more quickly kill him than his family curse.

"Well then, there is nothing for it. You must inquire at the house," Winn whirled on his friend, taking his foot and knocking the chair back to all four legs.

"What? Now? We were just about to eat," he whined.

"Nonsense, the bird still has to cook, and I will move the rabbit to a simmer. I still have to make a sauce."

"Sauce?" his friend asked expectantly.

"Yes, so you have plenty of time to call on mother and Cyn and find out who is there."

Winn all but carried him to the door by his shoulders and shoved him out into the cooling night air. He had the good manners to rub out the finger marks he left in the man's velvet coat before shutting the door in his face.

Not thirty minutes later, Reid was back, breathing heavy from his exertion.

"I will not speak a word until my plate is full and my cup refilled, twice." He sat down at his spot and hefted his cup toward Winn, who unceremoniously slid the wine bottle toward him and took up the plates to serve the now simmering dinner. Once they were both seated, his friend started. "When admitted to the parlor, your mother and sister were chatting with a woman; I would say close to your mother's age. It was, without a doubt, the older woman with your pretty partner from earlier. She was introduced to me as Lady Dorothy Lambert."

"If I remember, that is Zoe's maternal aunt."

"Quite right, or so I was told when introduced. It was the same woman we met on the road — the one who scooped up her charge and pierced us with reproachful glares. I got a similar one this evening. Your young lady was not, however, in attendance."

"She is not my young lady," Winn corrected. Why would he even say such a thing? They didn't even know each other anymore. A lot changes a person between the ages of nine and nine and twenty.

His friend grunted, as he shoveled rabbit and pheasant in his mouth, then closed his eyes in what Winn assumed was approval. Once recovered from his perfect bite of food, he commented on Winn's reluctance, "Well, if she isn't yours, I suggest you tamper your obvious interest, but soon my friend, or you may find yourself in the throes of a moral impasse."

"What in the world are you spouting on about?"

"You are smitten, any fool could see it. Now, perhaps your boyhood self was too, and once you spend time with the adult version of the girl, you will no longer be entranced, but if that is your goal, I will find some fortitude. Put as much effort toward thwarting your heart as you have been at finding a more interesting way to die." He chuckled at his speech and went back to eating without care.

Winn had nothing to say, and no argument to press with his friend. They had known each other too long for that. He had been smitten with the awkward and gangly Zoe. Not for her beauty, though he needed to admit, there were times even the stupid boy in him could see her potential, but it was her love of life he noticed. There was not a challenge she didn't meet. It burned him how often she would best him at a game or dare, but when she would smile at her victory, Winn could remember feeling that he too had won just getting to see her joy.

Hades have it. He might well be in trouble. Then a thought came to him. It had been twelve years, and Zoe was raised as the only child of a British diplomat in Rome, he thought Cyn had said once or twice. He was certain once she left after that summer, she would have been raised like every other deb. The chances were she would be haughty, self-serving, and spoiled. He would easily be off-put by her adult version, no matter how captivating her now- vibrant chestnut hair and green eyes were against her porcelain complexion. The line of freckles that crossed her nose and dotted each cheek just so could pose an issue though.

Winn grabbed the bottle from out of his friend's hand and poured a tall glass. His resolve starts now. He could not risk bringing Zoe into what was guaranteed to be another year of mourning in short order. He had enough guilt to work through before his death.

The next few days for Zoe seemed to fly by. She found planning a house party with marriage the goal not unlike helping her father plan a dinner party to get treaties signed. She was unfamiliar with those her friends and aunt were inviting, but she was learning.

"Lady Christina, Marquis Hall's second daughter, is two years into her come out and has several prospects, but the most likely is Earl Bancroft. He has the best connections, and she seems smitten. I sent them both invitations, and also Bancroft's cousin, Viscount Ronan. He is a very well-connected young man, who gained his title only two years ago, and I daresay would be very interested in a new bride who is so well versed in the political realm. He has claimed his seat in Parliament, tutelage would be welcome," Lady Burton explained.

Zoe looked to Cyn, "He is more than tolerable, and I have had discord with him on several occasions. He is intelligent and has a witty sense of humor, if not a bit cynical. I think he would impress."

Zoe nodded. They had been through the guest list every day since her arrival to help her learn names, titles, and connections. She had also taken notes to study when she was in her room at night since she had taken to waiting up, which annoyed and perplexed her.

After Lord Burton all but ran her down in his balloon several days ago, she had not seen him. Zoe had not asked where he was, because she didn't want to come across as anxious. Also, if she didn't mention him in front of Aunt Dorothy, perhaps she would forget about the incident and not mention that at all. So far, so good.

Her rooms in the family wing were near Winn's private rooms. In the morning, she is awoken to an army of footfalls, hurrying by her room to do their master's bidding. But she found his footsteps on the carpet resonated into her room when he retired for the night.

Her first night, she had fallen asleep and remained that way, far past the dinner hour. She woke to find a cold tray at her sitting area, and a pot of water for coffee sitting near the fire to keep it warm. As she sat in her dressing gown, eating like a starved child and just feeling blessed that her seat was not moving, either to the sway of the ocean, or the ripple of a well-worn road, the heavy thud, thud, in the hallway drew her attention. She scooted out of the chair and padded to the door, silently pulling it open. When she looked out, she glimpsed a well-muscled back and legs striding down the hall. He was in his shirtsleeves, with his jacket and waistcoat draped over one arm.

His breeches hugging his rump and thighs with every

step took her breath and sent her heart skittering around in her chest. His body, at least the backside, was made from activity. As she shut the door and went back to her supper, she considered changing her list and updating it with *a tight backside and thighs*. Cyn, she was confident, would approve, at least if she wasn't aware it was her brother who inspired the category, but she wasn't so sure about her benefactors.

Now, sitting by the fire in her rooms trying to remember which lady was married to Mr. Dufray, and did she have pugs or was she the daughter of a vicar, concentration escaped her. It was half ten and still no footfalls. Had he left for the city? Would he be present at the house party? She decided she needed to ask of his whereabouts tomorrow. If he were avoiding her, it was unfair that she drive him from his home.

She knew he didn't like her. They were at odds as children. If they went a day without quarreling over something or rather--well, she couldn't remember a day they did, so it was irrelevant. Just then, the constant footfalls coming down the hall sounded.

Zoe was out of her chair and to the door in a shot, but this time when she opened it, the light that would normally bathe her from the hallway sconces was blacked out. She was not, as usual, looking at the door across the way from her own, but she was staring straight at a crisp white cambric shirt, with the collar left open. Nestled between the pieces of the stark white fabric, slightly tanned, taut skin with a dusting of dark hair peaked out. He caught her nightly crime of peering at him as he walked down the hall each night, half-dressed.

"Good evening," Winn drawled. His deep voice seemed to

vibrate from his chest. She was so close. She took a step back because he made no concessions to remove his large form from her space. "May I help you?" his voice seemed to drop another octave, and it reminded her of smoke wafting from a warm, fortifying blaze on a winter's night.

"I, ah. Good evening, My Lord." She dipped an almost forgotten curtsey. "No, I heard a noise and was curious as it is quite a late hour." She knew she was caught, but a proper lady had to try at least to cover her duplicity.

"Are you so concerned for your safety, Miss Chase, that you are atwitter at every noise you hear?" He leaned heavily on the door frame and bent his head low to look her in the face. He smelled of wood smoke, night air, and a sharp scent that was probably whiskey, or some other strong drink. He was drunk. "Perhaps you would feel safer if I stationed someone in your rooms at night?"

"No, my lord, I am quite safe, just curious, as I said. I am certain I can defend myself if the need arises." She was wholly aware that she stood in front of Winn in her night-dress, with her robe untied and open. Not to mention her bare feet sticking out for the world to see. Oh, Lord! Heat flooded her face, rising from her neck to the hairline. "I am glad you are home safe. I shall now go back--" She attempted to turn and close the door, but his outstretched arm stopped the door dead.

"Hmm," he said, staring down at her as if trying to decide something.

"May I help you with something, my lord?" She asked, needing to move this interlude along. She could now smell a more subtle scent of shave cream, which just made the other fragrances more pleasing. His brown eyes had not changed from the boy she remembered, and she was sure he was using them to learn all her secrets. "My Lord," she said again, with as much assertion as she was able.

"Who are you, Miss Chase? Who have you become?" he asked, still not taking his eyes away. He reached up and wrapped a tendril of hair around his finger and began examining it.

"My Lord--"

"Winn."

"Winn, my Lord, I believe you have been drinking. Perhaps you consumed more than you should." At that, he laughed. Full belly laughed. He would wake the entire household. Luckily, that only comprised his family and her aunt at the moment. If this had been tomorrow night, as the guests began arriving, it would be disastrous. She needed to make sure this would not happen again. "I must insist that you take your leave, and not stop by my door again, My Lord."

"Do you believe in fate, Miss Chase?" he continued to play with the curl in his hand. "I do. I think we are all wrapped up in the act of a play that has already been written for us, but I also believe that if our will is strong enough, we can rise above our fate and lead our destiny to where we want. The problem with my theory is that we become complacent."

Perhaps he wasn't in his cups but has just fallen into madness, she considered, trying to follow his thoughts. She couldn't pull away; she was captured by his expression, his eyes, the small dimple in his cheeks when he speaks and smiles.

"I also believe that it challenges us at every turn. You like challenges, if I remember. Is that still true?" he asked, looking at her with a piercing expression.

"Yes, I guess, I do to some extent, wh--"

Before she could ask him why, he wrapped his arm around her and pulled her to him. He was warm. As her brain registered his large solid form connecting with hers, she had no time to react when his mouth came crashing down on hers in a heated kiss she was not expecting. His free hand found its way to the back of her head, cradling her as he leaned in and deepened the kiss.

Zoe's shock melted away, replaced by liquid heat. Every point of contact flared, and the sensation consumed her. As his lips covered her mouth and swept along the delicate skin, she couldn't help but soften to his touch. A sigh escaped her mouth, but his whiskey laced tongue replaced it. She met the challenge and leaned in, pushing up on her tiptoes, forcing his head to lift a bit. A voice, soft and almost inaudible, cautioned her. Warned of deep hurts and dashed dreams, but another voice-- that of her father to find the one who touches you in your heart-- drowned out the cautionary plea.

Zoe slid her once limp hands up his chest and grabbed either side of his shirt for stability, for she thought she might float off the lush carpet any moment. She worked to form a thought, make a plan, but her brain was a whir of heat, emotion, sensation. Could a person experience so much at one time that they expire? As if Winn heard her thoughts, as quickly as he pulled her into his embrace, she was unceremoniously set down and back a few paces from his large solid form.

He collapsed on the door jamb, breathing in heavy gasps, not unlike herself. Zoe stood off-balance like she was back on the ship as the waves pitched the vessel around underneath her. Can one get drunk by licking it off of her partner's tongue? Like she drank one too many champagnes at one of her father's gatherings, her head spun. She gained her composure enough to raise her face to see him.

He stood, leaning against the wall with a haggard, almost angry expression. Still drawing in deep breaths, like he had just run a race, he brought his hand up and ran it behind his neck, like it pained him.

"Wh--" She began almost leaning forward to see if she could help him. His raised hand stopped her words in her mouth. She unconsciously licked her lips.

"Stop that!" he growled, rubbing his neck.

"Stop what?" she demanded. She had done nothing but open her damn door at the wrong moment.

"That, that thing you just did," he snapped. "I knew this was a mistake. I knew it would be all wrong," he grumbled, looking at the floor. She had thought it quite amazing herself. She had been kissed before, but those kisses would be like milk-sopped toast compared to this one. Her heart, which had been beating wildly only moments earlier, seemed to seize in her chest, sending a wash of cold throughout her body.

She wasn't sure what this oaf was playing at, but she would not be part and parcel to it. She was too busy trying to find a husband and had no time for a ridiculous lark that would cause her nothing but embarrassment and pain.

"Well, My Lord, I am sorry it was not to your liking. But I would remind you I did not solicit it and I have had no complaints about my kissing before. I would suggest you work on your execution before you accost a poor innocent in your family quarters another time." And with that impassioned statement, she kicked him in the shin with her bare foot, sending him back just enough for her to shut the door in his face and turn the lock just in case he wanted the last word.

Zoe collapsed against the locked door and began to cry. Whatever for, she had no idea.

CHAPTER FOUR

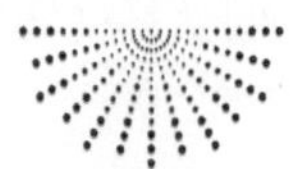

Zoe walked into the breakfast room the next morning with more confidence than she felt. Her late-night encounter had shaken her resolve. She could not sleep, but was unable to spend any of her mind on her notes. The kiss ran back and forth, filling her mind. What had sparked his need to grab her? Had she said something to provoke him? Why had she been so foolish as to open the door when she hadn't heard the footsteps continue down the hall?

She was innocent, however, but understood when a man was aroused. A woman did not spend time in Rome without learning what love or at the very least, lust, was. It was a warm and open place, where men professed their love of women. She was sure her mother would have liked them to be less obvious, but it wasn't England.

He had enjoyed the kiss. Zoe knew it. Why he was angry about it after, she didn't understand. When the sun rose, she got ready for her day. She looked over her notes with a clearer mind, but she knew she would be distracted for most of the day if she didn't force some other activity.

Zoe was brought up short when she entered the breakfast room to see the large form of Lord Burton behind a newssheet. Thankfully, the table was changed out from a simple round for more informal gatherings to an extended long table equipped to fit half of those from the house party. The room next door would be set up identically to this, so in the event, all the members of the occasion were breaking fast together, everyone would be seated.

She would have turned and run back to her room, locking the door and calling for a tray, but Cyn came up behind her blocking her escape. "Oh, so my darling brother decided to join us. How accommodating Winn," she chastised, as she looped arms with Zoe and all but dragged her into the room and up to the sideboard, groaning with delightful breakfast choices. Zoe, however, had no hunger. But just as she began the thought, her childish stubborn side spoke up and demanded she hold her ground and show him he had no affect what-so-ever on her in the light of day.

With new resolve, she took a plate and began filling it. Lady Burton warned that with guests arriving throughout the day, she would want to be mindful. As guests came and were offered tea or snacks, they would expect to join the other ladies and partake, but that was later, now it was time to show her shaky nerves who was boss.

Cyn made her way to the table, and to Zoe's surprise Winn never even grunted to his sister's barb. He remained hidden behind the paper, stoic.

"So, are you nervous?" Cyn asked as she slathered persimmon jam on her still warm roll.

"A little," Zoe admitted. She would be a liar to say otherwise. "Who do you think will arrive first?" she asked Cyn. Never having attended an English house party before, she wasn't sure of the protocol.

"Oh, that is easy, the mothers and the debs. The mothers will want their precious daughters to be present as much as possible in front of the gentlemen to get the best advantage."

"Oh," Zoe said, overwhelmed by the competition. She hadn't thought that would even be a component of husband-hunting. It all seemed so difficult to begin with.

"The eligible gentlemen will be here as late as possible, as they do not want to be paraded around like the prized goose at the butchers," Cyn laughed. "Irony is a funny thing. Which gentleman are you most looking forward to?"

Zoe was not ready for the question and popped a piece of egg in her mouth to give her a moment to compose an appropriate answer.

"I suppose you wouldn't be sure since you are acquainted with none of them. It is difficult just going by a list of attributes written by someone else. Not very romantic."

"I am thinking perhaps I am looking forward to meeting Viscount Ronan. He seems to fit with how I grew up, so we may get on well." At her admittance of the gentleman, Lord Burton swore, though quietly, and adjusted his paper.

"Oh, for the love of Helena, Winn, are you hungover? If so, you should have taken a tray in your rooms this morning. The last thing any of us needs is you skulking around like a thunder cloud because you drank too much. Honestly, you haven't even the decency to be available to our guest," Cyn spat with all the disgust of a mother, not a sister.

Zoe couldn't help but think if he had availed himself any more last night, she might be with child this morning, not eating scrambled eggs. The heat on her neck threatened to spread to her cheeks. She immediately began scolding her traitorous body. You will not blush. You will not blush, she demanded, over and over in her head.

The crisp snap of the news sheet being folded and then set down with a whack to show his annoyance of being spoken to by Cyn pulled Winn from behind the curtain he created for himself.

In the light of day, Zoe's dark hair blazed, and in the light, the sun glinted off some well-placed golden strands that sparkled like gold thread. When Winn had made it to his rooms last night, he continued to drink. He should have stopped, but he was either celebrating or drowning his sorrows, he couldn't remember anymore. For at least two nights, hence, passing her door, she would poke her head out and watch him continue down the hall, but why? Winn shouldn't want to know why, so he had purposely kept away from the house only coming home when he was sure everyone had taken to bed, but she wasn't in bed. It was like she was waiting for him.

"Miss Chase, welcome back to our home." He bent his head in a respectful sort of bow. Since he had ignored both women when they entered, he owed her that much. Reaching out his hand and she proffered hers, so he might kiss it. Winn hoped she would hold her composure and not turn into a fit of the twitters and get all red and blotchy like debs are prone to do.

"Thank you, Lord Burton. It is good to have returned. This is the only home in England that I remember, so this is a comfort." She had no hint of embarrassment, missishness, or even lust. Nothing. "I hope the racket in the night did not wake you. I know I had the devil of a time finding rest."

"What racket?" Cyn asked, looking concerned.

Was she doing this in front of his sister? Was she challenging him to acknowledge last night's kiss? The little minx. Not something an innocent deb, getting ready for her first house party should be playing at. On the other hand, he was any number of terms his sister would no doubt use in succession if she knew what he had done the previous night, only hours ago. He could feel his body reacting to the memory of it. He was lucky to have escaped before he had gone too far.

"I heard the racket you spoke of. I, as my sister so elegantly stated, was out with friends last eve, and when I returned, I inadvertently let one of the dogs into the house. The noise was undoubtedly a servant trying to coax him back downstairs, but once the mutt was taken care of, I slept well, with only good dreams to report." He studied her face for any hint of the innocent she was, and yes, there it was. One must know the signs. At the base of her neck in the hollow, which nestled a single pearl on a ribbon, was a wash of pink blush. Like a titan, he could see her willing it away and winning, but he had seen it. She had been affected last night.

As for his dreams, they were fabulous, but none could be discussed in current company, and he hoped none of which would come true because he did not need that kind of complication in his life.

"I am glad to hear that your sleep was not disturbed. I shall not be spooked next time one of your muddy mutts comes scratching at my door then."

"Oh, those things can be awful," Cyn assured her. "They are not mean if they were bathed on occasion,,, but Winn does not believe in training hunting dogs for anything but hunting, so they are undisciplined puddles of drool."

"Yes, I dare say most dogs are," Zoe agreed with Cyn, sending a tart little smile in Winn's direction. His sister had no idea they were speaking of two different creatures.

"I do hope you keep those beasts away from the house during the party," Cyn continued, with no hint of the undercurrent in the room.

"Dear sister, if you like, I will take them to the lodge and remain to be certain they behave."

"I do wish you could be as industrious in all your dealings as you are in trying to avoid this house party," Cyn snapped. "I would think you would want to assist our dear childhood friend in securing a fabulous match."

"Oh, dear sister, I do. I assure you I am eager to see Miss Chase well settled. I will be at your disposal as soon as the first guests arrive." He caught it as Zoe's brows knit together, and her smile turned downward for a fraction. Why? "But, as for now," he continued, "I must attend to my grooms. There is a mare ready to foal at any moment, and I must remain appraised of the situation." He rose then and tucked his newssheet under his arm. "Ladies." He bowed and quit the room before he asked Zoe why his comment bothered her. He felt the energy in the room change with her expression and damn it; he hadn't liked that. Not one bit.

He made his way out into the fresh morning air, his

thoughts heavy. His mother only yesterday had summoned him and gave him his marching orders for the remainder of the event. He was to be available at all scheduled activities and make it a point to be the first on Miss Chase's dance card if they decided on a ball, as well as making sure she was never without a group to converse with. Winn would report back to his mother those interested, and his thoughts on how to proceed with each gentleman.

The groom released the pregnant mare into the pasture and then watched her dance around in the morning dew, but his mind was drawn back to the kiss last night. His hope was it would lack something, anything would have been acceptable, but it had not. Winn could have swept her up in his arms and carried her to his bed. Making love to Zoe would be as much a feast for the senses as one drunken kiss and more.

He would be wise to refuse his mother's dictate and leave the country for the season. She would no longer tempt him. However, Winn had a responsibility to his family, and Zoe was considered family to his mother and sister. If he deciphered the best match for Miss Chase and helped to blossom that affection, this ordeal might be finished before he did something he would not be able to correct. A pressure in his chest appeared. The sweet, cool air tasted dank and mildly sour as he inhaled. Winn cursed loudly and continued down to the stable.

He was meeting Reid later before he had to play pretty to his unwanted guests. Luckily, Hayhurst was on the guest list and would come daily for the planned activities, but they would be under the watchful eye of society, so no more balloon ascensions for the time being.

The barn was dark, but the warmth from the horses made it inviting. Winn would need to have his horse saddled and saw a young groom ahead.

"Boy," he waited for the young man to acknowledge him. "Yes, you. I need my horse saddled while I check on the mare."

"Aye, milord. Right away, milord." And he hurried into the tack room.

Winn continued through the other side and into the paddock. "Good morning, milord," Drake, the head grooms-man, greeted him, "She is lookin' feisty this morn." He cocked his head toward the mare.

"Yes, she is Drake. I was watching her dance around on my way down. How far out do you think she is?"

"Close. Tis hard to figure these things to the day, though. I have set a groom to watch around the clock from here on out. Any sign, and I'll send word."

"Please do, no matter the time. Tell them to take the other entrance to my quarters and just come in and wake me. My mother and sister are getting ready for the house party so they may disturb the guests."

"Ah, yes, I was appraised of that fact last week. I emptied the carriage house to use as the stables for the guests and not bring Lady any undo stress so close to her time."

"Good idea," Winn agreed. He then stepped away from Drake and nickered, clicking his tongue. Lady pranced up to him and nudged him with her large, velvet nose. Winn rubbed under her chin and rested his forehead on the horse's. "Tis almost time beauty, then you will be back to galloping across the field with me. I promise it's a date." The horse whinnied and cantered back to the sweetgrass patch she had found.

"Ye have a way with um, milord, ever since you were a boy. Course, I'm not sure if it is with all horses or only females, that is among all species."

"It's horses, I assure you. Females, in any species, are very unpredictable and potentially dangerous to our well being. Lady," he swung his arm in the horse's direction, "just as easily might have pranced over and bitten me, but today she is in a kind, docile mood."

Drake laughed and turned to take the reins of Winn's saddled horse as the groom led him out of the barn. "Here you go. Riding far this morning?" the head groomsman asked.

"No, I am meeting Lord Hayhurst at his vineyard. I am helping him consider this year's crop today."

The two men said their goodbyes, and Winn rode out while Drake disappeared into the darkness of the barn. He was free for the moment, freer than in months. His other problem hadn't bothered him at all. He prodded his horse to speed up, so he might outrun those thoughts as well.

"How are you doing, dear?" Aunt Dorothy asked Zoe once all the women were settled in the solarium, soaking up the morning sunshine and enjoying the sweet smell of the various plants doing the same.

Zoe set her embroidery in her lap and looked up at her aunt. "To be quite honest, I am missing my mother. I know she had been looking forward to my season and coming home."

Aunt Dorothy patted her hand and blinked, Zoe assumed to hide her own emotion of losing her sister after so long an absence. "We cannot bring her back, but we will do all we can to make this a pleasant and productive experience."

"I know you will. I am not sad per se', just missing her."

"To that end," Lady Burton spoke up, "I have some wonderful news. I got word yesterday from a dear friend of your mother's, and she has agreed to join us and help."

Her aunt stiffened next to Zoe, "Do you think that wise?" She asked in a clipped tone that spoke more than the question posed.

"I think it very wise. You know Victoria always felt guilty about what happened and would have made amends if possible. They corresponded regularly, especially in the last few years."

"I am aware, but Victoria was too accommodating for her own good."

"Posh. I am certain Victoria would have reached out upon her return and would be thrilled that we all work together to give Zoe all the advantage we can."

"But her reputation may well prove to destroy her chances of a good match."

"Nonsense. Sarrafinna is welcomed into the most fashionable homes for visiting hours in London. Her special circumstances give her much in the way of leniency toward her choices." Zoe sat listening, but not following.

"Who is it you speak of, and what is the concern?" Zoe cut in. Both women pursed their lips and made annoyed little humph sounds as if bothered that she would need to ask. Zoe looked at Cyn, who seemed as curious as her.

Finally, Lady Burton spoke, "Lady Sarrafinna. She was your mother's dearest friend. They met during her first season and became fast friends, even though your mother was only a viscount's daughter and Lady Sarrafinna, the daughter of a Duke."

"Then, whatever could the issue be?" Zoe asked, knowing from her own experience in politics that a Duke's daughter was often above reproach, no matter the infraction.

"Well, my dear," Aunt Dorothy picked up where Lady Burton left off, "You see. After your mother and father married and moved from the continent, Lady Sarrafinna chose a very different path for her life. One that in most circles would have forbidden her from ever being welcomed into the drawing rooms of London."

Zoe couldn't imagine what it was. "Did she choose to work with the poor?" That was the noblest of causes, but from what she knew of her peerage, it would be frowned upon.

"No, sweeting," continued Lady Burton, "She became a courtesan."

Zoe sat, stunned. Her mother corresponded with a courtesan? Zoe conjured a picture of her most proper mother and tried to picture her sitting at tea with the only vision she could create of a courtesan. The two did not work.

"And she became a very successful courtesan at that. She is still a Duke's daughter. The family has never outright disowned her, so it becomes a very precarious point for hostesses. Lady Sarrafinna always conducts her business with the most discretion possible. In fact, in recent years, she has become quite a fashion icon in the Ton. Women may not want to be her, but they certainly would like to look like her."

"Lady Sarrafinna is coming here?" Cyn asked with awestruck enthusiasm.

"Yes, but that does not mean you need to spend over much time with her yourself," Lady Burton cautioned, "while she will help to bring some excitement to our little house party, and she will be a benefit to our cause with her knowledge, we cannot downplay her industry."

"Was my mother aware of her--profession?" Zoe asked, trying to settle on the correct vocabulary as not to offend, but to get her point across.

Both women looked at each other and seemed to decide on an answer jointly. Aunt Dorothy took the reins, "That, my dear, is not our story to tell I am afraid. It was your mother's. Perhaps if you speak with your father, but it was a very painful time for them both, so I would suggest letting it be."

"Oh." The idea of her mother and father ever having a painful time was unfathomable. They were quite happy, Zoe thought back. Theirs was a marriage of contentment. They smiled a lot and laughed. She wanted to construct her marriage to be as she witnessed growing up with them. She knew that what was on the surface, often was only part of the story. But as a diplomat's daughter, she was not afforded the freedoms that many children were, and so she spent most, if not all, of her time with her parents. She should know if they were happy or not.

"Well, when shall she arrive then?" Aunt Dorothy moved the discussion along, leaving no chance for Zoe to argue about the secret.

"She left early this morning. I got a messenger late last

night with her decision to come. She will most likely be the first to arrive, which should give us time to hear her thoughts. I sent her our guest list, so she might have thoughts upon arrival." Lady Burton explained. "I would expect her within the hour."

Zoe felt off-kilter a bit. She was not only getting ready to meet the men she would consider as viable husbands, but she would meet a woman who had a past with her parents and was a very notable courtesan. At that moment, Zoe wished she were back in Rome with her father, getting ready to dine with the warring factions of that country's very changeable government right now. She was confident the conversations would be more in her realm of comfort.

Cyn stood. "Zoe, what say we take a turn about the garden. I would love some fresh air before we all retire to the front parlor to await our guests."

Zoe set aside her embroidery and rose to lock arms with her friend. The girls said their goodbyes and continued into the sunlight of the late morning. Cyn plucked two parasols from a bin next to the door of the parlor, and they headed out.

"Better?" Cyn asked as they made their way out into the sweet-smelling garden.

"Yes, thank you. It's just all so much. I hadn't considered my experience with my father would not help."

"Oh, it will. Believe me, once you are set to mingle among the guests, your training will take over," Cyn reassured her.

"Whatever am I to think about this Lady Sarrafinna?" Zoe asked to get to the heart of the matter. She couldn't expect that an infamous courtesan would help her find a respectable match, but she was far removed from London society most of her life, so she could be wrong.

"She is like a great storm come from the sea," Cyn explained with mischief in her eyes. "She is the daughter of a duke who, after one season, fled to Bath and took up with another courtesan for some time, then sent her parents a letter saying she had chosen her life."

"Wasn't there a scandal?"

"I am sure there were many who would have liked a scandal very much, but her father is a very influential duke, and they never openly disowned her, so no one dared. According to my mother, she takes care not to bring undue attention to herself but has been known to use her father's title to her advantage when necessary."

"Oh." Zoe wasn't sure what to make of it all. She didn't want her come out to have any whispers of impropriety.

"She will not hurt your chances. As my mother and your aunt said, most men want to be close to her, and most women want her sense of fashion and her ability to capture an entire ballroom. She is more of a fascination than an oddity."

"I had no idea my mother had such a friend as her."

"Well, I am sure they were friends in their season, but your mother left with your father, and Lady Sarrafinna fled to Bath, so she was not so scandalous when your mother was her friend."

"Yes, I suppose that is correct," Zoe agreed, still trying to gather her thoughts about it all.

"So, what do you think of the list thus far?" Cyn asked, squeezing Zoe's arm in hers as they strolled among the spring flowers.

"Well, they all sound most acceptable, but I fear I am not familiar with any of them, or their families."

"Yes, that is difficult, because you cannot dismiss any based on your own bias. Have time with each gentleman to decide for yourself."

"I suppose I will," Zoe agreed, feeling the exhaustion of it all settle on her shoulders.

"Oh, now don't get all discouraged. A house party is a far better venue to see a man's true nature than a ballroom for only a few hours at a time. They get comfortable at a house party and cannot begin to show the pretty all the time. We will weed out the bad ones. Don't you worry." Cyn patted Zoe on the hand with reassurance.

Zoe hoped they would do just that. She wished her father had given her more time, or that she was previously introduced to each one, or that she could simply line them up and see which of them could kiss her with the passion of her kiss last night. That way she would find another who made her whole body sing just by touching her lips, and put Winn out of her mind. No one had found him admirable enough to put on the list, and why would she want him on her list, anyway? He was safe. That was all it was. She knew Winn. Well, the child that he was. She did not have any inclinations of the man he had become. The stories Cyn told of him in her letters could not be considered knowledge of his character. She could not muddy the waters with any inclination of a life with Winn. She needed to put that out of her mind along with the kiss. It was the only thing to do.

Cyn and Zoe made their way back into the parlor. After, Cyn recounted every detail about the men on the list one last time. It would not have been considered an acceptable conversation between ladies by the older women. Zoe felt like she had a better feel for the men. Cyn knew Zoe's character very well and therefore tried to frame her comments based on what Zoe would look for. Perhaps this would not be as daunting as she feared. They had just settled in again when Lady Sarrafinna's coach rumbled up the drive and caused a flurry of activity in the hallway.

CHAPTER FIVE

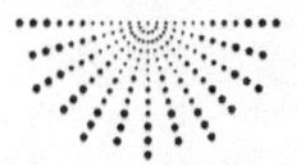

After only a few moments, the doors opened wide to the main hallway, and Peter, the butler, came into the room and cleared his throat. "May I present Lady Sarrafinna," he intoned with his dull practiced tone.

"Thank you, Peter. Please have my people fed, it was a long trek," she swept past the butler and seemed to fill the room with her vibrancy. "I mean, really Penny, isn't it time you moved your household to your London townhouse? Making us all traipse out to the country is exhausting." Her complaint was not reinforced by her tone or lack of enthusiasm for her host. She enveloped Lady Burton in a familiar embrace, as the rest of the party curtsied in deference to her higher station as a duke's daughter. She didn't seem to notice and grabbed each woman down the line for a close embrace.

When she got to Zoe, she inhaled deeply and brought her hand to her throat. "Dear Lord, you look so much like her," she whispered, tears pooling in her eyes. Zoe decided she liked Lady Sarrafinna very much if she saw her mother in her own eyes.

"Thank you, I take that as the highest of compliments," Zoe said and attempted to curtsey again.

"Stop that at once," Lady Sarrafinna commanded. "I allow some more crusty grand dames to curtsey because that is the price you pay for judging the daughter of a duke, but we are among friends, dear."

Zoe rose, and all the women got settled once Lady Burton ordered a meal be brought to the family salon, which would not be open to most of the guests. That would be a respite for them all during the gathering. As the women filed out, Winn was just coming out of his study and halted when he saw the first guest.

"Lady Sarrafinna, welcome. I was not aware you were joining our little party," he said, bowing and taking her hand. Zoe noted a hard glance toward his sister.

"Well, I am happy to attend. I adore your mother and sister, and to help the daughter of my dear, dear friend is the least I can do."

Once the pleasantries were finished, the ladies made to move along, but Winn stepped past Zoe to block his sister's progress up the stairs. "A word, if you will, please."

There was nothing in his voice to indicate he was angry, but the stiffness of his posture and the hard lines in his face made Zoe concerned. From behind him, Lady Sarrafinna turned only briefly, with a secret smile on her lips, then continued.

"Yes, of course, brother, Zoe, go on ahead. I'll meet you there."

Zoe nodded and continued to the stair top where Lady

Sarrafinna had held back. She looped her arm in Zoe's, and they began walking behind the others. "It seems everywhere I go, I cause a scene," she commented with humor.

"Oh, well, I am sure it has nothing to do with you."

"Well, aren't you the polite one? My dear, I am well aware I make men like Lord Burton very uncomfortable and with good reason."

Zoe felt her eyes widen as cool air hit them. "Why?" she asked with morbid curiosity. Had Winn and she been intimate?

"I represent to a man all of their worlds. It is quite intoxicating for them, and threatening."

"Whatever do you mean?"

"Most men work very hard to be proper in proper society and mixed company, such as yourself or the daughter of a duke. However, with a mistress, they do not have to abide the strict rules of society. They have it quite compartmentalized, you see. Don't you ever wonder why life is so broken up, instead of flowing one aspect into the other? It is in a man's design."

Zoe had wondered why things had to be so broken up. It made sense.

"I make a muck out of their carefully ordered world. Not a common light skirt, but nor am I the chaste daughter of a Duke. I am prepared to act accordingly in the bedroom or the ballroom. That unnerves them."

"But, surely their wives--"

"You have spent much of your life in Rome, where a woman is looked at very differently. In England, a proper wife is only in the bedchamber to bear an heir. Of course, there are exceptions, but alas, I do not get to meet those husbands outside of the ballroom, but I do not perplex them either. It is quite fun actually, unnerving the men of the Ton."

Zoe thought she would quite like to unnerve Lord Burton for his callous behavior in the breakfast room or be it last night in her bedroom doorway. Had he not then, the breakfast room would not have carried out so horribly. As the women walked, Cyn's voice raised in an angry, loud whisper, but she could not make out the words. Then came the distinct male growl of his lordship, again with no sense of what was being said. Zoe tucked her arm into Lady Sarrafinna's more tightly and continued up the hall around the corner, leaving Cyn to deal with her brother.

"Brother, I am surprised at you! I never took you for such an insufferable peer," Cyn spat. If Winn could put her over his knee, he would, but he was sure it would only garner him a black eye.

"I am not insufferable, Cyn. I have done my time in the capital. Lady Sarrafinna is the last person in England that can help ease Miss Chase's way into an acceptable marriage." When the carriage drew up, he was hoping it would be one of the twelve invited prize cocks for the party, but when Lady Sarrafinna alighted from her well-sprung carriage, he was appalled. When his sister informed him that his mother and Zoe's aunt thought it a good idea, well, the world had tipped for him.

"Winn," Cyn continued with a placating tone to her voice, "Lady Sarrafinna was great friends with Zoe's mother, and she has knowledge of the men on our list that may be helpful. Also, she is a draw. Once it was made known that Lady Sarrafinna would attend, we had several more responses arrive. She is a fashion icon, and her knowledge of national and world politics makes her a worthy conversationalist. I assure you it will not harm Zoe in the slightest with her appearance. Now you have to let me go. I need to hear what Lady Sarrafinna has to say about the list."

Winn was not convinced, and he liked Zoe being exposed to Sarrafinna less than he cared about his sister's virtue. That should shock him, he was certain of it.

"Fine, but if this takes a turn, do not think I won't point it out."

"As always, brother," Cyn agreed and turned to head to the family parlor with her guests.

Winn continued to the front of the house where a groom held his horse for him. He had intended to ride out straight away, but had forgotten his crop in his room. His mount was more fitful than usual, but Winn realized it had been a while since he had ridden this beast, so he decided to take the open pasture on his way to catch up with Reid and give the horse his head for a ways. Perhaps it would give him the chance to shake off his sour mood. The mood would not be as bad if not for the flashes of that damned kiss mixed in. That was what sent him over the edge. Why couldn't she have been a bad kisser? Why couldn't she have been not as lush and malleable in his hands, like she belonged there? Blast all women to hell! That would be his new motto, at least until his mother and sister could empty his home of the most intoxicating and infuriating females in all of England. He prodded his horse to pick up the pace.

The fresh air was exhilarating, and it began to repair that which Winn started to think was broken. This would be a long ride today because once the other gaggling debs arrived, his mother and sister would sink their claws in and force him to play the pretty to them all, but especially Miss Chase. He was every kind of fool to have kissed her. Prudence would have been the better companion, but he had never lain in that particular bed. All he had to do was find Miss Chase the best candidate for a husband. If he were in luck, there would be a proposal of marriage before the house party broke up, and he would not be forced to do the same in London. Winn did not care to spend his last weeks chasing Zoe's skirts.

Ahead he spied Lord Hayhurst waiting on the knoll. His most dear friend, Winn thought. He was not much about sentimentality, but of all his acquaintances, he would miss Reid most. That is, if you missed people when you were dead. Perhaps you would not. His friend was with him through Eaton, the first years on the town, and now ensconced in the country. If he were in a different circumstance, he could imagine his children playing with Reid's children. A flash of little chestnut-haired girls running amuck on the lawn had him jerking the reins.

At the sudden change in tack, the horse shifted under Winn. The saddle loosened. And, like a wheelbarrow dumping its cargo, the saddle slid to the horse's flank and Winn with it. He felt a moment of freedom from the restraints of the saddle's taut seat, but the knowledge he was falling from a large horse, galloping at a high rate of speed up a rocky hill, dashed his surprise. He had only seconds to make adjustments. If he let go of the reins, a fall was inevitable, but possibly there was a chance to try to stop the beast. In a last-minute decision, he dropped the reins and wrapped his arms around his head as best he could.

He could hear Hayhurst yelling and trying to come up

alongside his mount, but all Winn could do was wait for the landing, which he hoped would be quick, but his boot on the side he was on got stuck, and he did not make a single landing. Instead, he was being dragged and bounced from rock to rock, as the beast kept running, hoping to outrun that which was attached--Winn.

After what seemed like miles, Reid got the horse's leads and pulled it to a halt. The lack of movement was a pleasure to Winn. He laid on the ground with one boot still hanging from the saddle, trying to take stock. Nothing hurt so bad as to think it was broken, except perhaps his ribs, but he could inhale a great breath when his lungs worked again. Reid talked to him, as he worked to free his foot, but his voice was very far away and hampered by a terrible ringing noise that would not cease. His leg hit the ground with a thud, and Winn thought the only spot not already bruised, would now sport a whopper of a bruise thanks to the unforgiving rock pile he was on.

"Blast it, man, speak!" Reid shouted as his face filled Winn's vision. He was so close to Winn his breath warmed his face.

"Yes, yes. I'm fine--I think." Winn assured him but still did not attempt to move.

"Your head is bleeding, or your face. I cannot be sure, but there is quite a bit of blood," his friend announced. Winn knew the warm feeling of the thick trickle down his forehead, so he was not surprised. "Here, help me up." Winn reached his arms up toward his friend, "Slowly," he added.

Once in a sitting position, Winn knew his attempts at protecting his head were valiant, but not as successful as one would like. The horizon dipped and weaved around while

Winn tried to steady himself. He heard voices and footfalls of men running, which on the one hand was embarrassing, but on the other fortuitous that they were not further out, because Winn would not be returning to the stables without assistance. Once they all gathered, there was an initial attempt to yank him up to his feet, which only served to rid Winn of the very hearty breakfast he had eaten earlier.

"If I could just get up onto my feet, I am sure I can right myself and my stomach," he assured the assembly. Many of the men looked skeptical about the prospect of getting thrown up on, but the head gamekeeper stepped up, and in one painful, stomach-turning movement had Winn on his feet for a mere second. Winn's legs and his vertigo would not allow him purchase, so it forced him to lean heavily on the gamekeeper, but the whole company began the slow walk back across the field. About a third of the way, two young grooms came running from the house with a homemade gurney which Winn accepted with appreciation, as his head spun much less when not bobbing around the top of his neck. He closed his eyes and allowed his men to take the poles and carry him home. Before the blackness took him, he wondered if this was how he would go — death by a horse. There were far worse ways to die, but there were also far better. He knew because he had cataloged them. As he faded, his last vision was of him naked in bed with an ivory-skinned beauty with chestnut hair curled up to him.

Zoe was not accustomed to so much sitting. For the past year, she had taken on her mother's duties and was consulting with the housekeeping, cook, or doing the household books, or on occasion, helping to plan a gathering with her father's staff. There was only so much embroidery a woman could do. Lady Sarrafinna had eaten, then took a leave to rest and unpack. She took the list to go over it and promised to be back before the guests began arriving to have thoughts. Presently, Zoe was trying to concentrate on her embroidery, which was proving more of a task than it should be.

She set it aside and paraded around the room, looking at the different pieces of artwork and knick knacks. She found a sunny spot in front of one of the floor-length paned glass windows and admired the vast expanse of the pasture beyond the manicured lawns. It reminded her of Rome. She loved sitting on the verandas of the grand villas and looking out to the fields and vineyards beyond.

She watched as several men began running to the knoll beyond her sight. Her heartbeat quickened, and she watched with anticipation. Then, two boys came running from the house below her with what looked like a litter. "I--I think someone is hurt in the field," she said, looking over to Cyn, Lady Burton, and her aunt.

"What makes you think that, dear?" Lady Burton asked, not even looking up from her embroidery, but Cyn saw the concern on Zoe's face because she set aside her project and came up next to Zoe by the window.

"I saw several men running beyond the knoll, and then two boys are headed that way with a litter," she explained. At that, both older women disregarded their items and also joined the girls.

Zoe had lost hope of ever seeing who it was, when the group of men once again crested the small hill, with a prone body on the makeshift bed. The man wasn't moving, and even from far away, his face and clothing were covered in blood.

"Winn." The name escaped her before she thought better of it. It was one thing to have leave as a ten-year-old girl to call him by his Christian name, quite another as a grown woman. No one seemed to notice, as Cyn cursed and looked at her mother.

"What has the fool ass man done to himself this time?" Cyn asked as she spun on her heels and headed from the room.

"Cyn, there is no need for such language," Lady Burton chided, but followed behind her daughter. Zoe fell in step but wished they would all move faster.

"Is there no need for such language, mother? If not now, when? When the fool goes ahead and kills himself? Can I swear then?" Cyn spat back at her mother, angrier and more concerned. Zoe only wished he was not seriously injured. All the rest would sort itself out.

"I am sure it isn't as bad as all that," Lady Burton reassured Cyn, but all it got her was an annoyed humph.

The women entered the breakfast room, just as the men carrying Winn did from another door. It looked dire. He looked pale. What skin was not covered in blood was already covered in bruises. Zoe froze in the doorway, gripped by fear and heavy sadness. Only an hour ago, he was hale and hearty. arguing with Cyn. Now he was flat on the table with no sign of life. It reminded her of her mother after she died.

"Is he--" She asked just above a whisper, unable to finish the thought or the sentence.

"Naw, milady," answered a large, gruff man with a full

beard and hands the size of her head. "He's just knocked out, is all. Took a right good thrashing, he did."

"What happened?" Cyn asked with resignation in her voice.

"It was not one of his knock-kneed plans this time," Lord Hayhurst spoke up. "He was riding out to meet me, and he shifted strangely in the saddle, and it came loose sliding right sideways on the horse. Winn held on for a moment before letting go, to protect his head, but his boot was caught up in the saddle, and it dragged him as the horse galloped along. I got him stopped and had him sitting up talking to me by the time help arrived. He managed to--" Hayhurst stopped his story and looked at the ladies present, then turned red and was unsure how to proceed.

"Oh, for God's sake, man, just say it. There are not sensibilities present that are too fragile," Cyn prodded with annoyance.

"He threw up on his first attempt to stand," Reid continued. "After that, Hector got him on his feet, but he was not sturdy, and when he laid out on the stretcher, I think it was kinder that he blacked out. He is still breathing, and we heard him moan and mumble at times across the lawn."

"They will need to move him to his rooms. We are expecting guests in less than four hours. It would not be a fortuitous start if they were to greet their host, the lord of the manor, in the breakfast room laid out on the table," Lady Burton began giving orders. "Trisha, have the doctor fetched post haste. Tell him it is quite an emergency and may keep him here overnight." The maid bobbed a curtsey and fled the room to do her mistress's bidding.

"Thank you, gentlemen. Leave through the kitchens and

get a hearty meal for your trouble," she continued. The groomsmen and gardeners thanked her and made their way out.

"I know you have company coming milady, but I would like permission to come check on his lordship later if it is right with you," Hector asked. Zoe vaguely remembered Hector, and wasn't sure of his title on the property, but knew he had been here at least since her last visit as a child.

"Of course, Hector, just use the back stairs. I will let the doctor know you will stop by," Lady Burton assured him. With that, he left.

Zoe suddenly felt very ill. She wanted to run away and lock herself in a room with happiness and finish out her days there. So much tragedy in her life, she was ready for that to be over. Cyn took her hand, squeezing it. "Are you quite well?" she asked Zoe.

"I--I guess I am a little affected by the events of the day," Zoe confessed. "If you do not need me, I may go to my room to freshen up before the guests arrive."

"Of course." Cyn enveloped her in a warm, caring embrace and walked with her back up the stairs. She left Zoe at her door and continued to her brother's rooms down the hall.

Zoe closed the door behind her but did not move. She had removed herself, not because she couldn't bear to deal with such unladylike events, but because all she wanted to do was run into Winn's rooms and not leave until he sat up and told her himself. If she was locked in her chambers, perhaps she could control her urge.

CHAPTER SIX

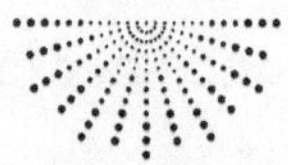

Zoe sat in the chair by the window to contemplate her evening events to meet her potential husband when a knock sounded on her door. She leapt from her chair, fearing Winn had taken a turn. When she opened the door, Cyn stood with a forced smile.

"I'm sorry. You must want to rest before all the guests arrive, but I was hoping you would come sit with me. Mother is too upset to sit and stare at my brother, unconscious, and I am not sure I can pass the time before the doctor arrives alone."

"Of course," Zoe said with what she hoped was a warm, understanding smile. The last thing she wanted to do was sit in Lord Burton's bedchamber and watch him lay on his bed. "Let me get my shawl and a book. Do you have a book or project with you?" She asked, knowing from hours spent sitting with her mother in her last days, having something to occupy your mind helps. When Cyn shook her head, Zoe reached for her embroidery basket.

Zoe linked arms with Cyn comfortingly, and the two marched down the hall. Three maids were bustling around the room, moving furniture that may impede the doctor having adequate access to their master. Another spread a blanket over him. Cyn folded the blanket at his waist.

"If it covers him, I cannot see his chest rising and falling. At least if I can see him breathing, the foolish man is not dead yet."

Zoe put her hand on her friend's shoulder. She understood precisely what Cyn meant. Zoe spent a good deal of time waiting for her mother to pass. She understood.

"He will be fine, Cyn. He is a healthy young man," Zoe tried to comfort.

"He is, but I have had enough. Mother and I cannot take anymore. It seems he is forever coming close to death, and every time preparing ourselves for the worst."

"Here, keeping your hands and mind busy will help to waylay the foreboding." Zoe handed the basket to Cyn.

Cyn looked at the basket, then at her brother on the bed, then at Zoe. "Oh, dear. I should not have asked you-- I was so insensitive, after what you went through with your mother's illness, and being all alone in Rome--."

Again, Zoe put a loving hand on Cyn's shoulder. "It's fine. Truly, I do not mind. I am aware of how tedious and tiring this can be. I am glad to be of support."

"Thank you. How have I suffered my brother all this time without you?" Cyn said.

The two sat down in chairs next to the bed, Cyn at Winn's

head and Zoe at his feet. They threw themselves into their various endeavors. Cyn, finding where Zoe had left off of the handkerchief design and Zoe diving into her current book of poetry. She only got through a stanza before she checked that Cyn seemed more relaxed, then she moved her eyes to Winn.

Asleep, he was just as gorgeous as awake, perhaps more. In sleep, his features were not drawn tight in a scowl — his full lips when relaxed turned up in a mischievous half-smile of sorts. The gash on his head was almost unnoticeable after the housekeeper cleaned the wound. She wanted to reach out and touch him, to see if his skin was cold, or if he was burning with a fever, but that would not be proper. Still, her hands gripped the book to keep them from doing just that.

If only he were on her list. The idea popped into her head before she could force it away. It swirled and ebbed around, before settling into a pocket of her mind and making itself comfortable. Her cheeks burned, and she glanced around at the still busy room to see that no one had noticed her internal discomfort. She decided it best to go back to her book and let all thought be done with.

After only ten minutes, both women jumped at the sound of Winn groaning and shifting in the bed. Cyn jumped to her feet, embroidery forgotten, falling to the floor. She leaned over him and put a hand on his chest to nudge him. "Winn? Winn, I'm here. It's Cyn, and Zoe too. We are both here." Cyn turned and motioned for Zoe to move to the edge of the bed and acknowledge her presence.

"Yes, Lord Burton, I am here. Do wake up. Will you?" she said with trepidation. There was no point in asking her mother to wake. She spent much of the day prattling on to her about life but never expected her to answer, which she did not.

"Winn. For God's sake, wake up, you fool," Cyn demanded.

In return, Winn moaned and blinked his eyes open like he was looking into the sun.

"Oh, thank God," Cyn said, bending her head to rest on her brother's forehead, for which she got a pained grunt.

"Ouch! You remember I hit my head, do you not? There is no need to reinjure me with your rock of a forehead, sister."

"Just rest, my lord. The doctor is on his way. I am sure your head is pounding," Zoe tried to comfort him as she slid herself between Cyn and the bed. The anger coming off her friend in waves was electric, and she thought it best to let her get some air. "Why don't we close the curtains to keep the glare down." She instructed the maid to see to their needs.

Winn blinked a few more times, then met her eyes with his. They were bright and sharp. He was quite awake and looked to be doing fine with no ill effects. Before she stepped back from the bed, he seized her hand in his and closed his eyes, turning his head away. As his breathing became more even, his grip did not loosen. That stupid little thought that had made a home in her mind earlier started to spread itself out, as her hand warmed in his.

Perhaps he was not as clear-headed as she first thought, and was mistaking her for Cyn, who had left the room to inform her mother and the others he had regained consciousness. Asking the maid to ring for tea, but instead of using the bell pull, the silly young girl curtsied and left them alone. She at least was not unwise enough to shut the door, so propriety was intact, Zoe thought.

"I liked it, you know." Winn's deep voice, raspy from sleep, pulled her attention to him. When she looked down, his head was turned toward her, and his eyes, open once again, were still clear and seeing more than they should.

"I beg your pardon, my lord?" Zoe asked, not sure what he was talking about.

"Our kiss, the other night. You think I was not happy with it, but that is just not true. I enjoyed it, more than I should have."

Zoe had no words. She blinked, her eyelids flapping like butterfly wings, but was unable to muster a smart retort, or even a tsking sound. She just looked at him. Then he smiled. Her heart flew to her ribcage, and her cheeks heated to an uncomfortable level. The idea from earlier settled in and grew roots. She knew a bad idea when she had one and would need to purge it as soon as possible.

"Well, I ah..." she still could not come up with a comment of any kind, and when he squeezed her hand and began rubbing his thumb in the center of her palm, her legs became wobbly.

"Dear Lady Cynthia, I am sorry for the wait. I was helping Mrs. Denton. Terrible gout, poor woman."

The voices were behind her. The doctor had arrived, and Cyn was with him. That meant she could escape. It would be wholly improper for her to stay while the examination took place.

"I understand, Doctor Liam. It is not as if you have Lord Burton as your only patient. However, I am certain that Winn paid for your daughter's dowry and wedding with his foolishness."

"Well, I prefer a patient that is strong and keeps healing. Better for business," joked the doctor.

Providence, thought Zoe, as she took the chance to make a hasty retreat. "Ah, my lord, the doctor has just arrived. I will leave you in his more capable hands. I hope to see you at the festivities once you are feeling more the thing." She wrangled her hand from his, as he did nothing to loosen his grip, and curtsied. She gave Cyn a sympathetic look and left.

Once she entered the solace of her room and shut the door, she once again felt her heart slamming against her chest. She needed to marshal her emotions. She was about to meet a group of men that had been carefully chosen as potential husbands. It would not be prudent to be preoccupied with a foolish man with no intentions of marriage. She took a deep breath and stepped toward her dressing table to see to her appearance before making her way downstairs, but a knock on the door stopped her.

It was Lady Sarrafinna. She was tall but elegant and filled the doorway with an energy that Zoe could only imagine having. "My dear, I assumed you would be here alone since Lady Cynthia is seeing to her brother. Might I have a few moments of your time?"

"Yes, of course. Please come in." Zoe wasn't sure what Lady Sarrafinna could want to speak about. She was intimidated and in awe of a woman who, despite having every advantage as a Duke's daughter, chose her own way. It was unsettling for a young woman sent home from Rome to pragmatically choose a husband as dictated by her father. "Please," she motioned toward the small sitting area, and both women sat.

"My dear, I wanted to speak with you in confidence. I

well know the care your aunt and Lady Burton are taking with your betrothal, and I am also well aware of your obvious desire to do as your father and family want of you."

"Yes, I am fortunate to have such generous sponsors," Zoe answered as she knew was expected.

Her answer, however, garnered a sigh from Lady Sarrafinna. "And that is what I mean. You are so worried about doing what is proper, have you given any thought to what you want?"

"Beg pardon?" Zoe was not sure how to answer that.

"Do you even want to marry?" Asked Lady Sarrafinna in a businesslike tone.

"Well, yes, I want to marry. I mean, that is-- I mean no disrespect--" She stammered, realizing her words may have insulted London's most famous courtesan.

"Oh, my dear, do not spend any moment worrying if you have offended me. I have been set down by the most formidable and came out rather unscathed. I made my choices and have never looked back, but they were my choices. If you truly want to marry, then my next question is this. Do you have a man already in the running that has not yet made it onto the list?"

Zoe's cheeks heated again, though she didn't know why, but didn't want to consider the events of the last day or so. "I know not one from here, save for my aunt, Cyn, and Lady Burton."

"Is there no boy from Rome then? Perhaps a visiting diplomat's son that you took an interest in?"

"No." Zoe thought quickly of all the diplomats and their families that she had become familiar with. Not one gentleman of her age stood out as a candidate — not one.

Lady Sarrafinna looked hard at Zoe before nodding. "Very well then, I will continue to help you. But you must know that I will never be part of a scheme to force a girl into marriage, no matter how advantageous the union might be, if the girl is not a willing party."

"Of course, I would never think that you would," Zoe assured her, not knowing why Lady Sarrafinna so adamantly admitted that just now.

"They made me aware the carriages are arriving, and the guests will be awaiting your introduction once they have settled in and cleaned up from travel," Lady Sarrafinna said as she rose. Once Zoe followed, she pulled her in for a comforting hug. "You are about to enter a stage that your upbringing as a diplomat's daughter has only partially prepared you for, my dear. As women, we do not have armor per se', but we do have pretty dresses, ribbons, and baubles. I would suggest the mauve and pink chiffon, with some lovely pearls if you have them." And with that, she swept out of the room, taking the energy and most of the air with her.

Zoe went to the bell pull to call for her maid to help her change dresses and don the new creation that had been airing out and left hanging on the wardrobe door. Zoe was not sure now how to go forward. Lady Sarrafinna made it sound like a war, not a friendly house party. If that were so, Zoe thought as she sat at the mirror to check her complexion, Zoe had the best list of generals on her side than she could imagine.

Winn's head, shoulders, neck, and well-- everything-- hurt like it had been dragged behind a horse. He sat on the side of the bed, cataloging his aches. He was certain tomorrow he would be sorer and would find bruises in places he didn't know could bruise.

"You should be abed, you fool," Reid commented dryly, as he perused the shaving kit the valet had set aside.

"I am expected downstairs," Winn answered tightly, as he allowed his man to force his boots on. Every movement jarred him.

"You are not. Not one person in that suffocating drawing-room would expect you after your ordeal to attend them." His friend walked toward the windows with his back to Winn. "You are going down there for her."

"For whom?" Winn asked, with true indigence in his voice.

"You know who. I haven't decided if this compulsion is because you want Miss Chase married or if you are taken with her." He turned and gave Winn an assessing stare that would have made him squirm if it wouldn't hurt so much. "I am going with the latter. I believe my friend has fallen to the only real curse known to man."

"And-- ouch!"

"Sorry my lord, it may be prudent to leave off the coat this evening." The valet tried to coax the offending piece of clothing off, but Winn would not have it.

"No, just do it as quickly as possible. I am sure once on, it will not trouble me."

"Now, Hayhurst, what were you babbling about? What curse?" Winn tried to put all his attention into his friend, as the valet yanked, pulled, and pushed, finally getting the coat into place. Sweat was forming on his upper lip, indicating his level of exertion.

"Love, my friend. You have found love."

Winn could not help but laugh. He was cursed, but not by such a foolish thing. Miss Chase had grown rather lovely, but he had the impression she would have expectations of his behavior, and about their relationship. Namely that her husband does not die before they read the banns. Winn was not in love.

"That's it, no port for you this evening. Come, let us go greet my guests," Winn said as the valet stepped back with a nod of approval for his work. Tonight would not be easy. He still felt nauseous, and he hoped no one wanted to shake his hand or expect him to move.

"Yes, let's. I'm eager to mingle," Reid said with humor as they made their way out of the bedchamber and down the hall.

The sounds of voices chatting could be heard well ahead of seeing the doorman at the entrance. Winn waved him off from announcing him. Perhaps he could slide into the room and survey the goings-on before noticed — no such luck. One gentleman, brought to his home as a potential suitor, and one Winn had warned Cyn against putting on the list, made eye contact straight away. Fabulous.

"Burton!" he chirped with surprise, "shouldn't you be abed, resting? Quite a horrid accident," Lord Seller asked as he walked up to Winn and grabbed his hand with a hearty shake. Winn clenched every muscle so as not to crumple to the floor. The motion made his head spin, and his stomach roil. Perhaps Reid had been to the point in suggesting he stay abed.

"Seller, good to see you, chap. I'm a little stiff, I'll admit, but nothing to keep me away from my guests. How was the ride out?" As he allowed Seller to pander on about his new matched bays and how they alone could make a trip seem like floating on a cloud, Winn scanned the crowd. It only took a moment to find Zoe, with her dark locks piled high atop her head, almost spilling out on to her mild white shoulders. A bevy of guests, mostly gentlemen, surrounded her. As he knew to be the case, she was handling the attention and the assortment of admirers well.

"So, Seller, why are you not with Miss Chase, getting to know her?" Winn asked, hoping to find out anything about his interest.

"Ah, yes. The lovely Miss Chase. We spent some time together earlier this evening. Enchanting young lady. A bit of a political bent to her, however. I am sure it comes from being dragged all over God's creation as a diplomat's daughter. Not sure she whets my pallet enough."

"I see," said Winn, trying to hold his smile at bay. "Women like Miss Chase will most likely muddle many a man who is not comfortable with such a forward-thinking woman."

"I do not care what her bent is so long as she keeps it to herself. I will never understand why women think they can speak on such matters as the cost of wheat, or any of the social issues of the day."

"Yes, well, was splendid chatting, Seller, but I need to make the rounds. Please help yourself to my private stock." Winn motioned for a footman to get Seller whatever he wanted. Satisfied that Zoe's personality would most likely force the more undesirable suitors to tuck tail, he found his way to his sister. Reid followed.

"I will not even ask you, dear brother, how you are feeling," Cyn commented as she stood next to an open window in the overheated parlor with a glass of champagne. Winn knew her snipped comment was a thinly veiled warning about his antics.

"Is there no way to convince you, dear sister, that I was innocent in this farce? I was seated in the saddle properly and was not even attempting a jump of any kind," he petitioned. Hayhurst handed him a glass from a passing waiter, and Winn took a soothing drink. Champagne was not his first choice but worried that anything stronger might force him to leave his guests. Perhaps the bubbles would help his throbbing head. Hoping to steer the conversation away from his total lack of consideration, as his sister would claim if given the time, he turned to the guest list. "Has everyone arrived then?"

"Yes, it surprised me when the last name on the guestlist rolled in late this afternoon. We had no late cancelations. Well, except for Lord and Lady Sutton. They will be coming late, but they are to make the party more balanced, nothing more. Mother and Lady Sarrafinna are thrilled." She motioned to the grande dames of the event, including Zoe's aunt, all lined up on the settee, with approving looks all.

"Humph," was his only reply.

Winn turned his attention to Zoe across the room, chatting with several young men animatedly. "How are we doing? Should we expect a proposal as soon as the breakfast table tomorrow?" Even Winn could hear the sarcastic bent to his words.

Cyn looked at her brother with an expression only a sister can impart. Part annoyance, disgust, and curiosity all in one. After a moment of silence she finally said, "She is faring exceptionally well. All who meet her seem enthralled within moments. Of course, we know how exceptional she is, but to see so many others, it is heartening. I do think you will have to wait longer before kicking everyone out of your home, sadly."

Another grunt escaped Winn's lips. Luckily, Cyn thought him merely a bad host not wanting people in his country home, not that he did not like the fact so many men-- eligible men-- were being introduced to the finer points of Miss Chase. He wished he had remained upstairs in his rooms. Perhaps he could claim his headache was just too much. Before he could formulate a proper plan, however, the current cause of his unease stepped up to Cyn. She smelled of rose water and mint. Fresh like the spring evening. Had he just gotten a whiff, it would not have been so difficult, but Cyn's open window allowed the evening breeze to carry the intoxication across his nose like a flowing brook.

"Oh, Cyn. Thank you so much for this," Zoe said breathlessly. "If I did not have to scrutinize every gentleman during our conversations, this would be a fabulous way to meet interesting people before the crush of the season."

"I am glad you are enjoying yourself. Are they all interesting, or are there any that seem more interesting than others?" Cyn asked with a conspirator's grin. Winn wanted to walk away, needed to walk away. He did not want to hear who Miss Chase was already considering, but his feet would not move, his mouth would not interrupt.

"I am not sure. I have only spoken to everyone once or twice at most, and they are all amicable and well versed in all things social. There are a few that I think are standing out as not potential, however," Zoe said with a frown, and guilt dancing in her eyes. "I feel like the most horrid of horrid individuals trying to find fault in some poor innocent man."

"Few men in this room, or the whole world, are innocent enough to be free from the scrutiny of their faults," Winn assured her, liking the bent of the conversation even more.

"What Winn is trying to say," Cyn stepped in to assure Miss Chase, "is that no man is perfect, and those faults that jump out at you, may be the reason your marriage will not be a success if you ignore them now, after only marginal contact."

"Yes, I am sure you are correct. It just seems cruel."

"Do not fret, my dear. Those men you feel guilty about are assessing your potential as a wife. They are most likely not looking at your character in their assessment," Winn said dryly, draining his glass and motioning to a footman for another. In his estimation, there were few men that deserved her guilt and fewer still that should take her time to consider them on any level. "My suggestion would be, if you have any reservation or question about one of your suitor's character traits or ease of communicative ability, then you should scratch them post-haste. No point in wasting valuable time."

"Is 'communicative' even a word, brother?" Cyn asked, eyeing him. Winn downed his second glass and placed it on a nearby table.

"Of course it is. If the man cannot or will not carry on a conversation on any topic Miss Chase brings up, then they must be struck off the list. Do you understand how many hours a husband and wife will need to converse in a lifetime? No topic should be off the table, or they will run out of conversation before the honeymoon has faded. Sad, sad reality of marriage." Winn went on until he noticed Cyn looking concerned. "You know, I think I may have attempted too much too soon after my ordeal. I think I will go the rounds, then make my way back to bed. I will see you ladies on the morrow, more myself, I am certain." He bowed to the women and made his way around just as he said, hoping to find the door as quickly as possible, before he let too much show, even for him.

CHAPTER SEVEN

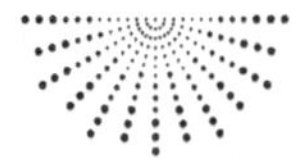

Zoe woke early, as was her custom. When she at last hit her pillow, it was close to, if not past, midnight. But even as she laid in the darkness, stretching her toes to just tap the end of her bed, energy flowed through her. Her trepidation was the order of yesterday. From worrying about a list of unknown men to meeting a famous courtesan-- then Winn's fall from the horse. But after the evening had ended and Lord Hayhurst escorted her to the family rooms, her trepidation had fled.

Now, she felt hope. Hope that there could well be a suitable match for her in this group of suitors. Lord Ruthaford was handsome, and well versed on commerce law and trade issues throughout Europe. She was also partial to his kind eyes. Lord Seller, a viscount, only just having inherited the seat after his father's death, was good looking, but distant when attempting a conversation. Lord Seller had been among those not as excited to hear her opinions on anything political. She couldn't strike him off her list, because when Winn entered the parlor last evening, Seller was the first guest he interacted with, even before acknowledging his mother and sister. If Winn felt him that important a man, it would be wise to hold judgment for a bit longer. She knew it essential to follow her heart, but she also recognized the importance of connecting to a man on the rise.

Zoe slid out of bed. The cold floor stung her feet, and a draft tickled up her legs under her nightdress. She ran to the bell pull, then hurried back to the warmth of her comforter to await her maid. The poor girl burst into the room, still tying her apron. Her hair was pulled up in a tight knot, save for a few loose strands, and her eyes even appeared heavy-lidded.

"Oh, Mary, I am sorry. Did I wake you?" she asked, not accustomed to waking before the servants.

"Tis quite all right, Miss. I like starting my day young. I get more done that way."

"Do you know who else is about?" Zoe asked, wanting to know who she might run into so she could be ready with possible topics of conversation.

"No one, Miss," the maid answered in a surprised tone as if no one in their right mind would be about at this hour. "Cook is up, and said that when you are ready, she can have a tray sent up."

"Well, I would prefer a tray to Lady Burton's parlor if you don't mind. Once I am dressed. No need to make two trips below stairs."

The maid nodded and tried to hide a yawn as she stoked the fire back into a warm, glowing blaze. She began sorting through the new dresses in the wardrobe. "How's the blue muslin this morning, miss? I think it will contrast lovely with your complexion in the morning sunlight."

"That sounds fine," agreed Zoe, as she abandoned the covers for the warmth of the fire.

Once dressed, with her thick hair piled atop her head framed by a blue ribbon to match her dress and small button earbobs, she made her way down the hall with her diary and a book of poetry. She would go through the list once more and record her initial thoughts about each suitor. First impressions were important, she knew, so best not to forget them.

When she entered the parlor, several candles already lit the room, and the fire was burning cheerily in welcome. Lady Sarrafinna, who had been busy at her portable writing desk that had been set up the previous day, looked up in surprise.

"Zoe, I was not expecting any company much before nine o'clock, and only then, the older set."

"Oh, I am so sorry for disturbing you Lady Sarrafinna, if you like I will leave--"

"Nonsense, come make yourself comfortable. Am I to assume you are always an early riser or are you up because of troubling thoughts?"

"I confess, I was always awake before the rooster. My mother used to be so perplexed by this. Many a day, she grumbled that if it not for her dastardly daughter, she would have been abed, enjoying her slumber." Zoe had forgotten that memory until just now and smiled at her mother's jib. "Then, she would say that nothing made her happier than to awaken to my bright face every morning."

"Your mother was not one who liked early morning

outings. I remember that well." Lady Sarrafinna smiled at the memory.

"Please do not let me interrupt you. I planned to settle in and go through my thoughts of last night so that I can refer back to them."

"I would love to hear your thoughts, but please, you should get them figured in your mind first," Lady Sarrafinna reassured and went back to her correspondence, which Zoe noted seemed quite extensive with a large and growing pile of letters waiting for the post.

The women sat in silence as each worked on their own. Mary brought Zoe's tray and left only to return with one for Lady Sarrafinna. Zoe munched on a scone and only drizzled honey on her page once, that she wiped off and licked from her finger. The tea was strong, which she liked. That led her to wonder if the men drank tea, or preferred the more bitter coffee which was spreading throughout the world. She made a mental note to discuss the merits of British tea versus coffee at some point when appropriate.

As she recounted her evening in her diary, the parts that were most vivid were after Winn arrived. She must have been relieved to see him upright. He looked quite the mess when they brought him in after the accident. She had been talking with three of the younger gentlemen on the list, and all noted Winn's arrival with an air of awe and reverence. Zoe would bet all her embroidery needles that those men looked up to Winn for his crazy schemes and adventures. The biggest thing, Zoe thought, that kept Winn off her list. Life was too short to make foolish decisions and risk dying.

"There," Lady Sarrafinna said, with the click of the ink

well being closed up. "Sometimes correspondence is exhausting."

"Yes, I think it can be quite tedious if it isn't of a personal bent. I often helped my father with his correspondence once my mother was no longer able. Some days we would be hours at the task," Zoe agreed.

"You must have been quite a helpmate to your father as he dealt with his duties and your mother's illness," Lady Sarrafinna said with compassion in her voice. "It was a great burden for your father, and one I am sure you helped to lighten a great deal."

"I suppose," Zoe agreed, though she had not thought about it in that way.

"You look a perfect mix of the two. You have your mother's coloring and your father's features," she said with a nostalgic air to her voice. "Your mother and I made quite the sight when we would enter a ballroom together. Her milk-white complexion and deep chestnut hair contrasted with my darker Spanish complexion and raven hair. We were the talk of the Ton during our season."

Zoe laughed at that image. "Oh, I am certain there would have been no doubt about that."

"So, what have you discovered about our list of young suitors?" Sarrafinna asked, changing the subject.

"Not as much as I would have liked," Zoe admitted. She would not acknowledge that after Winn entered the room, she could not account for anything the other gentlemen had conversed about. Something she needed to work out for herself.

"Unfortunately, that is what happens, or you end up with

more questions than you have answers. What are your first impressions of the top of the list?"

"Well, Lord Ruthaford seems interesting, and he seemed interested in what I had to say. He also has kind eyes. Mr. Smythe is interesting, but he seems distant. Lord Seller seems a bit green, but he appeared off put by my knowledge of politics."

"Yes, it was a shock to the family when his father passed. It was not a shock to anyone who had seen his gout in recent months, however," Lady Sarrafinna explained.

Zoe recounted what she could remember of all the men. Those who seemed attentive or too attentive, and also those who seemed almost aghast at her political knowledge.

"I was afraid of that, with several of the men on the list. Lady Burton means well, but she is from a different time. So is your aunt. They would not consider that, but those you mentioned, with Seller being at the top of the list, were the ones I would have warned you against. You seem to have good instincts, my dear."

The door opened, and Mary came in to collect the trays. "Thought you'd like to know that some of the house is stirring. Five women have asked for trays, and several of the gentlemen are talking about riding out."

"Oh, thank you. Should I go greet them?" Zoe asked, not sure of the protocol.

"No, you are fine to stay here until Lady Burton is awake and receiving. You should defer to your hostess."

"Besides, Miss, his Lordship is up and making plans with the other gentlemen. I doubt they will still be about if you were to scurry there now."

Zoe thanked the maid, and she left with the empty trays.

"Hmm," Zoe turned to see the older woman giving her a knowing look.

"What?" Zoe said, confident she couldn't have given anything away in that exchange.

"You must remember that your complexion opens you up to observation if you cannot control your blush, my girl."

Zoe's hands flew to her cheeks. Heat rushed through her when the maid said Winn was up and about but didn't consider the ramifications.

"Why is the lord of the house not on your list?" Lady Sarrafinna asked, with a twinkle in her eye that Zoe did not trust.

"Well, he-- I, that is--" Zoe was lost. She wanted to scream. He was all wrong, but her heart would not allow such nonsense. She looked at Lady Sarrafinna for a quarter of help, but there was none. So Zoe squared her shoulders, took a deep breath, and decided the truth was all there was for an excuse. "He could be, well-- when I was ten, I think he was the only one on the list, but we have grown up so far apart, and we are at different places."

"How so?" Lady Sarrafinna asked with genuine interest.

"When we were in Rome, I didn't have many acquaintances of my age. There were some, but the political climate, then the kidnapping of a diplomat's daughter in India--"

"Oh, yes, Lady Braveton. That was horrible, just horrible. I met her recently at a ball. Lovely woman, quite happy now. Married and settled."

"Cyn said that as well. They may be attending but at a later date."

"Yes, you are correct. Max, Lord Sutton, does not like

crowds over much. I am certain Giselle is having to coax him into coming," Sarrafinna prompted.

"Well, my mother was my only companion. When she got ill, I tried to remain positive and would sit with her day in and day out, chatting with her, reading to her, and just keeping her company--" Zoe knew her voice had trailed off to a whisper. She cleared her throat and looked into Lady Sarrafinna's warm eyes. Her own were now shimmering with tears, she was sure. "Until the day I realized I had been the only one chatting, the only one commenting on a character, or replying to articles in the fashion news. I witnessed my mother lose the life within her. I watched it fade."

Lady Sarrafinna reached out her hand and covered Zoe's, which sat on her lap, trembling.

Zoe looked at the older woman's hand on hers to finish her reasoning, "I spent so long living in a world of the dying. I--I just can't bind myself to a man who takes life with such contempt." There, she had said it aloud. She felt horrible as soon as the words were given flight, but it was the truth.

"Ah, you mean His Lordship's apparent need to flirt with death at every turn." Sarrafinna settled back in her seat and brushed out her skirts as she nodded in understanding.

"Yes, I mean, can you believe?" Zoe went on with more zeal at finding someone who seemed to understand. "The first time he met me on this trip, it was in the middle of the road, and he ran me over with a hot-air balloon that came to an awful end once he evacuated the contraption. And Cyn told me that just days ago, an angry donkey almost dispatched him with a solid back leg jab."

"Yes, the curse has wreaked havoc in the Burton line for as long as I can recall," Lady Sarrafinna explained. "If there ever was a curse. The men of this family are determined to find death on their terms."

"Do you believe there is a curse?" Zoe asked, skeptical of such nonsense.

"I believe they believe in it. I am certain there is a much more logical explanation, but no one has bothered to take the time to search it out."

"I can't imagine no one has looked into it," Zoe countered.

"Perhaps they have, and found nothing, but it has been my experience that most people just go through life allowing it to happen to them. They deal with their circumstances like they are foregone conclusions. You need to guide your own life through different things, but if you give a horse his head, you will wind up in a fox hole for sure. It is the same with life, my dear."

"So, you think I should put Winn back on my list?" Zoe asked with more hope in her voice than she would have expected.

"If, that is to say, he was ever on your list, I would not count him out altogether. You have only just been reunited. The interest in a beautiful woman will make men go against their nature if that pull is enough." Lady Sarrafinna looked at the clock on the mantel as it struck the hour. "Oh, will you look at that. I must get this mail out as soon as possible if it is to leave on the early coach. You will excuse me, won't you, my dear?"

"Yes, thank you for taking the time to talk with me." Zoe rose with the courtesan, and they embraced.

"I hope it helped. I do not feel that I am able in my circumstance to assist you in the rounds, but private consultations and conspiring is well within my realm." She squeezed Zoe in one last embrace, grabbed her letters, and hurried out the door to find a footman to deliver her mail.

Zoe sat back on the couch and considered her conversation. Winn was attracted to her, but she was uncertain he would come around before her father arrived. If no choice was made, her father threatened to do so for her. She would figure out how to entice Winn to overcome his foolishness or find a suitable husband among the choices in front of her. Perhaps there was hope for a happy union after all.

"So, what say you, Burton? Are you throwing your hat in the ring with the rest of us?" Lord Ruthaford prodded, as most of the men in residence attended a showing of Winn's horses in the stables. He had two mares almost ready to give birth and would love the opportunity to make a sale. Reid already laid claim to one of the unborn ponies, but to sell the other one would bring him a good payday to put back into his breeding operation.

"What? For Miss Chase? No, I think my mother has corralled enough poppy cocks for her to choose from, don't you agree, Ruthaford?" Winn shot back as he motioned for a groom to bring the stallion father of the soon to be ponies up to a canter in the paddock.

"Perhaps we should all be concerned about what her great flaw is, if you, yourself, are not interested," quipped Seller. "I mean, your families are great and long friends. It would make more sense that you step in to unite the two. What is wrong with her that you are staying away?" He asked in such a cynical tone, Winn imagined tossing the wastrel into the paddock and letting Phoenix trample him.

Winn laughed, giving him time to school his emotions and his tone to reply. "Nonsense, it is not I that has stepped back. See, I was not this much of a gentleman as a young boy, and well, I put a bad taste in her mouth. A woman's scorn and all that." The other men all laughed and nodded in agreement. The last thing he wanted was for Zoe's chances of making a good match ruined because of his presumed lack of interest.

"Lord Burton," called Hector from the other side of the barn, "might I 'ave a word?"

Winn excused himself but was sure they would not miss him, as the men were well enthralled with the stallion and the mare to the unborn babe. He smiled as he made his way to the darkness of the main tack room. He would get something out of the house party after all.

"Yes, Hector what is it? Did you find anything?" Winn had asked the groom to see if he could come up with any reason his well-trained horse would shy and how the saddle ended up not being tight. He knew it was tight because he hefted on it himself, as every time he got in the seat.

"I did," He said with a bit of intrigue. "When I put the saddle up, I looked it all over and see what I found stuck to the underside of the saddle, pushed between the fabric and the leather?"

Winn walked to the window for better lighting. It was a dogwood branch. His father had a border created around the berry bushes, to keep deer and vermin from eating all the berries. The dogwood had a lovely white flower, but its beauty hid large sharp thorns that covered the branches from flower to trunk. As a child, Winn experienced their wrath more than once. "You say it was between the fabric and the leather?" Winn asked.

"Aye, it was put in there in such a way that I don't think it would have pricked him until you began riding in earnest, then the thorns would have found their way through the fabric and every time you landed the seat he would have been in horrible pain," the groom said with a grave expression. "Someone wanted 'ta see ye hurt, My Lord," the groom added, which Winn thought unnecessary and unsportsmanlike. "Also," the groom walked around to the strap that held the saddle on, "I found this." He pointed to the hole that would have held the buckle secure.

Winn studied it, and sure enough, just above the buckle hole was a clean knife slit from the next hole to just short of it connecting the hole being used. It would have held fast at first until Winn started jumping around in the saddle, compromising the integrity of the grip. Winn's head swam. This was not an act of the curse. Someone who wants to hurt him did this. Or, more potentially, kill him.

"My lord? Sir? Lord Burton, are ye quite all right?" asked the groom. Winn could not respond right away, for all that was going through his head.

"What? Ah, sorry, yes, Hector, I am fine. But looking at this, I am not supposed to be."

"I agree, milord. Someone has plans fer you that are not good a'tall."

"I concur. From now on, I know it will be a lot to ask, but I need you to be the only one who tends Phoenix. Do not leave his side until I am mounted and on my way. There will be a handsome stipend for you this month, my friend," Winn assured the man, who taught him how to ride when he got his first pony.

"Pah, no need fer that milord. I was going to suggest just that. No blackguard will kill ye' on my watch. That should be reserved fer your wife," he jested with a hearty belly laugh. And considering which way Winn's thoughts were going in that arena as of late, he was certain Zoe would make at least an attempt throughout their lives together, if that came to pass.

"Thank you, my friend," Winn said with a big smile and slap on the back for his groom.

"Why so happy, milord? We just figured that someone is trying to kill you," the groom asked, confused.

As Winn turned to leave the tack room to rejoin his guests, and potential murderer, he spoke over his shoulder, "Because Hector, a curse is deuced hard to get the upper hand on-- but a living, breathing, murderer, well, I at least have a sparing chance to end this once and for all."

Winn's head throbbed as he stepped into the brightness of the day. It hurt from the large egg-shaped knob protruding from the back of his head, it hurt from the sun-- because apparently, one's eyes become sensitive when they have bounced around in their holes like billiard balls-- and it now hurt from trying to piece together at least the last eight months. Could it be possible there was more afoot than a simple curse from an angry witch? It also hurt from unbidden thoughts of Miss Chase, not to mention all the images playing havoc with his psyche that were wholly inappropriate. Hot need spread from his shoulders, down his body, and into his hands and lower. Damn, he hated house parties.

CHAPTER EIGHT

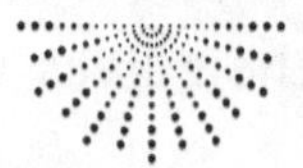

Dinner was a festive event after a day filled with many planned activities. After the gentlemen returned from their ride, there was a picnic at the lake with lawn games and conversation. Lord Burton had joined, but it was evident his mind was elsewhere. Several times Zoe spied him looking sullenly out onto his guests, who dispersed on the lawn partaking in varied entertainments. Cyn assured Zoe that it was his usual expression when forced to behave like a lord, but it troubled her still. His customary easy smile and quick wit seemed absent.

Now, as Zoe sat with Lord Ruthaford across from her, Mr. Smythe on her right, and Cyn to her left and Lord Seller across from her, she could see Winn seated at the head of the banquet table. His head was bent in deep conversation with Lord Hayhurst and Lord Ronan, now and then scanning the guests, but then back to his conversation.

"Is the quail not done to your liking Miss Chase?"

"What? Oh, yes, it is delicious," she answered Lord Ruthaford's concerned question. "It is just that I do not eat well when I am tired. Today's activities, however fun, were taxing." She smiled and took a small bite to assure all she was fine.

"What of the food in Rome? Was it tolerable?" asked Mr. Smythe as he buttered another roll.

"It was quite good. The climate is so that fresh vegetables are always in season," she answered, not wanting to insult her guests, but the full-flavored, fresh variety of food was one thing she missed from the only home she had ever known.

"I cannot imagine that it is healthy for you to consume fresh vegetables all year round," snorted Lord Seller.

"I have to say that cook's scones far out rate any vegetable dish abroad. I was in heaven this morning. Some things are just better from England." Zoe hoped this would temper any ill will to her preference in Roman cuisine. It seemed to work, because all in earshot nodded and agreed that to be true.

Once the conversation became louder than the clinking of silver to platters, Winn rose. "I think we should take this party to the study, gentlemen. The port will be served there. Ladies, we will rejoin you in mother's parlor."

The women rose and, in a group, made their way to the parlor for sherry and a collection of small cakes set out for the guests' pleasure. Lady Sarrafinna linked arms with Zoe, and they paraded around the large room to stretch after sitting so long at the table.

"Well?" she asked Zoe.

"It seems the original first choices are still the most attentive. Lord Proctor excused himself from the group when Lord Ruthaford asked my stance on the upcoming vote in Parliament and has not approached me since. Lord Seller may be growing a distaste for my free-thinking mind but has yet to fall off the chase," Zoe explained.

"Hmm, I am not surprised by Lord Proctor, very traditional. In fact, he would still wear a wig if it would not gain him jibs at his club. As for Lord Seller, I have not heard he needed funds, but his family is highly secretive in their accountings. I will put in some requests for those who may have more information than I. We do not need you dealing with that sort of thing."

They continued walking while Lady Burton instructed the staff on setting up the card tables before the room filled.

Lady Burton then gave each woman her seat assignment to make sure the tables would be even. Once the men arrived, she instructed them where to sit as well. They all made their way to their designated spot. To Zoe's surprise, Winn walked over and slid his large frame into the place to her right. Zoe looked around to see if any man was standing, looking perplexed at Winn, but apparently Lady Burton had assigned him.

Winn bent over and whispered, "Mother must be attempting to create a situation where one of your suitors must spend time without you, so he will know the heartache of missing you." Then he winked at her. It was not overt, and only Zoe had seen, but the brute was toying with her.

"Or, perhaps, your mother has decided we would match well, and she is playing cupid," Zoe shot back.

The look of surprise and fear made her swallow a giggle. Winn motioned for a footman and asked for a drink.

"Would you like anything?" he asked before sending the footman on his way.

"No, thank you. I do not think it would be wise to get to know people while drinking."

"Really? Hmm, I usually find it more appealing than being forced to do it sober. People are so much more interesting when you have been drinking," he assured her while he picked up the cards and began nimbly shuffling.

"How should we partner up?" Cyn asked, bringing both Winn and Zoe back to the bustle of tables settling in to play. "I suggest ladies against gentlemen."

"Oh no, you don't," Winn snapped. "I will assume since I know you are a more than proficient card player that your dearest friend would also be more than competent at play as well. We should do couples. Zoe and I, as it would not be fair to the other team that my sister and I team-up. We have played as teams far too much for it to be fair."

Cyn and Lord Deming agreed to the pairings before Zoe could argue. She preferred pairing as Cyn suggested, but it was not to be. And when had Lord Deming sat down?

"Well, I hope you are proficient at cards, as I do not care to be at my sister's mercy," Winn quipped.

"I am certain I will hold my own, Lord Burton. Please deal so we might begin."

Winn and Zoe won the first three hands, then lost the next two. The evening passed pleasantly, with Winn's customary humor and relaxed style making Zoe more comfortable with every hand. Lord Deming, for his part, was an accomplished player and had an easy smile, if not a bit quiet. After several games, the older set in the party said their goodnights, leaving only the youngest house guests and a few servants to keep propriety. The gaming tables were then forgotten, and the party dissolved into small groups or pairs, finding quieter spots for conversation. Winn, to Zoe's surprise, had neither excused himself to leave or found others to converse with.

"Are you finding it exhausting?" he asked her as he handed her a lemonade from a tray.

"Am I finding what exhausting?" Zoe asked, nervous about giving an incorrect answer.

"This, just all of this. Having to be the smiling, accommodating debutant at all times." He tucked her hand on his arm, under cover of his gloved hand. The heat coming from his arm and his hand warmed her side. Drat, she remembered Lady Sarrafinna's warning about her complexion giving away her sentiment. Her chest heated. Before Winn commented, she jumped in.

"I am terribly warm. Could we go onto the patio or near a window? I fear my complexion is rather ruddy when it is stuffy." Without question, Winn turned them toward the open glass doors and out onto the patio.

"Better?" he asked with concern, looking into her face.

"Yes, much, thank you. And, no, I don't find this all so exhausting," Zoe admitted. "What I find exhausting is trying to read something into every conversation, look, or remark from men I still don't know well enough to read. I do not understand what I am looking for, yet they all know exactly what they are looking for, but do not share it with me," she ended with a heavy sigh. It felt good to voice some frustration that she was experiencing.

"Miss Chase, you are considering what your suitors want to be some invisible entity, but it is straightforward."

"Really?" she asked. Winn turned them down a path leading away from the house.

"Yes. Lord Ruthaford is looking for a wife to give him an heir, as they all are. However, he is also looking for a wife with a background such as yours. He is hoping to move up in the ranks of the House of Lords. He will need a wife who can carry herself aptly in the realm of the political elite. You are a perfect specimen. I dare say, he all but drooled when the prospect of grabbing you surfaced."

Zoe looked up at him with large, round green eyes. He knew the intelligence that spoke to him at every turn. "I find it difficult that men would have such a simple list of requirements for a life partner." She blinked but did not turn away. She was determined to find a love match, but allowing the men to continue with their quests for a glorified secretary would be disheartening.

Winn strolled them along the candlelit path close enough to the house to be proper, but far enough so they had some privacy. He wanted her alone with him, he needed just Zoe. The compulsion drove him past his common sense. He would never compromise her because he could never give her what she wanted, what she deserved-- but the need to have her all to himself burned. "That, my dear, is the fundamental difference between men and women."

"What is?" she asked, allowing him complete control of their meanderings.

"Men have plenty of friends or life partners. Women are looking for a confident and friend. You, as a species, tend to over-romanticize marriage." The tug on his arm was the only indication she had stopped following him.

"I beg your pardon?" she said, with her head cocked off to

one side, quite like one of his hounds when he sits by the fire and talks to them. Her green eyes pierced him with a look that begged to defy her.

"You," he gently tapped her nose with his finger, because--well he didn't know why he just did, "are romanticizing marriage too much. You need to see it as one would a business deal."

"Pah, marriage is anything but a business deal, my lord." She answered with an annoyance that only a woman could, but she continued following the path and allowing him to lead her through the garden.

"I fear you are mistaken, and I also fear that you are setting yourself up for utter disappointment if you think it otherwise."

"I do not have to think it; otherwise, I know it tis." she insisted. "What do you remember about your parent's marriage?" she asked.

"Not very much. My father died when I was very young, and mother never remarried."

"Well, I have many fond memories of my parents' relationship and can emphatically declare it has nothing to do with business. If you don't suit as a couple, then you have no business getting married. My parents loved each other. They saw each other at their worst, and still, they loved each other."

There it was-- the passion he remembered in ten-year-old Zoe Chase. Her cheeks were lit up, and her eyes sparkled, filled with her pique. He had heard rumors about her parents' relationship, but wasn't sure what she knew of its inception. It was not for him to comment on.

"That is a true find to be sure." He turned onto a smaller,

darker path. Zoe didn't appear to notice. "I have never considered what the day to day of the marriage relationship would be, as I do not intend to marry."

He felt her stiffen on his arm, and her steps slowed but didn't halt. "You plan on letting your family name and title die with you? Do you not consider that selfish?"

The question and her almost saddened tone when asking it sent shock waves through his veins and slammed his heart into his chest. Righteous anger built within him. Yelling and railing would not get him to his desired outcome this evening, though, so Winn took in a calming breath.

He forced a small chuckle and tried to explain. "It must appear that way too many on the outside of my family nightmare, I suppose." He turned again onto another small path, leading away from the house. "Most people just consider my responsibility to my title. They see it as my duty to create an heir. What they do not consider is how that heir will be affected at five when I die, and he is forced to grow up without the love and support of a father." The last bit of his speech came out clipped. He had dealt with many an angry grande dame that saw to lecture him into marriage, and he had to deal with it silently, but with Zoe he felt safe to open up, to explain why what he was choosing was the opposite of selfish. Especially now that this determined, fiery, brunette swept into his life. Now he saw the ultimate sacrifice it truly was.

"I, I never thought," she said, while tucking her body in closer to his and taking hold of his hand with her free one. The one resting on his arm gripped it and heat shot through Winn. From his booted foot to his ear, his body burned on the side she walked on.

"Yes, well, I doubt most people do. My father lost his father very young, and then I too lost mine. Whether it was to the blasted curse, bad timing, or just ill luck, I do not intend to put another child in that predicament. No matter how much I would like to marry."

"So, you would like to marry then?" Zoe asked, with a tone Winn didn't quite understand, although his body reacted to it.

"No, yes-- it is more of a complicated matter than a yes or no."

"I am no expert, my lord, but I believe that is the essence of marriage." She giggled, and he couldn't help but break out into a smile.

"Yes, I suppose you would be correct, Miss Chase." At that moment, they had reached his destination. Deeper into the gardens was a chokecherry tree in full bloom. The white blossoms hung heavy on the branches, and their sweet smell was almost cloying in the warm night air. Cyn adored this spot, and because of that, the servants most nights hung glass jars with candles in the branches to illuminate the place for anyone who would like to come and enjoy. There had been a bench brought from the patio and set back, hidden at first to walkers along the path. You would have to know what you were looking for to notice anyone there. Perfect.

Zoe stopped short and gasped. "Oh, my. This is beautiful." She looked at Winn with a question.

"Not I. This is Cyn. She is the romantic. She loves this spot. I didn't think she would mind if we borrowed it as she is no doubt busy being the shining hostess. Come." Winn led Zoe deeper under the tree to the awaiting bench. He waited for Zoe to sit and arrange her skirts, then he took the seat next to her. The bench was tight. Two women would fit comfortably, but with his larger frame, he had no choice but to rub his thigh against hers. He noted a red tinge to her neck and cheeks and realized her milk-white complexion would not allow her to hide a blush. That information could come in handy. They were not so deep into the garden that they could not be back in a moment's notice. Sitting under the tree, they could hear the dull murmur of conversation and voices, but if caught, it would not matter how close they were, it would not be enough. "If you are uncomfortable here, with me--"

"No, not at all," she jumped in to assure him.

"I feel required to remind you that we are spitting in the face of society rules. I would not want to see you compromised." As the statement came out of his mouth, his mind filled with visions of Zoe compromised all over him. He stifled a growl with a cough and shifted as much as space would allow in his seat.

"Winn." His Christian name on her tongue sounded like rain pitter pattering on a frog pond. Comforting. He licked his lips. "If I were worried about any of that nonsense, I would have stopped you when you first stepped off the main path. You appear to have forgotten that I spent a summer running through these gardens with you."

"Of course." Not sure what to say next, the fact she willingly went astray made his heart race even more.

"So, Lord Burton, what have you dragged me from my potential suitors for? I assume tis very important."

"No real reason. I just could no longer remain in such dull company. I thought you would like to see this spot and have a moment to yourself."

"Ah, but I am not by myself, am I?" she asked with more knowledge than she should have, or was it hope? Damn, why should he care at this moment? His hand slid up her arm and her shoulder to the nape of her neck — the skin, soft as silk. Her pulse throbbed a quick little tattoo on his palm, making his heart quicken. That he could make her blood rush at a mere touch was a good sign. She wanted him.

Without any more consideration, he bent his head and pressed his lips to hers. The feel of her warm, plump lips giving way and molding with his own ripped a heavy sigh from him, and one thought above all else became apparent. His. She was his. She had been his since she was ten. And, beyond all logic, he would make sure she remained his. The anguish of it would have taken down a lesser man. He would grieve his lousy luck later. Right now, it was about this kiss. Winn closed his eyes and allowed himself to be pulled in.

Night birds sang, and under her eyelids, she could see the play of the little candle lights in the trees swaying in the gentle breeze. The right side of her neck tingled with heat and radiated down her body, stopping in the most delicious places. This is what her contemporaries in Rome spoke of. Every sense she had heightened. She was awake, but more awake than she had ever been. Had the dratted man stopped at rubbing her neck, she would have needed to take a breakfast tray in her room tomorrow to give the blush enough time to wash out of her-- but this kiss.

"Mmm," she heard herself murmur. Winn growled in response and wrapped his free arm around her waist and lifted her onto his lap. Now close enough, she wrapped her arms around his neck and leaned in to make sure he didn't pull away. The growl he made low in his throat sent vibrations humming through her.

"Do that again," she managed to say, while keeping her lips on his. Before he answered, he had slipped his tongue into her mouth, sending a new wave of sensations through her.

"Do what again?" he asked as he withdrew from her mouth, trailing kisses from the corner of her mouth, down her jaw, and ending under her ear lobe.

"That noise you made," she said, letting her head loll back, enjoying this kissing as much.

"You mean this noise?" he asked, as he took her ear lobe into his mouth and growled low in her ear.

"Yes. Oh my, yes. I like that," she admitted, with her eyes still closed, trying to catalog every movement. That was when she felt his departure. Where there had been no air between them, there was a slight breeze creating a barrier. Zoe did not like that. She forced her heavy lids to open and met his stare.

"What? Did I make a faux pas? I am sorry, I am very new to all this--"

"No, no, you did nothing wrong. I am certain in this realm you could never make a miss-step. I am certain you will be a natural." He was breathing heavy and bent his head, so it rested on her forehead.

"Then what is the matter? Why did you stop?"

"Because if I have one complaint, Miss Chase, it is your enthusiasm. A man must not allow his enthusiasm to get away from him in these matters, but yours seems to be taking mine on a tide, and I am concerned it will get away from me. I am afraid we would both be unhappy with the consequences."

She slid her hands to wrap around both sides of his neck and tried to read him. "I don't understand, I--"

"Zoe, you have to know how attracted to you I am. I know the kiss the other night was not gentle, but you had to suspect it, and you must feel it now. If I don't stop, I may not be able. It would be the end of me to hurt you." He pulled back and took her hands from his neck, settling them in her lap before standing and walking to the tree trunk, with his back to her.

She knew full well where this would lead, and knew the consequences of that, but didn't care. She would never try to trick Winn, but if that were how it happened naturally, she would not be ashamed. Her father said to go with her heart.

"We need to get you back," he snapped. He pulled a handkerchief from his pocket and walked over to a small fountain that she hadn't noticed until now and dipped it in. "Here, put this on your neck near your pulse point. It will cool your blood and help your color to calm." He offered his hand to help her rise. The walk back to the house was in silence. Zoe was not skilled enough in this venue to know what to say, so she remained silent. The knowledge of how attracted he was to her buoyed her spirit. Perhaps Lady Sarrafinna was correct. If he wanted her enough, he would leave all this curse nonsense behind, and with it the dangerous lifestyle.

When they returned, Cyn caught their eye and gave them a look that said they had arrived in time. "There they are. I told you they were down on the open path. I told you if we called, they would be here straight away." Zoe heard a noise behind her. Coming directly from the path they were on was a footman and a maid walking a respectful, yet proper distance behind them. Zoe would owe her friend for the rest of her life for this little farce.

"Yes, we were at the frog pond searching for peepers. Apparently, living in the city in Rome does not allow one to experience such a cacophony, and Miss Chase was curious." He turned to the servants. "Thank you, Paul, and you as well, Mary. You may go back to your duties." The servants bowed and curtsied and made their way back to the house.

"Well, that was exciting," Mr. Smythe announced. "Next time, Miss Chase, please allow me to escort you to visit the wildlife, perhaps a walk in the orchard tomorrow?" he asked while taking her hand and kissing it.

"That would be lovely, thank you," Zoe conceded.

"Good night then. Until the morrow," he answered and made his way out of the large parlor. The other guests said their goodnights as well and left. Winn made sure he was among the first flow of gentlemen who Zoe assumed were making their way to the library, not their chambers. She wondered if any of them would have the nerve to question Winn. When she watched his stiff posture as he walked along with Mr. Smythe, she was sure they would not.

"Well, either you two have impeccable timing, or you are the luckiest fools in the world," Cyn said as she locked arms with Zoe and headed toward the family quarters. Zoe had no answer because she had had no part in any of the coming or going. She would admit to being a full party to what happened between times, but that was it.

"What no defense? You drag my brother out to the

wilderness and attempt to compromise him, and you can't even speak for yourself?" Cyn jested.

"Drat you, Cyn. Now I'm blushing and for no reason whatsoever."

"Do you get as hot as you do red when you blush? That must be painful if you do," she teased.

"We did nothing untoward, Cyn. I promise. I would never try to trap your brother--"

"Stop. I know you would never do that. I can hope, but you are too good of a person. His fool mind needs a good straightening out, though. I was certain he had not taken you too far. I assured everyone you probably needed some air, as the parlor had gotten rather stuffy. And you appeared at the perfect time, with escorts none the less."

Zoe smiled, meekly at Cyn. She wanted to ask if she had sent them on the trail to fall in behind them, or if Winn had planned so well that he had them stationed. She doubted it, because she was the one who asked to go into the garden for air. He could not have orchestrated that. Zoe looked over at her friend, and Cyn winked at her and leaned into her in a friendly embrace. At Zoe's bedroom door, Cyn bent to embrace her and in her ear whispered, "Sleep well, my dear friend. It is as if we are already sisters."

Cyn continued down the hall without a glance back, and Zoe was left standing by her door, agape. Cyn knew something, but was she getting information from Winn, or were they being so obvious?

Zoe's maid, Mary, had the fire crackling and her night rail laid out. She had been waiting for her. Zoe allowed Mary to get her out of her dress and stays, then into her night rail. As her hair fell free of the pins, her scalp tingled with relief, but the tingling brought back her sensations during the kiss.

"Are ye cold, Miss? I can add to the fire afore I leave," the maid offered.

"No, no, that is fine, just a chill. It has already passed. Thank you for all your help, but I can finish up."

The maid collected her things and put them away, leaving her alone. In the quiet of her room, her predicament sat heavy with her. Her aunt and Cyn's mother had worked very hard to put a whole collection of eligible men in her company. All these men were looking for a wife, as she was looking for a husband. It was the perfect situation for a woman in her position. Still, she wanted the one man in the company that did not want the same thing as her and blatantly disregarded the only thing every human being should hold precious--his life. Her heart told her he was her future, but her mind reminded her that his future might not belong. Head now pounding with all that she must consider, she rose from the chair and snuffed the candles. The low, flickering glow from the fire was enough to light her way to the bed.

Sinking into the overstuffed mattress and billowing covers, she nestled her head into the bank of fluffed pillows cocooning her. Set away from the real world outside her doorway,She closed her eyes and imagined the bedding as Winn's arms encircling her and holding her tight to him, out of life's storms, protecting her. A contented sigh escaped her lips, and she nestled down even more. The sleepiness tugged on her until she realized how exhausted the evening made her. Not to mention, how much she coveted her time alone, to be able to sleep without worry that she might say or do the wrong thing, or the constant anticipation of Winn walking around the next corner. Before she gave in to the tiredness, she was sure she heard footfalls coming up the hall, pausing at her door, then continuing down the hall toward Lord Burton's rooms. Suddenly her bed wasn't quite so cozy and not as warm as it could be.

CHAPTER NINE

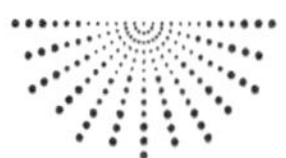

"What is our next step?" asked Reid as they rode through the west pasture. Winn had sent a boy with a note requesting an early morning ride, just the two of them. After a double inspection of the tack and the horse, the head groom allowed Winn to mount. "Winn? Hello?" Reid asked when he didn't get an answer.

"Oh, sorry, next step? Damned if I know. With the notion I was cursed, I accepted my fate. I am having some difficulty with this notion that that may not be the case. Where would you start?" Winn asked, hoping his friend would help to order his thoughts. From the moment he entered the parlor with Miss Chase last night, his thoughts had been more like vignettes of his most ardent fantasies. None, to be honest, would help him with this current situation. It only made him frustrated and confused more than usual.

"Well, we need to decide if we feel this is happening from someone invited to the house party, or if it is someone in the neighborhood. With your other brushes with death, would you say they were self-inflicted, mere accidents, or something more?" Hayhurst thought out loud.

Winn forced his mind to focus on the topic. He had left the house well before anyone had risen to avoid having a fresh image to war with. If he could steer clear of her, perhaps the current images would fade. "I would say half and half. I would call none of them accidents. They were caused by my own self-confidence or something else altogether."

The sun was just coming over the copse of trees in front of them. Winn forgot how much he loved the morning. Did Zoe like mornings? Many women of the Ton never saw the sunrise. He pulled himself back to his friend. If this situation didn't get resolved, whether Zoe liked mornings was irrelevant.

"They did not all happen here, correct?" His companion motioned to the surrounding area.

"No, actually until the other day, any of them not self-induced happened elsewhere. In London, at my club, oh, that time at the horse race in Britton."

Reid shook his head. "That one almost had you."

"Yes, to be between two randy stallions with a mare close by. Death by stud fight." Had he not thought better of it and jumped into a stall that had not been cleaned yet, they would have trampled him. As it was, both handlers walked away with some nasty injuries.

"At the time I was aware, but refresh my memory, what were you doing in the stables?"

"Looking into purchasing one of the studs in question. After receiving incorrect directions to the stud's stall, I wandered into an area that was roped off."

"Who gave you directions?"

That was a good question. It had been over a year ago. Winn had been enjoying himself, so he was into his cups. Not overmuch. He never allowed himself to get sodded, but any amount of ale will impede one's memory. Who was he with? "Who were we with that weekend?" Winn asked to get his friend to help remember.

"Anyone in the horse world or anyone interested in horseflesh was there. I daresay, most of the men present here were at that weekend. We were with Lord Granger. Deming came late. I remember he had papers or something to go over with his solicitors. Then there was Frasier."

"Oh, right, Lord Frasier was the reason we all got together that weekend."

"Yes, the old boys from Eaton, he had said." Both men laughed as their horses meandered next to the streams heavy with winter runoff still.

"Frasier gave me the initial directions because he was the one who introduced the owner to me; they were acquaintances from Scotland. I made it to the stable, but the main doors to the barn were shut. With luck, Seller and Smythe were coming around the corner after having looked at a mare one was considering. They directed me to that spot."

Both men rode a bit, saying nothing. Could there be a murderer, or at the very least attempted murderer, at his mother's house party? And why would Winn be a target?

"Can you remember if any of them were present for any other incidents?"

"Not immediately, no. Since I turned nine and twenty at least three that come to mind, the one at the race being the most recent. Let us put him on the list and pay close attention. It is one thing to put me in danger, but if someone is fool enough to try to kill me in my own home, he is putting my family at risk, and I am not having that."

"Agreed," Reid intoned as they rode into their destination, the hunting cabin.

As the men dismounted and let their horses leads drop, because the fresh clover would keep them close around the hunting lodge, Winn asked, "Will you be over for dinner and festivities tonight?"

"I am, unfortunately, present for the whole of your house party. Your mother guilted me and helped her cause by also getting my mother on board. I am to be present at all events starting at luncheon and going throughout the day until the guests find their rooms."

Winn noticed he had been present at most of the activities but hadn't realized he was thereby order of his mother. He cocked a brow at his friend.

"Oh, don't you do that to me. Your mother when determined is a force. She pointed out the fact that a good portion of her family meal budget includes my presence, so if I am comfortable to partake in family dinners, I would be expected to help in this endeavor."

"My sister had nothing to do with this?" Winn asked. His friend's cheeks blazed, and he hmphed loudly as they made their way into the lodge. Winn sauntered to the fire to get it ablaze, and Hayhurst unboarded the windows for much-needed light.

"Your sister was absent when your mother cornered me," he defended.

"Of that, I am sure, but what I meant was, would my sister's presence have anything to do with the fact you allowed yourself to be dictated to by a woman with gray hair and a cane?"

"I have no idea what you are talking about, but while we are on the subject-- were you hoping to be caught last night by a guest so you would be required to marry Miss Chase and therefore not admit your stance on marriage is incorrect, or was she trying to trap you?"

"Neither. Zoe was warm and needed air. As we walked and talked, we got further back from the parlor doors than we both expected. Did you send the servants on a hunt?"

"Cyn's idea. Once she realized the two of you were missing, she sent me to find two servants to wait in the shadows and pop out behind you. Sneaky, that one." Winn couldn't deny that.

"Have you broken the fast?" Winn asked.

"No, I had a friend rouse me from my bed before dawn. I would have eaten gruel for a week had I considered waking my cook at such an hour." At that warning, Winn swung a bag from his shoulder to the table. Inside sat a wrapped ham shank from breakfast the day before, and also fresh biscuits with a hunk of cheese, and a large bunch of grapes. "Breakfast is served."

"You are handy to keep around. I'll give you that. It only marginally makes up for the trouble you cause, but tis enough," Reid complimented.

"I will make a point to shadow Smythe today and this evening see what he is getting himself up to. Out of the choices, he seems the most capable of something nefarious. I am surprised he hasn't just said his goodbyes. The looks he gives Miss Chase when he thinks no one is looking are of the utter disgust category. There is no way they would suit as a couple, anyway. I rarely see Miss Chase choosing to single him out for conversations."

"Yes, I have noted that. Smythe is not so progressive that a woman with a mind of her own would be attractive."

"Well, in the chap's defense, his family has not had the best of luck in the rumor mill or any other. He only just got their reputation restored from something that happened years and years back, and there is a rumor of substantial debt heaped on him from his grandfather and then his father. I'm not even sure Miss Chase's dowry would be enough to get him to square."

"I had heard that as well. The notion that someone seeks a wife based on her potential profit, and not her as a person, perplexes me. What must a marriage like that be like?" Winn thought out loud.

"I know you eschewed all things marriage, considering you do not plan on living past your birthday and all, but even you must understand that is the way of things."

"I am very aware, and that is one reason among many to steer clear of any talk of marriage, or brides, or weddings. Perhaps it is just that I have a sister, but the thought of Cyn spending the rest of her life with a person who wanted nothing more from her than her money makes me consider murder myself."

"Your sister would never allow that."

"Oh, I well know, but what happens when I am gone, and she is still without a husband? I am leaving both my mother and sister set up so they will never want for anything, but there will still be those who try to press the matter. It makes my blood boil." Then, to consider what poor Zoe is going through as we speak, Winn thought. She was attracted to him and could not deny her physical reactions. She might not understand her feelings, but she wanted him just as much as he wanted her. Yet, he was aware she disapproved of his life choices. Disapproved of what she called blatant disregard for the life that he had. He knew a lot of his adventurous ways were sparked by his hope to control his destiny, but to be honest, he was always the boy who needed to climb just a bit higher in the tree to see what he could see. He doubted he could curb his wildness all together and wasn't sure he wanted to give up that part of himself for another.

The morning chill did not seem to want to give way to the warmth of the sun, as Zoe stood in the entry hall, waiting for a maid to fetch her warmer shawl. Zoe was fooled by the sunbeams dancing across her pillows, waking her at dawn's first light. Now, waiting to explore the gardens with Mr. Smythe, she would need something to ward off the chill.

"I am so sorry for the wait. I did not realize how much bite there was to the morning air today," she apologized to her companion, waiting by her side.

"An apology is unnecessary, Miss Chase. I admit I was surprised myself. This old behemoth of a building holds the heat nicely, so it was disconcerting when the chill struck me in the sun. Nevertheless, I am at your disposal."

"Ah, there she is, Jane, thank you so much for fetching that." Before she could take the shawl, Mr. Smythe took it from the maid and wrapped it around Zoe's shoulders, making sure it draped around and settled before he let go.

"No worries, Miss. Have a good outing," the maid said, before heading back to her duties.

"Ready?" Mr. Smythe asked with good humor.

"Yes, let us go explore the gardens," Zoe said.

The cloying smell of roses assailed her senses as they entered the large formal garden from the west.

"They lined this side of the gardens with roses to keep the deer at bay from the orchard," Mr. Smythe was explaining. Zoe wanted him to intrigue her. He was kind and not unhandsome to be sure. They had assured her that all the men invited had means, or at least the potential, for taking care of a family. She had no real delusions about marrying an Earl or Duke. She was too inconsequential for that. Her father was well-liked and respected, but lacked the family backing and title to make her known to them, not that she cared about a title. She wanted her heart to be engaged. Oh, why wasn't her heart getting engaged with Mr. Smythe?

"Are you interested in horticulture, Mr. Smythe?" she asked, trying to engage her heart by force.

"Not overmuch. I spent a great deal of time with my mother as a boy before I went to Eaton. They could not afford a nanny and save for my schooling as well, so my mother took on the task. She loves flowers, so I spent a great deal of time playing in the garden and overhearing her discussions."

"I didn't have a nanny either," Zoe admitted. "My mother wanted me close to her, and didn't think handing me off to a nanny would accomplish that. I am very fortunate for having spent such a large amount of time with her." Well, Zoe thought, at least they have that in common. Many of the people in her circle would not understand not having a nanny. Perhaps all she needed to do was spend quality time with each suitor to get to know them in a more personal way, instead of just on a conversational level.

Zoe hadn't seen Winn at breakfast and was told by Cyn, without having to ask, that her brother has taken a leave of absence and run off. He would be back for dinner and evening activities, but would for the foreseeable future not be available during the day. She had to wonder if it was him giving her space to do just as she is now, getting to know her suitors, or has he hatched a new wild scheme for ending his life fashionably? Zoe huffed out a breath and squared her shoulders. She would prove to her heart that Lord Burton was not the only man capable of setting it aflutter. It was crucial to give each of her suitors her undivided attention and not a wit of consideration about Burton. If he was stepping back after the physical encounters they have had, he must not be as interested as she had hoped last night.

After what seemed like a longer than usual visit to the garden, Mr. Smythe escorted Zoe back to the house in time to settle in the parlor with the other guests for an afternoon of charades. Lord Ruthaford seemed to be the next in line to parade her around the parlor on his arm. He was a very genial sort of fellow with good manners and kind eyes, Zoe thought as they walked the perimeter of the large room, once both had been called out by Cyn.

"If I am to be honest, I detest charades," he admitted, dipping his head low to whisper his confession in her ear. His comment and his breath on her earlobe made her giggle.

"Why ever do you have such strong emotions toward a game, Lord Ruthaford?"

"Well, I have never excelled at such a fast-paced game.

Then there is all the shouting," he explained as Miss Lightfoot, another young lady of her benefactor's acquaintance, jumped up and yelled the winning answer.

"Miss Lightfoot seems very accomplished at the game," Zoe commented.

"Yes, she does. Perhaps I should press her for some pointers," he dryly intoned.

"I dare say you could ask me for pointers if you are in need."

"I would say nothing to disparage a lady. But for total fairness, I must point out that you are currently walking the perimeter with me after having been thrown out yourself, while Miss Lightfoot is clearly showing her expertise in the matter of Shakespearian dramas."

"Why, Lord Ruthaford, I am certain I should be offended and hurt. It is hardly gentlemanly behavior to call out a lady's faults while touting another's accomplishments," she said with mock disgust, but her chuckle waylaid any indication that it upset her.

Both laughed, and then Zoe made her confession, "I have to admit, I as well do not care for charades. If you have something to say, you should not have your voice taken from you. It sets a terrible precedent for young women." She held her breath, wondering if her statement might be too progressive and feminist for Lord Ruthaford.

"I had not considered that Miss Chase, but I see how a game taught to young impressionable girls in the nursery could lead them to believe that their voices should not be heard." He tucked her arm into his a bit snugger and laid his hand on hers. "You will no doubt keep your husband, whoever that will be, on his toes. It is refreshing to meet a woman who can speak on so many topics, and yet not come across as trying to be a man. You know what you are talking about, but still spin it in a way that gives a man something new to consider. Well played, Miss Chase, well played."

They continued walking and discussing the topics of the day, until Cyn pulled them back for another round. Soon Zoe, unable to take the ridiculousness of the game any longer, suggested a walk to the stables for all. It had warmed up and she suggested that fresh country air would do them all well before luncheon. The women dispersed to grab their shawls and hats, and the men to get their walking canes. It was decided to meet on the patio in fifteen minutes.

Waiting on the patio for all to assemble, they watched a new carriage rumble up the drive. "That must be Lord and Lady Sutton," Miss Lightfoot explained to Lord Seller. "They responded they would be delayed in their arrival."

The coach stopped at the bottom of the long stairs leading to the door. Cyn broke from the group of onlookers to greet the new guests. A giant beast of a man stepped out first and turned to help his wife out.

Zoe had heard of Lady Sutton's ordeal within India with her father. It was one of the reasons her father sent her back to England. Lady Sutton had dark hair that shimmered in the sunlight, and the markings that were rumored to cover her body from her time in captivity were more understated than Zoe thought they would be.

Cyn brought the couple to the top of the stairs to introduce everyone. "I would like you all to meet Lord Sutton and his wife, Lady Sutton."

"Hello, I believe we are acquainted with almost everyone from last season, but I am not familiar with you," Lady

Sutton said directly to Zoe. "You must be Miss Chase." Before Zoe could curtsey or reply, Lady Sutton pulled her in for a tight hug. "I feel as if you and I are already friends. We share a kinship as children of diplomats."

She let Zoe out of the embrace and stepped back. That was when Zoe noticed the slight roundness to Lady Sutton's belly. She was with child. That could explain the late arrival. It would be rude to point such a condition out, so instead she replied, "I feel the same way. I hope we can have time to get to know each other."

To that, before Lady Sutton could answer, her husband leaned into the conversation. "Lady Sutton will be most excited to chat, but at present, we must settle in, and she will be taking a nap before the evening festivities."

"Of course, it must have been a long trip for you. We were just heading down to the stables, so the house will be quiet for some time." Zoe finally got in a curtsy, and the couple said their goodbyes and retreated into the house.

All those taking air were present, and the troupe headed down the path, all with new things to discuss with the new guests having arrived.

CHAPTER TEN

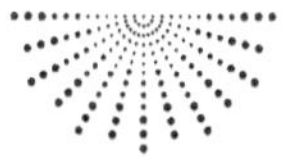

Cyn had outdone herself for the afternoon. Zoe drew in a deep breath, taking in the fresh air. If she had to suffer one more parlor game, she would have expired from frustration.

Only half of the party joined them on the lawn for archery. Many of the women decided instead to walk the gardens, hoping to run into Lord Burton. Or so Zoe surmised. Little did they know he left the manor last night, and to her knowledge had not yet returned. Where he disappeared at night was a puzzle Zoe wanted solved.

"Would you like some pointers, Miss Chase, as to a proper stance?" Lord Selling came up behind her, startling her out of her wayward musings.

"Oh, Lord Selling, you startled me. If you would think I am in need, one should always attempt to improve in all endeavors," she answered, turning with her bow and arrow toward the target down the hill.

She knew this was part of the courting ritual, to feign helplessness to allow a gentleman to get close, but it grated on her nerves. Zoe was, in fact, an excellent marksman. It was an activity her father allowed at their villa for her to pass the time with. He even called in an instructor.

The memory was interrupted with the hot breath of Lord Seller covering her ear and neck as he leaned in to see her vantage point.

"Good, good, now spread your legs a bit to give you a more solid stance."

Zoe did as directed, knowing it would not improve her balance at all. In fact, it would most likely result in a missed target, but an opportunity for Lord Seller to continue his instruction.

"How is this?" she asked, getting more annoyed as the lesson continued. His instructions were tiresome and incorrect. After more directions, she adjusted herself to her comfortable stance, drew her bow, knocking Lord Seller out of the way with her elbow as she did, and let the arrow fly. The whir of the arrow had a pleasant sound, but not as satisfying as the thunk of the arrow hitting its target in the center and Lord Seller coughing and mumbling something that sounded like a curse. Zoe swung around to the applause of the group and the dismay of Lord Seller. "Thank you, sir, you are a fine tutor. I am certain all the ladies present will want instruction now."

Cyn covered her face with her fan to hide the smile. They had spoken often in letters about Zoe's love of the sport. She stepped away to allow others to fill the shooting stations and found her way to Cyn.

"I was hoping you chose to shoot the arrow and not beat the man over the head with it instead."

"Now, Cyn, I think I played along quite well."

"Yes, you did... until you didn't," she pointed out. "In fact, I had them set up that shooting station for you so you might showcase your ability." She pointed to a station to the far left that stood empty because of the distance to the target.

"Do you think I should, or would it be too presumptuous and showy?"

"Part of attracting a husband is attracting the right husband. If you love archery and are exceptional at the sport, will you be willing to feign stupidity for the next odd years?"

"Well, since you put it that way," Zoe agreed, watching arrows fly off in every direction, only reaching the target occasionally. Zoe made her way to the empty station and tried to ignore the looks of the other guests, particularly the men, as she readied the bow. After calming her body and focusing on the target, she let the arrow fly, hitting the target a bit to the left of center.

Applause came from the others, and she nodded her head in recognition. She noted Lord Seller was not as happy about her shot as everyone else. She would have to make amends later and assure him she had not meant to mock him as she was sure that would be what he thought.

After several hours of archery, which also included a light fare on the lawn with good conversation, the group began to disperse for quiet quarters and to prepare for dinner.

"Are you coming, Zoe?" Cyn asked

"Ah, no. You go on ahead. I'm going to help collect my arrows. I overshot a few and am sure I know where they are."

Cyn waved her off and followed the other guests into the house.

"Ye don't 'ave t' worry boot helpin' t' find the arrows lass," a doorman said.

"Nonsense. I know the direction I overshot them in, and therefore it will be done more quickly. Besides, did you notice how quiet and peaceful it is out here?"

The footman laughed and went about cleaning up. Zoe meandered down the long lawn and around the hedges where the target was. Three arrows did not hit their mark and hopefully landed close to where she saw them go. As she wandered through the ornamental fir trees and undergrowth of the less maintained part of the area, she heard a loud rustling from behind her. Too large to be a chipmunk or squirrel, Zoe rose to standing but froze in place, hoping whatever forest beast it was would pass her by. The rustling got closer, until Winn emerged from the denseness of the forest-- jacket slung over his shoulder, cravat hanging on either side of his chest undone, and his shirt hung gaping, exposing his lightly hair-dusted chest for full view.

"Oh, my," Zoe said before she could pull it back. Winn had not noticed her until the words slipped.

"Miss Chase. What in the devil are you doing skulking in the garden?"

"Skulking? Me?" His arrogant tone rode on the same nerve Lord Seller had been dancing on all afternoon. What was it with insufferable British men? "I am helping to find the arrows that overshot during the entertainment today. I might ask why you are skulking in the recesses of the forest half clothed?" She curled her arms at her chest. It gave an air of disgust while hiding the fact that her hands were shaking with a desire to see how soft and springy that hair truly was.

Before Winn could parry with a clever set down, they both heard the familiar whir of an arrow just in time for Winn to yank Zoe from harm's way. The arrow made a solid thunk into one of the fir trees and wobbled, dispersing the energy from the impact.

"I would hope you would be wise enough not to search for loosed arrows whilst someone is still shooting."

Zoe shot Winn a withering look. "Well, of course, I am not searching for arrows while someone is still shooting. Everyone headed back to the house, and it was just me and two doormen left." She only just got the last word out when another arrow followed the first, but this one decidedly set off to the new direction of where they were.

"Jesu, come on," Winn cursed, grabbing her hand and running while ducked down back into the woods. Once under sufficient cover, he turned and began to check her for injuries.

"I am fine. Thank you. I'll appreciate you not manhandling me."

"Right, sorry. You don't appear injured."

"No, I am not. Who would be so foolish to be shooting without checking the safety of the area first?"

"Who, indeed? Stay here," Winn demanded, and crept back out to the edge of the forest at a different angle.

"Who do you see?" Zoe whispered as she came up behind Winn, jumping him. She appreciated all he did was give her a look of reproach and not a lecture.

"No one. They fled."

Winn stood, stepping out into the open, and the two

made their way up the lawn. In the grass lay an abandoned bow and quiver of arrows. They had cleared away all the targets, and no other sign of the afternoon's activities existed. Winn grabbed the weapon, and they walked toward the house together.

"Oh wait, your jacket--" Zoe realized when she looked up and saw his broad shoulders bare, save his shirt.

"No, bother. I'll send someone to fetch it. I do not think it wise for us to terry in the open."

"You are probably correct, if someone was aiming for one of us."

"One of us. Why would someone be aiming for you?" he questioned.

"Well, I believe Lord Seller is sufficiently annoyed with me."

Winn laughed at that. "My guess would be Lord Seller is sufficiently annoyed with more than half the female population at any given time. I don't want to prick your ego, but I'm guessing he has already put you out of his mind for the time being."

"Perhaps I should be more offended than relieved, but I confess to the latter more than the former."

Winn chuckled. At the door leading to the kitchen was a large pile of all the targets and archery equipment waiting to be put away. Winn added the stray to the collection and led her around the house to the main entrance.

"Was there someone helping you find the errant arrows?" Winn asked.

"Yes, a doorman. I don't remember his name."

"So, he abandoned you in the yard without so much as an

explanation?" The question was more an accusation with a hard edge to his voice.

Zoe couldn't help but think this Winn was Lord Burton. Not Winn, the easy-going jokester-- but Lord Burton, the hard, demanding Lord of the Realm.

"I assure you I will deal with that. Now, you most likely want to ready for dinner. I will leave you to it." It was then she realized they were at the foot of the staircase in the entry hall. The man could addle even the most jaded of women's brains, she swore.

"Yes, of course." She turned to leave, but he stalled her with a hand on her arm. She turned back.

"Do not mention this to anyone, please. It would not be prudent to upset the other guests."

"Of course, you are correct."

"Well then, see you at dinner." And he walked from the room.

"My brother tells me you two had some excitement when I left you."

"He told me not to tell anyone," Zoe said with a great deal of annoyance in her voice.

"My brother has many faults, but keeping things from me is not one of them."

"I will bear that in mind."

Cyn smiled and took a drink of her port. "When it comes to you, however, I am not sure he tells me the truth of the matter."

"What is that to mean?"

"Nothing, other than I believe he is interested in you." Cyn put up a hand. "I am aware you have been adamant in your refusal to accept the notion of the two of you because of his lack of respect for his own life, but you have to admit he did not in the least provoke today's incident."

"Yes, well, in that you are correct." Zoe sipped her port and looked around the room to make sure they were far from interested ears. Most everyone else sat at the gaming tables spread around the room or sitting in small groups talking about the outing planned tomorrow to the abbey ruins. "I must admit I am leaning toward this being more of an attempt to harm than a mistake."

"Perhaps it is clearer why we cannot dismiss all of Winn's dangerous encounters as his own doing?"

"It will not help your cause of finding a husband if you continue hiding behind the furniture chatting with your friend," Lady Sarrafinna said as she joined their little group, stopping the tract of the discussion, which Zoe was not at all unhappy about. She must have given Lady Sarrafinna a long-suffering glance because the older woman laughed. "Are you not finding any of the gentlemen present sufficient options?"

"Oh, not that. I like many of the gentlemen present; it is just that..." How did one explain it? "It is just that I am tired of having to work so hard to plan my next comment or making sure I keep my expression serene and friendly."

Both Cyn and Sarrafinna nodded in understanding. "That is understandable. Have any of the gentlemen asked to escort you to the abbey tomorrow?"

"No, but I have not spoken to them since Cyn announced the plans. I would rather not attach myself to one person so that I might converse with many."

"I heard Lord Proctor and Mr. Smythe talking about finding you, so if you would like to avoid that sort of invitation, I would suggest retiring sooner rather than later," Lady Sarrafinna warned.

"I am sorry to interrupt, but I must bid a farewell to my sister." Winn came from nowhere, and all at once, Zoe's senses jumped. He smelled of shave soap and whiskey.

"I thought mother instructed you to be present for the evening activities," Cyn pointed out, annoyance full in her voice.

"She did not state that I had to be the last one abed, though. I played two games of whist and lost both to Seller, who was cheating. I am sure of it. Then I stood while mother and the other chaperones waxed poetic about the upcoming group of debs. I have done my penance, and I beg you to release me."

The women laughed, but it intrigued Zoe. She was certain he was not spending the night at the manor, and hadn't since their last intimate encounter, but where he was staying was a mystery.

"Will you be attending the trip to the abbey tomorrow, Lord Burton?" Lady Sarrafinna asked.

"Yes, mother has insisted to even the numbers, and I am interested in talking with Lord Sutton about the farming technique he is trying on his lands."

"Well, brother, thank you for your suffering this evening," Cyn released him. He bowed to the group, but Zoe couldn't help noticing he never looked away from her, and his eyes burned as his gaze fed from her. Like a touch, she tingled and heated from his attention.

"Zoe was just talking about retiring as well. Would you be a doll and escort her?" Cyn jumped in before he could escape.

"Of course, if you think it will not be untoward to our guests."

"I wouldn't think so, but just in case--" Cyn waved over a doorman. "Please escort Lord Burton and Miss Chase to her rooms. Lord Burton is escorting her on his way to his chambers."

"Of course, my lady."

"Oh, well, good night then. I will see you in the morning." Zoe took the arm Winn offered, and the party of three left the room.

"Escaping as well, I see," Winn said with laughter in his voice.

"No, not escaping. I am just tired."

"That is why you hid behind the furniture, not once taking a turn about the room with a single gentleman?"

"If you were in attendance at all during the day, you would see I have all but ground a rut in your hardwood taking rounds around that room. There is not one more knick knack to be considered that I don't know intimately."

Winn threw back his head and laughed. "My dear, I hope you find your husband during this house party, or you might die from boredom and frustration going into the season."

She loved his laughter and the fact that he was always so quick to laugh at life. It washed over her, making her feel cared for. "Here we are," Winn said, stopping in front of her door.

"Thank you. I will bid you good night then." Zoe did not look into his eyes for fear of getting lost, but the insufferable man would not respond until she did so. What she saw-- the raw desire heating his gaze-- seized her lungs and sent a rush of heat through her. However, Cyn's assigned chaperone took his job seriously and hovered only feet away.

Instead of leaning in for a kiss that Zoe knew they both wanted, Winn raised her hand to his mouth and, turning it over in his hand, placed a lingering kiss in the palm. "Good night, then."

"Yes, good night."

Winn had opened the door and handed her into her room, after which he headed down the hall. How could one gaze and a simple kiss on the hand make her legs refuse to work? She wandered into her room, taking off her gloves and rubbing the spot where the kiss landed, marking her. After a moment, her earlier thoughts about nighttime travels popped back into her head. They were not leaving for the abbey until late morning, so he would have time to return and dress if he so chose.

Zoe rummaged to the bottom trunk in her closet until she found what she was looking for-- a pair of breeches and a cambric shirt she had donned occasionally in the country when her father would bring her to a friend's vineyard for holiday. It was more comfortable walking in the vineyard without worrying about ruining her gowns. Tonight, they would help her follow Winn in the woods with no fear of tearing or getting tangled in brush or trees.

No one downstairs would be the wiser, and once she fed her curiosity, she could come back and slip into her bed. It was foolishness, but something in her had to know. She scolded herself, because this was none of her concern, nor would his whereabouts ever be her concern. He never will be on her list of potential husbands, so this was a ridiculous endeavor, but her brain seemed to not be in charge at this juncture. She sat in a chair by her door, until she heard footfalls coming down the hall that passed her room. Winn.

Once she thought he would reach the servant stairs at the end of the hall, she rose and quietly opened her door. Once sure she was alone, she slipped out of her room, determined to learn more about Lord Burton's nightly endeavors.

CHAPTER ELEVEN

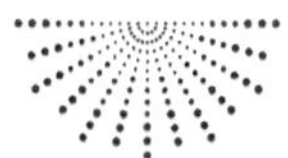

The almost full moon lighted her way onto the lawn and back toward where Winn had come from earlier. She just glimpsed him disappearing down the trail into the woods.

Zoe's soft-soled boots made no noise on the thick carpet of grass, and once she made the trail, the well-worn path was free of debris that might give her away.

Hanging back far enough to keep sight, she watched as he scooped up the jacket forgotten earlier. So he did not send a servant to fetch it. Curious that. Did he not want anyone to know where he was heading off to?

As he walked along with a decided spring in his step, she took the time to admire his physique. Upon last seeing Lord Burton, he was a boy of but one and ten years old. There had been no inkling at the time that his shoulders would broaden so or that his hips would be so trim. Still, she remembered how her heart would flutter when he agreed to partake in some activity with her and Cyn. His eyes had not changed, she decided.

When she looked at Lord Burton as an adult, it was a young, mischievous boy looking back at her. The one always quick with a smile and always ready for a dare.

As they ventured further into the woods, the roar of rushing water consumed her. They were near the river, which ran through the property. As children, they were forbidden anywhere near the river without supervision. In the middle of the summer, it quietly meandered along its path slow enough for them to find a deep pool and stay cool from the summer warmth. But in the spring, with the heavy runoff from the snow, it could prove dangerous.

Ahead she glimpsed him veering from the path to the right. Once there, she followed down another moss-covered stone path leading to a bridge and a hunting lodge in an opening in the forest. She held back and watched as Winn busied himself with cutting and loading his arms with wood before slipping into the two-story cabin, closing the door behind him. After a few moments, the first puffs of smoke cleared the chimney, and the windows lit up as he lit candles. It appeared he was in for the night, but would he be alone, or was he expecting a guest?

"Are you trying to get yourself injured or ruined?" The deep husky voice came out of nowhere. Zoe, despite herself, yelped and jumped forward away from her intruder. When she turned, Winn stood leaning against a large tree trunk, arms folded, and his aristocratic brow risen in annoyance.

"You should not sneak up on people, my lord. Tis very ungamely." Her heart thundering in her chest refused to calm.

"I could say the same, but you were not as adept at sneaking as I. What in the devil are you doing out in the middle of the night dressed... well, dressed like a damned man? I would think today's little adventure would prove to you that all is not as safe as it would appear here at the manor." Winn pushed himself off of the trunk in one fluid motion and sauntered toward her. Her blasted heart picked up its pace.

"I, um, well, you see, I--"

"Don't," Winn had reached her, and before more nonsense came from her mouth, he placed a finger on her lips, silencing her. "Don't lie. If nothing else, our childhood friendship deserves honesty."

"Yes, I was following you. I have been aware since our last," Zoe searched for an appropriate word and landed on, "encounter... you have been leaving the manor every evening. My curiosity got the better of me."

"There. Was that so difficult?" He had gotten closer. How? Zoe couldn't remember him moving, but he was leaning into her now. His face but a breath away from her own. A twig in the distance snapped, bringing them both back to their senses. "Come."

He walked past her and out into the opening. It took Zoe a moment to gather herself and turn to follow. Once inside the lodge, the coolness of the night became plain as the warmth of the cabin stung Zoe's cheeks and seeped into her britches. It was a rather cozy place with comfortable furniture placed around the room, and a large, well-worn table standing in front of the fire. Strewn around the main room were piles of books, some neatly stacked, others more haphazard or fallen over. She picked up a volume closest to her; Comprehensive Collection of Curses and Other Folklore.

She picked up another, and another and all in that pile were a study in curses, witches, and other folklore.

Winn bent to stir the fire then turned to give her a pointed look.

"Have you found anything to comfort you in these?" She couldn't think of anything else to say and decided he wanted honesty. She did not believe in curses and such things. There was a logical explanation for everything if you just dug deep enough.

"Not really. Nothing useful, at least."

"Are all these piles of books research?" she asked, looking around the room, trying to calculate the number of books staring at her.

"Not all, but many are. I keep them here because they upset mother and Cyn. They believe I should just live my life and not give any credence to the curse."

"And you disagree."

The fire beckoned. Zoe warmed her hands, and that is when she noticed the heavenly scent coming from the pot hanging on a hook inside the hearth. She bent in to get a better sniff.

"I believe that a man should be in charge of his destiny. Now whether that be choosing the way of their death or fighting fate, who's to say? Would you like some?" he asked, rising and grabbing two bowls from a shelf on the wall along with two hand-hewn spoons.

"I would. It smells divine. Did cook send it along for you?"

"You wound me. I made this stew myself earlier today. It

has fresh wild vegetables and a freshly caught rabbit. I also have a small kitchen garden out the back with herbs." He pointed behind him to a back door, which she realized he utilized to sneak up on her.

"I apologize. I was not aware you are a culinary master, Lord Burton." She giggled as she bowed before him.

"I would appreciate it if you kept it to yourself. Only Hayhurst knows of my skill. Cyn would never let me off if she found out. Here, I made skillet bread as well."

Winn ladled out a hearty portion of stew and handed her a roll from a rack on the other side of the hearth she hadn't seen. Both took their meal and settled at the large table. Neither spoke for a few spoonfuls, enjoying the hearty fare.

"This may be the best rabbit stew I have ever had."

"Tis the spoon that makes it taste so good. No dingy silver to taint the flavor," he said with a straight face.

"Is that so? In that case, I may announce at the house party that I intend to swap out my husband's family silver for wooden utensils." Winn laughed at her declaration.

"That would be a sight to see all the men deal with that. Please let me know when you plan on doing that, so I can be present."

"You mean not here hiding?" She asked over the buttery skillet bread. They stared off for some time.

"I'm not hiding. I spend a great deal of my time at the lodge as it is. People are just here to see it now."

"No. You are hiding. You didn't spend nights here when I first arrived. Only after our last kiss." She knew it was impolite to point such things out, but she needed to know who he was lying to, her or himself.

"I am giving you space," he answered, but bent back to his meal without making eye contact.

"Space for what?"

"To find a husband. That is why you are here, why they all are here. I am not looking for a wife, so it would be unfair of me to dally around taking time you could spend..." He trailed off without finishing his thought.

"What? Kissing other men?"

"Perhaps, if that is what you choose. I haven't given you a choice as I remember, so it would be a nice turn of events for you."

The fire popped, and Winn went back to eating, done with the conversation.

"I've been kissed before, you know. You are not the first and any kisses thus far that I have accepted have not been forced-- Including yours."

"I won't marry you."

She stared hard at him. They both wanted the same thing. The air was thick with the attraction. Electric. She had not and would not try to trick him into marriage. Besides, she already set him off her list because of his wild ways.

"I never asked you to marry, and frankly, you are not on my list of possible husbands. If we kissed until dawn, I would not want a proposal from you."

"Well, that will hearten my reserve on long winter nights," he said dryly, then chuckled and shook his head.

"I did not say I wasn't attracted to you. I am very much. I am just certain we would not suit day to day. Zoe Chase is too dull for your interest to remain over time, and I do not care for your lackadaisical respect for your life and safety."

"Miss Chase, I hope that you are not proposing a

dalliance before you choose a husband," He said with mock horror, but Zoe couldn't ignore the desire banked in his eyes, not unlike the fire crackling behind her.

She chose not to answer and gave her attention to her meal. After selecting a husband, she would not have a lover. To her, once married, one was loyal to their spouse. But as long as she did not ruin herself completely, there was no reason not to indulge with Winn. Perhaps if she spent time with him, it would help to calm the thoughts that would pop in her head, when such things should not be popping.

"You cannot be serious," Winn said with shock and perhaps anger in his voice. "It would ruin you."

"For heaven's sake, I am not suggesting we go as far as all that, but I am also certain there are--" How does one say such things in a ladylike fashion? "Activities couples can partake in that do not lead to ruin." She waited for his reply, which did not come. He continued to stare at her with a strange mix of confusion, desire, and something else that she couldn't put into words, but that wrapped her in a sensual fog. His spoon remained half-raised with broth dripping back into the bowl. "Well, say something."

He blinked. Then he blinked again, finally letting his hand put the spoon back into the bowl. He leaned back in the chair with his hands resting on the table. "I am not sure what to say or do. I should throw you over my shoulder and return you to the manor in your room, alone. Safe."

Zoe's heart was beating in her chest, and her breathing was ragged. Perhaps she misplaced her attraction for a mutual feeling. If so, she just made an utter fool of herself and could never greet him in public. He rose and walked around the table to the fire, where he added a few pieces. He then turned and took her by the shoulders, leading her out of the chair to her feet.

"If I was wrong--" She started hoping to end her suffering in the silence.

"Oh no, you don't. You do not get to put such a suggestion into the ether then attempt to retract it from embarrassment."

"Well, if I was mistaken and you are not attract--"

He cut her off again with his lips crushing her own. This kiss was as crushing and overpowering as the first night when he was in his cups. All of Winn's ballroom manners were absent. He took from her all he wanted. When he pulled her to him, what air she was reserving in her lungs came out a whoosh. The thin cambric shirt she wore gave no protection to her breasts as her dresses did. She felt the roughness of his jacket rubbing, sending heat with every scrape of her nipples. She groaned low in her throat, and it broke the spell. Winn broke the kiss and set her aside only to grab her arms again when she teetered from the onslaught of sensations.

"I am fine. Truly, you can let me go. Sorry." She stood silently running her fingers across her bruised lips, willing the sensation to remain. "You are correct. This is not a good idea."

"I did not say this was a bad idea. I am not certain it is a good one either, however," he said, turning from her, making the distance between them greater. Zoe stood the silence for as long as she was able.

"So, what say you, Lord Burton, to this next adventure? This new challenge?"

Winn stood in his oasis, his private sanctuary where he could be himself and nothing more or less, staring at his current problem, Zoe Chase. Perhaps his version of the family curse would kill him with desire. He wanted nothing more at the moment than to take her right there in front of the fire. Every muscle in his body taut with but one aim.

If he took her up on her suggestion-- which by every fiber of his lineage as a lord of the realm, told him no-- but if he did, would he have the control to stop short of her total ruination?

He moved around the room because not moving was proving uncomfortable. His lips still throbbed from his kiss, which was neither soft nor loving. It was hungry and demanding-- and Zoe met him at his game and kept the pace. Never having been so affected by a woman, he should run.

This battle of wills was a constant tragedy running through his thoughts from the moment he ran her over in the road. He would not marry. He refused to leave a young wife, with possibly an heir to this cruel world when he died, and he *would* die. At this point, he was becoming less sure it was a curse, but until he could figure out who was behind it, there was still a good chance he would meet his fate.

At the same time, saying no to Miss Chase was not a talent he possessed. He was not born with that particular skill and honestly, did not care to acquire it. If he could die after seeing her face in the throes of release, he would be able to meet his maker with a smile.

"If I were to agree to such a scheme, we would need rules."

"Rules?" she asked with her usual caution. It made Winn smile. Nothing would ever be comfortable with her.

"Yes, all the best dalliances have them. It protects both parties and their interests," he said, facing her from across the table. Not an insurmountable barrier, but one that would require significant effort to launch over.

"Are you well versed in dalliances then?" He noted the tremor in her voice. He didn't want her to think ill of him, but he couldn't allow her to fall in love with him and abandon her search for a husband.

"Well enough, yes."

"Oh, well, then what are our rules?" This time a hint of sadness in her voice hit him in the chest. He cleared his throat and pushed on, ignoring his own growing emotions.

"Well, for starters, if I get word from anyone that you seem not to be interested in finding a husband any longer or that you are rejecting all eligible suitors, I shall cut ties with you at once."

The look she shot him was instant and impactful. "I beg your pardon? You do not have a right to dictate my life choices, sir. I am a grown woman." Winn thought her hands planted on her hips was a good tactic.

"Madame, you misunderstand. I am protecting myself. I have informed you that I will not marry, but I am nothing if not a gentleman. So if you were to get attached to me, I would feel obligated to make sure I protected you. It has been my experience that people rarely realize they have fallen until they are too far gone to do anything about it. This will make sure that does not happen."

"Very well. Do I get to make a rule?"

"Of course."

"Then, you are no longer allowed to avoid the house party during the day. You will attend every event or activity your mother and sister have planned, and you will take part."

Winn felt his jaw clench. If he were to be involved with Zoe in the evenings and forced to be witness to her flirting and courting with all the men at the party during the day, it would be madness that killed him. "Fine, but if my estate falls into ruin, it will be on your conscience."

"Any other rules, Lord Burton?"

"For starters, when we are alone, I am Winn. Not my lord, or Lord Burton. Winn. And when we are alone, I will call you Zoe." She nodded. "And, I will dictate the meeting times, places, and limitations. However, if we are doing something you dislike, you are to speak immediately, no virgin modesty or apprehensions."

"Why do you get to choose?"

"Because I know the workings of the estate, and if we are to keep your reputation intact, they cannot find us out."

"Very well," she said, making her way around the table in a slow sashay. His mouth went dry, watching her hips sway in the tight-fitting trousers. Women must wear dresses to save men from insanity. "Now what?" she asked as she walked up to him and laid her small delicate hand on his chest. Her large green eyes filled with specks of amber lighted by the firelight looked up at him.

Without saying a word, Winn lifted her and sat her on the table while he stood between her opened legs. "This is as good a place to start as any." He bent his head and again took her in a kiss — this one he controlled more, sending her into a fog of desire.

His hands did not remain idle. He worked on the buttons of Zoe's shirt to free her breasts that were not bound by any stays or covered by a chemise. He slid the shirt to the table and stepped back to see her bare from the waist up. Just as he had imagined, she was perfect. He stepped back into the circle of her arms and dipped his tongue into her sweet mouth, but this time both hands covered her breasts. She was as responsive as he knew she would be. Her nipples puckered in his palms, and her weight leaned into him more.

"Mmm," she let her head fall back, and he replaced one hand with his mouth. She arched toward him, and he took all she offered. He moved to the other breast. A shot of liquid desire shot through him when she wound both hands in his hair, holding him to his task. Damn, she was responsive to his touch, but unfortunately, his body reacted in kind.

Breaking from the embrace, Winn stepped back, trying to drag in enough air to not pass out. This might prove more difficult than he thought as he took in her form sitting, legs open and arms leaned back, still naked and on full view. Zoe's eyes were ablaze and heavy-lidded with her own need. Her hair was loose and wild around her shoulders. This was a vision he would use to get through his days once she was no longer his.

"Well, that was pleasant, but tis time to get you back before you are missed."

"I won't be missed until morning. I called my maid off earlier in the day for her nightly duties. She won't check on me until the morning." The look of disappointment was almost enough to send his newly minted rules to ash, but he could not.

"That is good, but we don't want to overstimulate you on our first encounter. If you leave now wanting more, you will be enthusiastic next time."

"I thought the purpose of a dalliance was mutual satisfaction. How do I know if I am satisfied?"

"We will get to that, my dear, no need to be so greedy, love." He stepped forward and lifted her shirt back onto her shoulders as she bent to buttoning it. Winn understood her frustration in needing satisfaction. It was clear for the foreseeable future he would need to bring himself to his own release. Sighing at the thought, Winn lifted her from the table to her feet. "Shall we?" he asked, offering her exit into the cool night air.

"When will we meet again?" she asked.

"Hold on." This was a bad idea, the worst, but it didn't matter. He ran into the lodge and came out with a key. "This opens the back door. I will send you a message when it is safe, and this will allow you access if I am not here yet."

She took the key after looking at it with a mix of excitement and trepidation. "Thank you. When will I hear from you then?"

"I haven't figured this out yet, but I will." He walked past her to get some distance and so he didn't ogle her hips swaying in the moonlight all the way back to the manor. His home stood dark and silent in the wee hours of the morning, but Winn would not chance her reputation.

"This way," he whispered, leading her along a path next to the lawn, to the side door of the house. "Do you remember this door?" he asked in hushed tones.

"Yes, it leads to the stairs for the servants. It will come out in the gallery."

"Good. Now quick, quiet feet, my lady." He kissed her on the forehead and opened the door for her to slip in. As soon as the door closed, leaving him alone, it hit him. "Tis a good thing, I am so concerned about her not falling in love with me because it would be a losing endeavor for myself," Winn said to the wind. He was in some genuine trouble. Trouble that if an early death didn't come soon, he was confident he would spend the rest of his life wishing he had.

CHAPTER TWELVE

It was clear why Winn made her promise she would continue her search for a husband at the house party. Not that she had any plans to quit her husband search, but with Winn present at all the house party activities, she might well leave off her flirting. It was at the least embarrassing and at the most, humiliating.

Winn sat on the lawn with his sister and Lord Sutton staring at her while she played pall mall with the group. He watched her interact with every man on the field. She decided if he was cheeky enough to give her pointers the next time they met she would box his ears — insufferable man.

"I say, Miss Chase, is there a sport or physical activity you are not exceptional at?" Lord Seller asked, his frustration evident.

"Yes, I am not good at riding, Lord Seller. I love horses, but never had much need in Rome for practicing."

"Pity," said Lord Hayhurst, "riding is one of life's true pleasures."

"I am afraid I will have to take your word on the subject," she answered.

"I love riding," Miss Lightfoot interjected. "My papa gave me my first pony before I could walk."

"And you, Lady Sutton? Were you able to learn to ride while abroad?" Hayhurst turned to include their newest arrival.

"I adore riding. My sister and I were taught on Arabians. I am getting used to the more docile creatures here in England." She looked down and patted her rounded belly. "Well, for the time being, I am not riding at all." Everyone laughed.

"Well then, I will just have to resign myself to doing tolerably well at Pall Mall," Zoe declared. She doubted she would ever be comfortable atop a horse and did not see it as any great loss. "If you will excuse me, I would like some refreshments." She made her way to the table, groaning with picnic fare.

"I can't help but notice Lord Burton has become a fan of lawn games." Lady Sarrafinna came alongside her, making her jump. "I am sorry, my dear, I did not intend to startle you."

"No, it is not you. I am not fully myself today," she said, putting a glass of punch to her lips. "He is spending time with Cyn. It is good to see."

"Indeed." Lady Sarrafinna nodded with an expression telling Zoe she would have to do better than that.

"Excuse me," Lady Sutton came alongside them, and all

the ladies stopped and curtsied. "I just want to make sure I didn't offend you."

"Me? Oh, heavens, no," Zoe answered with her warmest smile. "Please walk with us."

A cheer went up on the field, making everyone glance to see. Zoe considered making a run for it. Lady Sarrafinna intrigued her. She knew her mother, and they were friends, but nothing more. Her parents never spoke of England and their life before marriage.

"Who is working their way to the top of your list thus far?"

Zoe understood she was changing the subject as not to embarrass her. "Oh, well, I'm not sure any are rising as much as some are sinking."

Sarrafinna and Lady Sutton laughed at that, and Lady Sarrafinna locked her arm in Zoe's, taking a turn around the lawn. "That is one way, I suppose, to choose a husband, but that does not show me a passion for one particular man. I am certain your mother and your father want you to marry for love and passion, not taking the one who is the least desirable."

"You are correct, of course," she agreed. "But I can't imagine a great love or passion appears overnight. It should begin as a list of common interests and easy conversation, and from there, it will grow."

"Love can form that way, but love with great passion is not like an ember that burns slowly. It is more like a firecracker that explodes in your mind and body and changes your perspective forever."

"How so?"

"When I was a girl, my father brought me to Vauxhall gardens, and I saw my first fireworks display. I can not gaze at the night sky even today without seeing how it would be improved by a firework or two. Passion creates a situation where once you have a taste, you will forever search for it again. And if it slips through your hands, you will be forever changed, and no experience will be as dazzling as it could have been."

The last was said with a knowing that made Zoe's heart ache for the courtesan. Did she have a great passion and lose it? Has she spent the rest of her life wishing for it? Zoe had no experience with such pain because her parents were in love. They were true partners.

"I have read that passion fades. It burns fast and dies even quicker."

"Come now, darling. You were raised in Rome. Italians are passionate about everything in their lives. You must have been witness to marriages of great passion."

She supposed she had and just never found it something worth noting. As a girl, one is not considering passion in her marriage.

Lady Sutton did not offer any advice on the subject, but walked and listened.

"Lord Burton, Lord Sutton, would you care to stretch your legs and take a turn with us?"

Before Zoe could form the protest, Winn was on his feet, and Lord Sutton was at his wife's side.

"Please, call me Max. I hate formalities of any kind," Lord Sutton said.

"Very well, Max. How are you liking being back in society?" Lady Sarrafinna asked as the small group meandered around the tables set for luncheon.

"Like a too tight smelly boot," he responded and gained a swat from his wife on his arm.

Lady Sarrafinna laughed, a musical sound. "I know that shoe well. I may have the match to yours. 'Tis a burden we must bear, but you are the luckiest of us all, you have your beautiful wife to guide you.

Max nodded, "She is the only reason I have returned. I spend most of my time trying not to do anything to embarrass her."

The warmth from Winn's arm spread up her arm as she listened to Max talk of his wife with such love. Passion may very well burn here before this house party came to a close. Just his general nearness sent shivers along her spine. Her nipples puckered at the remembered attention the night before.

"I was just discussing the importance of choosing the right marriage partner. Lord Burton, don't you agree?" Lady Sarrafinna turned on Winn and his face colored.

Zoe lost a step fearing Lady Sarrafinna would use the word passion. She might well burn up in her shoes if she had. Winn looked over to check she was steady before answering.

"Oh, I would agree. I am not searching, but if I were, I could not bind myself to someone I did not pair well with."

"Will you be attending Parliament this season?" Lady Sarrafinna changed the subject.

"Yes, that is the plan. It is a responsibility I take seriously."

"Max?" Lady Sarrafinna asked.

"I will. I had not decided, but I have been persuaded," he said again, looking at his wife. If there was one thing children of diplomats dispatched abroad were well versed in, it was politics.

"Miss Chase, are you current on the major items to be faced by Parliament this season?" Sarrafinna asked. Many of the other guests had left the game and were joining the conversation.

"Not as well as I would like. I have been begging the servants for the news sheets once the gentlemen are finished with them, but either they are not taking my request seriously, or they do not believe it is suitable for me."

Lord Burton stopped the little procession and looked down at her with serious eyes, "Why didn't you ask me?"

"I didn't care to bother you and feared you might consider it not appropriate. I am sure it will not take me long to come up to snuff once in London."

They continued their walk and made it back to where Cyn sat under a parasol smiling brightly up at them. Zoe broke from the group and took the chair Winn had been occupying. "Thank you, Lady Sarrafinna, for the chance to stretch my legs."

"You are most welcome, dear. I hope we will have time to talk later. Now, I must check on Lord Worth and see if he is up from his nap. He so hates the long travel to get to the country. He takes time to recoup."

Max and Lady Sutton made their way up the lawn to the shade of the house as well.

The group said their farewells, and Winn also jumped in with his excuse for leaving. Zoe couldn't help but smile at the fact he had not made it one full day without hiding away. "I too must bid you farewell for a time. I have some matters to attend to in my study but will be back for drinks in the parlor."

"Well, now that they are gone. What on earth was Lady Sarrafinna doing? Playing matchmaker?"

"Perhaps. Lady Sarrafinna sees something between us that isn't there, I fear, just the familiarity of childhood friends," Zoe said, hoping it sounded surer than it felt.

Cyn's expression said she knew more than she let on. "Well, I will say that Mr. Smythe certainly knew of your time with Winn. If nothing else, my brother's decision to be more present in the day to day has sparked even more interest in you from the others."

Zoe's cheeks flooded with heat. "Why on earth would Winn's decision to be an active participant in the house party make me more interesting?"

"Because dear, they think Winn is interested in you, and they are all aware of his choice to remain unattached. If we can persuade him to take an interest, then you must be more."

"Hm," Zoe understood the logistics of it, but she didn't care to be a prize fish at a market. She had nothing constructive that would not make her frustrations clear, so she just sat contemplating the others milling about eating, and she noted that Miss Lightfoot and Lord Seller found a kite they were preparing to launch. She considered her feelings about seeing one of her suitors with another woman. Nothing. It did not send any emotional response whatsoever to her brain. In fact, they made quite a handsome couple.

Zoe was exhausted from the previous night ,and having to keep track of all the men and make sure she didn't show favoritism to one over another yet didn't help.

"If you will excuse me, Cyn, I would like to go rest a bit before the party moves into the parlor."

"Are you feeling well?" Concern filled her friend's voice.

"Oh, yes, quite. I am just tired. I did not sleep well last night, and I wish to be at my best later."

Assured there was no chance Cyn would start showing her undue attention and muck up her plans with Winn, she excused herself and found solace in her room. Laying on the bed, staring up at the canopy, she replaced Lord Burton in the scenario with Miss Lightfoot. Her response was swift and unsettling. Her chest tightened, and the air in her lungs seized at the idea of seeing Winn with another woman. It was a good thing she decided she chose to have a dalliance with a man who vowed never to marry. She could grow to a ripe old age with her soon to be husband and never have to watch Winn across a ballroom cater to his wife.

Zoe turned to the window and noticed a package on the table next to the reading chair. That was not there when she left her room this morning. She jumped off the bed and sat in the chair with the package in her lap. It was wrapped in plain brown paper but tied with a white ribbon and a sprig of lavender. She inhaled the lovely scent.

Setting the lavender aside, she untied the package and the paper fell open, revealing what must be at least the last month's worth of news sheets from London. They had been newly ironed and organized by date.

Winn.

Tears sprang to her eyes, and her heart flipped. Damn him for being considerate. She could not become attached--but she had made the same complaint to every man at the house party, and none of them even offered to hunt down the most current one. Most dismissed it, and a choice pair said they would hate for her to gain a headache from all the thinking it would involve. Those were the two that had sunk to the bottom at the moment. Winn acted. He was not asked and had nothing to gain by doing such a kind thing.

She opened the first, most recent news sheet from this morning's post to find a white vellum note slid inside.

'Tonight. Use your key.'

He didn't even sign his name, but he didn't need to. If she didn't get some rest, she was apt to fall asleep and never meet him. Zoe left the news sheets to go back to later and cuddled down, anticipating what Winn had in store for them that evening. She fell asleep with the knowledge this would not end well, no matter what they both told themselves.

It was wise Zoe asked her maid to make sure she woke in time to dress for drinks in the parlor. When her maid woke her, she didn't remember falling asleep.

"Miss Chase," Lord Ruthaford greeted her as she entered the parlor, all smiles and kind words. "I looked for you after Pall Mall, but Lady Burton told me you went to rest. I hope you are feeling as radiant as you look."

She allowed him to take her hand and lead her into the room. "Yes, I am much improved. Sometimes a nap is just the thing one needs."

"Oh, I agree. When I am at home, I do like a nap now and again. Would you like some wine or port, perhaps?"

"Wine would be lovely, thank you."

Lord Ruthaford deposited her near an open window,

letting a warm breeze circulate through the room. She got a whiff of lavender and immediately searched the room until she found Winn, who had been staring at her. She mouthed her thanks, and he nodded, tipping his glass in her direction, then turned back to Lord Hayhurst, Lord Sutton, and Mr. Smythe.

"Here you are."

"Oh, thank you." Lord Ruthaford stood with his drink in hand, waiting for her to start the conversation.

"Are you attending Parliament this season, Lord Ruthaford?"

"Yes, of course. Several topics need to be considered seriously."

"Lord Burton said much the same thing. I am less aware of the governmental issues of England than I am of Rome."

"It must have been fascinating to be raised learning so much about a foreign country," he said, with genuine interest in his voice. For the first time, someone was listening to her. Other than Winn-- she stopped cold. Winn did not count. He was not on her list, and she was not on his. As much as she enjoyed their time together, it was not prudent to include him in her contrasts of other eligible men.

"Lady Sarrafinna, how are you this evening?" Ruthaford greeted her as she joined them. Zoe came out of her head and curtsied.

"Very well, thank you, Ruthaford."

"And how is Lord Worth? I know he detests long travel."

Lady Sarrafinna smiled. Zoe decided this was a man Lady Sarrafinna cared about. She had not asked Cyn much about her, but her curiosity was getting the better of her.

"He is doing well, but not ready to appear just yet. Perhaps tomorrow."

"Good. I haven't spoken to Worth since the last time I was in London. It will be good to catch up."

"Have you met him, Miss Chase?" Ruthaford asked

"No, I have not had the pleasure."

"Oh, you will adore him. Well versed in politics and for his age, he is open to women's ideas about such things."

"I am certain he will find you enchanting, my dear. He is looking forward to meeting you. I have told him about you," Lady Sarrafinna assured her.

"I look forward to meeting him, as well."

"Miss Chase, not to change the subject, but I have to leave in the morning for business but will return in two days. I was wondering if you would do me the honor of pairing with me for cards after dinner tonight since I will not have the opportunity to enjoy your company until my return?"

"I would like that, thank you for asking."

"Very well," the young lord said. He tipped his drink to his lips, but it didn't hide his smile. She quite liked him.

This meant, however, she could not come across as distant or distracted, and already she was looking forward to her other evening entertainment.

"If you will excuse me, I need to speak with Lord Burton about something before I leave." He bowed to both women, then left to join what was beginning to be all the men in the room.

"Well, that was promising," Sarrafinna said.

"Yes, I quite like him. He seems kind."

"He is. I would give my approval if you chose him. There are many good qualities in him."

"Yes, I think so as well," Zoe agreed, catching herself staring at Winn when she should have been staring at the man standing next to him. "I do hope to find someone here, so I do not have to begin this again in London."

"That would be fortuitous, I agree, but no need to worry too far ahead. We will find you the right husband, I promise." She sipped what looked like whiskey in a glass. Not a lady-like drink to be sure, but Zoe decided it suited her. Perhaps once wed, and no longer forced to be the epitome of an innocent maid, she too would make her drink of choice whiskey. What would Lord Ruthaford think of that? She sipped her wine and decided he would like it just fine.

Cyn joined their little group with Lady Sutton in tow. "This is why house parties are so difficult to host. The men never understand that the purpose of these activities is not to find a corner and talk about those things men do."

"Oh, let them be dear. They have all done well to play the pretty all day with our sex. They will be more agreeable after dinner if you allow them some time. Besides, it does not appear any of the eligible young ladies are neglected."

"I know I am not feeling ignored. I quite like the space," Zoe admitted.

"Of course you do," Cyn said dryly, "I blame my brother. It is him all the men are drawn to. When he is not in attendance, they are all more agreeable."

The women laughed at that and spent the rest of the time before everyone quit the room for dinner, talking about how Zoe's list was coming along and the fact that Lord Ruthaford was an excellent choice to lead the race.

Zoe waited in the hallway for Cyn to give directions for the set up of the parlor after dinner to the footmen. She had no desire to get caught by either Mr. Smythe or Lord Seller on her way to ready for dinner.

"Did you see the note in the package I left for you?" Winn's voice from behind her made the two glasses of wine she consumed dance and flutter her mind.

"Yes, I did, and thank you so much. It was thoughtful of you."

"Yes, it was, wasn't it?" Winn whispered with a gravelly tone to his voice.

"I will not be there when you arrive, but the fire will be going, and there will be wine. I will arrive as soon as I am able."

She nodded, not sure what she could say.

"I am excited to continue where we stopped. You will enjoy what I have planned for us."

"Winn, weren't you leaving?" Cyn stepped out of the parlor just as Zoe thought she might burn to the floor. Desire sent a thick haze to her brain, mixing with the wine. How was she to ever get through cards this evening with his words dancing in her mind? Drat him.

"I am. I was just giving Miss Chase some pointers on cards this evening. Don't forget, my mother cheats horribly," he said to her, making her smile when she looked up. He gave her a wink with Cyn still at his back.

"I was aware, but thank you for the warning. If I do bet anything, I will make sure whatever I lay as a bet belongs to you."

Winn bowed to her and his sister and left.

"Shall we?" Cyn asked, and both women headed to dinner. Tonight would prove to be a lesson in patience, Zoe was sure.

CHAPTER THIRTEEN

The night air cooled Zoe's cheeks as she followed the path behind the shrubs lining the lawn. It was easy, because the house was still ablaze with light, unlike their return last night when everyone was asleep.

As soon as she could whisk herself from the activities, which wasn't until the elder Lady Burton declared the games over, she found her room and called for her maid. Not wanting to start talk below stairs, she knew it was impossible to call her off two nights in a row. She claimed a headache from all the card play so that the girl would not dally and allow her to get some rest. The moment the maid closed her door, Zoe was out of bed and changing clothes.

After being around people most of the day, the silence in the forest enveloped her like a blanket. She took the time to consider her current action — nothing about this made sense. At the worst end of outcomes, they would get caught. No matter what they were doing, it would spell disaster.

Winn would do the right thing and marry her, she was sure of that, but he would never love her. No, she would choose not to marry. It worked for Lady Sarrafinna, after all. She would not trap Winn and cause him to see her as his demise. At the less public, but no less devastating side of the coin, they do not get caught and the house party ends, thus ending their little game. Zoe must find a husband. Which would be fine, but the one sticking point is the matter of her emotions.

She came into the clearing and she could smell the smoke from the chimney, but the other parts of the house were dark. Zoe made her way around to the side door and used the key Winn gave her. Inside she fumbled around, still not familiar with items. Her mind was otherwise occupied last night. In the open main room, once she lit the candles on the table, her heart stopped racing, as there were not as many strange shapes and shadows playing tricks on her.

Not sure how long it would be until Winn arrived, she settled in and read. Going to one stack of books, she plucked one off the top and sat to read it. It was titled *The Mystery of the Burton Family Curse*. Oh, Lord, there had been a book written? As she read, she noted lines underlined with ink and notes made in the margins, with other scraps of paper saving pages. Zoe realized Winn was studying how his father, grandfather, and great grandfather died.

It was quite a mystery, she admitted. How could three men in three different generations all die before their thirtieth year? Turning back to the beginning of the book, she started from page one, a history of the Burton title and name. She read, taking the time to read any notes, and tried to consider what Winn may have been thinking.

"Good evening." A deep voice filled the air.

Zoe jumped. "Oh, my. I am sorry I didn't hear the door." She looked up and realized right away the deep voice did not belong to Winn. "Lord Hayhurst, I ah--"

He raised a hand. "Your secret is safe. Winn sent me. There has been an incident."

"Incident? Is anyone hurt?" She sat up, the book forgotten.

"No, thankfully, that was not the outcome, but he asked that I escort you back to the house. I just need to put the fire out first."

He crossed the room and quenched the fire. "We will have to wait a bit to make sure it doesn't rekindle."

"Yes, of course," Zoe answered, feeling very exposed.

"I am loyal to Winn, Miss Chase. I have no intention of letting your time with him escape. It is none of my business, and as long as I see Winn happy, that is all I care about."

"Of course, I never considered--"

"Yes, you did, and you would not be such a smart girl if you didn't. All Winn said was that you and he were meeting at the lodge, and I needed to get you. I know Winn enough to know he is not particularly excited about ruining young women, and I know how much respect he holds for you."

Zoe could do nothing but nod, the emotion caught in her throat. After a moment of silence, she changed the subject. "So, what was the incident?"

Hayhurst gave her a harsh look. His jaw tightened. "Winn and I had just left the office of his solicitor. The man regularly rides to London and planned to deliver some correspondence for us." He turned to stir the fire again and douse it a second time. "As our carriage made its way back along the road leading to the manor, a bull came charging from a nearby pasture, jumped the wall, and rammed our carriage, breaking an axle. Then the beast continued to ram the rig, so we could not escape, and the driver could not set us free. I will admit it was rather unsettling.

"Oh my. What are the chances of such a thing?" Zoe said with horror. "It is amazing either of you survived."

He gave a bitter chuckle, "I will not say I do not put my life in danger being friends with Burton, but it is never dull."

She then remembered the book on her lap. "Is there any chance this could have been the curse?"

Silence filled the room, and Zoe decided Hayhurst would not answer. "I would like to hope no. I have been steadfast that there is no such thing as a curse. However, when these things happen to Winn, I must admit it becomes more difficult to set that theory aside."

"Have they caught the bull?"

"Yes, the owner was called, and a group of men got it corralled. They are housing it in a rock grain silo for tonight. Once there is adequate light tomorrow, we will examine him."

"What will you be looking for?"

"Perhaps he was wounded or poisoned. There are some plants and roots that, if eaten in enough quantity, could make an animal wild. We will have to search the field."

"Do you think this was an accident?"

He rose, satisfied the fire would not relight, and snuffed the candles, plunging them into darkness. "I am not sure. I do not want to consider that someone is trying to kill my closest friend, but at least that gives us something to fight. A curse leaves us with very little recourse."

She felt his arm on her shoulder, and she stood, tucking

the book under her arm and taking his hand with her other. He led the way outside and back to the house. Once the house came into view, she noted there were still many lights on, more than should be. She looked at Hayhurst. "If I try to sneak to my room, I may be caught."

He smiled a smile reminding her of Winn's mischievous grin. They suited one another. Hayhurst was blond and a foot taller, with a very slender build, while Winn was dark and still tall, but not as so, and his build was broader, more substantial.

"Follow me," he said, and they continued around the house to what looked like just another panel on the side of the framing. But when Lord Hayhurst pushed it in a particular place, it popped open. "A priest hole. This leads to Winn's chamber. He said to tell you there was a dress in the chair. He cautioned to make sure the hallway was empty before leaving his room."

Zoe nodded because her mouth was as dry as if she had a mouthful of cotton. He gave her a small shove, and the door shut behind her, taking the light with it. She felt around, and in front of her was a staircase. She wound up the tight staircase, using the wall for support, and decided total darkness was preferable to seeing all the things that might be in the stairs with her. At the top, a small sliver of light broke through at the bottom of a door. Sure enough, Zoe emerged into the dressing closet of Lord Burton. On the chair lay a very respectable nightdress and a robe, perhaps Cyn's. Quickly, she dressed and then made her way through his room to the hallway door. She listened for some time before deciding it was safe, and peaked out a sliver of an opening. Everything was clear. Zoe hurried down the hall until she was in a spot that would not cause questions.

After dressing into a serviceable gown and pinning her hair, she made her way to the family parlor, but it was empty. That must mean guests are also involved. She descended the stairs and heard raised voices as soon as halfway down. When she entered Winn's study, it was filled with guests and family alike.

"Oh, dear. I was hoping we would wake no one else. I am so sorry." Cyn met her at the door, all concern.

"Tis no bother, what has everyone in such a state?"

Making eye contact with Hayhurst, who had made his way back and next to Winn, he hid a small smile. Her cheeks burned, wondering what Winn told him about their meeting at the lodge. She had not considered what would happen if someone found out.

"There has been an accident," Cyn explained with stark worry on her face. Zoe realized at that moment what a toll this family curse was taking on them all. She enveloped her friend in an embrace.

"Is everyone safe?" she asked, already knowing the answer.

"We are all hail," Winn answered her from across the room, lifting his glass. That was met with all glasses raised and a resounding "here, here" by the collective.

Winn drained his glass and made his way to where they were standing.

"I am sorry to have inconvenienced you this evening," he said, looking down at her with an odd expression. "Thank you for coming down to check on us."

"I am just thankful no one was hurt."

"It was a blessing, that is for sure."

Winn's expression grew darker, and his eyes filled with desire. He was thinking about their lost moment, and his eyes on her made her hot and uncomfortable.

"Well, if everything is well and there is nothing more to do here, I will find my bed again, my lord." She curtsied.

"You make a good point, Miss Chase. There is nothing more anyone can do before the dawn. I wish you a good night's sleep." Winn reached down and kissed her hand.

Zoe said her goodnights to Cyn and a few others close by and made her way back to the family suite. It was miraculous that no one was hurt, but she still couldn't help but feel cheated for her night's plans. The room was dark but lighting a candle would be a waste. She found her way to the bed and laid down on the large mattress. What was she doing continuing such a foolhardy game?

When Hayhurst entered and told her of the crash, her body froze, and fear chilled her bones. Winn not being in the world was worse than her living in a world where he still existed, but she was married to another. She would be happy being away from him, but she couldn't live if he were no longer on the earth. She was lost, and she knew it. Her emotions were engaged long before this night.

The doorknob turned and she lay still, praying it was Winn and Winn alone. The choice to retire to his bedroom was decided when he looked at her in the parlor, but the thought of his valet was not one she considered until this very moment. She heard the door shut, then three footfalls that stopped in the middle of the room. She lay there a moment, then sat up.

In the room's darkness, Winn stood still and large in the

space, staring at her. He said nothing and made no move to go to her. The shame covered her like a blanket. She should never have thought this a good idea. Winn was an upstanding man. He was sure not to bring his dalliances into his home. Feeling the weight of her sadness, she slipped off the bed and attempted to leave him.

"I am sorry, this was very presumptuous of me, and I see now what a bad idea it was. I will leave you, my lord."

She made her way to the door, but as she went to pass him, he reached out a hand and pulled her to the side and into his large form. He said nothing but leveled her with a kiss. This one was not demanding, but tender. After a long moment, he released her lips and pulled her into him in a strong embrace. They did not speak, just stood there and held each other.

"Thank you," he whispered into her hair after a long moment. "I had feared my chance to spend time with you was killed this evening, but it is hazardous for you to be here. What if my valet followed me to help me get ready for bed?"

"Yes, well, I may not have thought that many steps ahead. For that, I apologize. I should not have come."

"I am glad you did," he said, kissing her on the top of the head. He released her and lit a few candles, then took off his cravat. His coat was off him by the time she made it to the parlor. Winn disappeared into his changing room and came out wearing a loose pair of sleeping pants and a wrapper tied at the waist.

Zoe's mouth went dry, and her skin heated from her toes. Perhaps she could convince herself it was not her emotions that were engaged, but her physical reaction to his male beauty. She cleared her throat and returned to the bed, sitting on its edge. She hoped Winn at least had an ounce of control because she knew she did not.

Winn watched Zoe cross his bedroom and perch on the edge of his bed. When she left the parlor to find her bed, the loss cut through him. It took all his strength not to reach out and pull her into his arms. After that, his next drink turned flat on his tongue, and he depressed at the thought of finding his cold bed alone.

Yet, here she sat. No other woman would be so bold. When he entered his room and saw her on the bed, he froze, not sure she was real. His first thought when the bull rammed his carriage was of Zoe being stranded at the lodge alone.

Now, sitting on the edge of his massive bed that dwarfed her, he was overcome by how dainty she was. Every part of her was feminine and small. The urge to protect her surged in him. He should send her back to her room. It was dangerous enough for them to meet at the lodge. The danger of them being caught amplified in the manor, in the middle of a damned house party. Then there was the need to protect her from him. Would he be able to stop before he ruined her tonight? Making matters worse, right now, he wasn't sure he cared. The idea of seeing her every night when he entered his chamber sent a calm through his body.

"I am glad you came here, but you must understand how foolhardy this is."

"Yes," she answered. "But I needed to be sure you were

unharmed and realized you would not admit to anything in front of all your guests. I will leave if you would like."

"No." He answered before thinking better of it. "You are here now, and it will take time for all the guests to settle back in. At this point, it will make more sense to wait until closer to dawn."

She stepped up to him and placed her hand in the opening of his dressing gown. The warmth of her touch shot heat throughout his body. He closed his eyes to memorize the softness of her hands on his chest. The calmness she brought to his mind was not the same for his body. Her hands were like fuel on a fire. He stood the onslaught until he had to join in. Winn took her face in his hands and bent it to meet her mouth. He kissed her, drank the very life from her breath. Weaving his hands into her hair and pulling the mass free from the loose knot, the scent of roses assailed him.

Zoe had untied his robe and already divested him of it. He took no time to scoop her up in his arms and place her back on the bed. Making to sit up and unbutton her gown, Winn stopped her.

"No, darling. I do not think that a good idea tonight." She looked at him with concern. "Tis not you, but I am not sure if I see you in my bed naked, I will have the control. Don't worry, love. We will still enjoy each other," he promised, placing a kiss on her forehead, laying her back onto the pillows. He followed her, straddling her legs and leaning down, elbows on either side of her head.

Zoe remaining fully clothed did nothing to quell his need for her. He wanted nothing more for the rest of his life than to have her underneath him, naked and warm. Never had a woman made him need so much. He bent to kiss her, hoping if he closed his eyes, he could wash that vision from his brain. Zoe reached up and wound her hands into his head, holding him into the kiss. She was innocent, but her instinct called to him at a base level.

Winn eased his body onto hers, connecting them from top to bottom, the lace of her bodice chaffed against his chest. How he burned for her soft breasts pressed into his chest. He moaned and turned them, so she was lying on him. Her weight was not a demand on his body, and Winn would happily sleep with her draped over him every night. Her weight grounded him and covered him with warmth like nothing else.

Her hands slid down his sides, leaving a trail of chills on her way. In return, he reached up and cupped her bottom, pressing her into his erection. To her credit, she made a little moaning sound and began to wiggle against him. "Darling, that is not a good idea," he said, after ripping himself away from her luscious mouth. "As much as I approve, it would not do to spiral my need for you any more than it already is. I hope to send you back to your room unaffianced by the morning light."

She stopped and looked at him with an odd expression, but he didn't take the time to think on it. He laid her to the side, for more access to her breast. Even through the bodice, her nipples were hard and demanding him to touch. Unable to control the frenzy building in him, his hands moved to her thigh and slid up, taking her dress with it. When he reached the curve of her bottom, his breath caught. God, she was perfect. Every part of her body fit into his embrace.

At the feel of his hand on her bare bottom, Zoe tilted her

hips into the side of him. He survived his carriage being attacked by a bull, but this slight innocent woman might kill him in his own bed before the night was done. The heat from her core beckoned him, and as he found his way, she opened with no hesitation. Oh, Lord.

"May I touch you?" he asked, not wanting to shock her or, worse, force her to comply if she was uncomfortable.

"Yes," she said through heaving gasps. "I want to touch you as well."

She was candid in and out of bed. Winn took a moment to loosen the drawstring on his pants and wiggled them down to his knees. He remained still as she reached out and explored his erection, squeezing his eyes shut to the sensation — pleasure mixed with the pain of resistance.

"Oh, Gawd Zoe."

She stilled in her exploration. "No, love, you are doing it exactly right." Then he captured her mouth to muffle her sounds as he found her center and inserted a finger. Her hand slowed, but as he began a slow-motion, she relaxed into the bed and began her ministrations anew. How long they remained in each other's arms playing and learning, Winn was unsure, but he would never forget when Zoe's eyes shot open, and the look of utter desire burned deep within them.

"Winn, I--"

"Shh, love, let it happen. I've got you." He kissed her parted lips and whispered in her ear until the first waves of her orgasm washed over her. He leaned up to watch the release play across her face in the moonlight. Not one to disappoint, he kept the pace until he was certain she knew what an orgasm was. He withdrew and held her in a tight embrace as she floated back to earth, gasping. He would pay for this tomorrow, and no doubt need to take care of himself, but that didn't matter now.

"I--"

"Did you like that?" he asked, smiling into her hair, knowing the truth of his question.

"Yes," she said breathlessly. "What was that?" He heard the awe in her voice.

"That was me bringing you to pleasure, love."

"Oh."

He had her tucked into his body with her head resting on his chest, no longer able to see her face. They lay in silence for a bit. Winn feared too much conversation would lift the spell, and it would be over.

"Does that happen every time?"

He smiled at her naivete. "Well, I cannot speak for other men, but it does for me."

Again, silence. She was an academic at her core, and this a new experience she no doubt had no prior lessons in or even conversations to help prepare her.

"Will it happen with my husband?" The question was almost a whisper, and Winn sensed a sadness in it. Another man doing with Zoe what he just did, made every muscle in his body fire. Not a man to contemplate murder, but he could be persuaded if another man ever touched her. Then reality set in. She would have a husband that was not him. Not because he thought she would choose another, but because he made it clear that he was not an option. He took himself out of the running.

"Well, I cannot say. Men all have different levels of talent and different ideas about what is appropriate with their wives, but if the two of you are compatible, then you will most likely suit well enough." The words were acid on his tongue, and his heart withered in his chest as his ears heard his own words. She was better off with another, and despite the pain in the coming weeks, he would continue to keep his word. But whenever spying her across a crowded ballroom, Winn would be reminded he was blessed with her flushed, desire -riddled face first. That would have to be enough.

She didn't have an answer to his comment but snuggled in next to him. Winn flung a blanket over their heated bodies and stroked her hair until she was asleep. He should sleep, as well. His body needed relaxing after being thrashed around inside his carriage. He wanted to have every memory of this moment saved. It would be the closest he would come to a wife sleeping next to him after making love. It would not be prudent to repeat this at the manor. She would never go in his bed again. So tonight, he would catalog every moment for those cold nights not long from now.

CHAPTER FOURTEEN

Breakfast was a quiet affair. Most of the men left at dawn to go with Winn and Lord Hayhurst to see the damage and inspect the field and bull. Many of the women took a tray in their rooms, knowing there would be no men to impress. After being woken in the dark and ushered out of Winn's chamber, but not before he held her in his arms at the closed door and kissed her until rational thought left, she found it impossible to go back to sleep and now sat with restless energy.

"You seem unlike yourself this morning, my dear," observed Lady Burton, as she sat eating her toast points with honey and butter on them.

"I didn't sleep well, I guess," was Zoe's awkward answer. She managed to sneak a look down the table at Lady Sarrafinna, who seemed to see through her thin mask. The woman knew things about things, and Zoe knew she was lost if she attempted to hide anything from her.

"I think the excitement of the evening had us all up late," Sarrafinna defended Zoe. "I know I found it difficult to relax after such an ordeal. I even had Lord Worth still awake to set me at ease. The poor child was alone in her room with no one to comfort her."

The mouthful of light as air eggs sat like a rock in her mouth. She washed them down with a gulp of milk, but it didn't work and only caused her to cough.

"Oh my, are you well, dear?" Aunt Dorothy asked.

"Yes, sorry, I swallowed my drink wrong is all."

Lady Sarrafinna added nothing more to the conversation after that, and Cyn breezed in, changing the tone and subject altogether.

"Well, after all the unsettling activities of yesterday, I thought we should all find time today to sit in the parlor and go over Zoe's list and multiply our efforts toward her top three. There is a top three by now, isn't there?" she asked, looking at Zoe.

"I, well, um, yes, I suppose so." Unfortunately, it would be untoward to ask each of those gentlemen what his aptitude was for making his wife's toes curl and giving her the feeling of being flung into the stars every night. These answers seemed to be paramount now to solidify her choices.

"Wonderful," Cyn clapped her hands together, seeing victory in her future.

"I hate to dampen the spirit, but I wonder at why Zoe seemed hesitant to claim a top three," Lady Sarrafinna pointed out, and Lady Burton and Aunt Dorothy nodded in agreement.

"Yes, my dear, you seemed to hesitate," her aunt spoke up.

"I would hate for you to make a hasty decision. There is always the season if none of these gentlemen suit."

"Thank you, aunt, I am aware I do not need to make a final decision, but there is no reason to be short-sighted because I am apprehensive. The men who would be my top three are upstanding good men, so we can at least acknowledge their standing."

All the women nodded, though Cyn was less enthusiastic. It was decided to start finding ways for Zoe to spend more time with Lord Ruthaford, Mr. Smythe, and for the time being, Zoe didn't have a clear third. However, they all agreed that Lord Seller and Zoe would not suit and therefore be struck from the list. Zoe thanked the women for all their help, but Lady Sarrafinna wasn't having it, by the expression she gave. If she hurried, she might get a glimpse of the carriage after the accident at the stables, so she finished eating and excused herself.

Zoe was not ten paces down the path to the stables when Lady Sarrafinna called to her.

"Miss Chase, I was hoping you would accompany me to the stables to view the wreckage. I have not been to the stables here in so long. I do not want to get lost."

"Yes, of course," Zoe answered. "You don't ride?"

"Oh, yes, I do. I am quite accomplished, but I do not dare leave Lord Worth for long, as he may need something."

The caring in her voice struck Zoe. No one spoke of it, but they all knew she was Lord Worth's mistress, not his wife, yet Sarrafinna showed sincere concern for the older man. Zoe hoped whichever man she chose she would share such emotions toward him. They walked for a few moments in silence, but it did not last long.

"Zoe, you are a smart girl and observant, so you well know that I too am observant, and in my vocation, it is imperative I be able to read people. There is one left off your list. I believe you would have him in your number one spot."

Zoe said nothing. She couldn't either discredit what Sarrafinna said, nor defend her reasons for leaving him off.

"Lord Burton is a good man, Zoe. A bit wild for sure, but that will wane with age. He would--"

"He won't have me," she blurted the words. With the words came the tears welling, threatening to make her a watering pot. Zoe cleared her throat to get past the emotion. "He has told me he doesn't intend to marry ever no matter how tempting the woman. I am not leaving him off the list. He took himself off. My father expects me to choose a suitable husband by the time he returns home. There is no time to chase someone who does not want to be caught."

"My dear, I am sure if you--"

"No, I am sure that short of putting him in a sordid position, he will not." This conversation needed to end. It was landing too close to her raw emotions and things she had no right to be considering. She could not fall in love with Winn, and to consider swaying his mind would make for an unhappy ending for her.

"Very well, my dear, it is clear you considered your options. It is well-advised that you step away lest your emotions get involved. Messy business, emotions." Lady Sarrafinna wrapped Zoe's arm inside hers and laid it on her arm, patting it in a motherly way. "All will work out as it should. Forcing the matter will not help. You have this well in hand, I can tell."

The rest of the walk was silent. Zoe needed to rein in her

emotions in case Winn and the other gentlemen were at the stables. Sarrafinna allowed her the space to do that. Once at the stable, the mangled carriage sat in the paddock, and Zoe froze with a realization about how horrific the outcome might have been.

"Oh, dear," whispered Lady Sarrafinna.

"I had no idea. I mean, I knew the accident shook them, but still," Zoe said, tears again filling her eyes.

"Good morning, ladies. Come to examine the carnage?" Hayhurst came from behind the pile of wood and metal. He was all smiles and warm welcomes this morning. He walked up to the women and saw the tears in Zoe's eyes. "My dear lady. We are all hail, regardless of what this apparatus might say to the contrary. I assure you."

She cleared her throat. "Well, yes, I am aware. I did not realize how miraculous that was until this moment, though."

"Good morning," Winn shouted as he crawled from what appeared to be under the wreckage. "Found it Reid, and it still works. I would have been angry if I had lost this. It is my favorite, after all," he said with a wide dimpled grin as he held up a pocket watch. He joined the group, and his smile slipped as he too caught sight of the tears threatening to flow forth.

"Miss Chase, whatever has you so upset?" Winn asked, confusion and concern evident in his expression.

Had he asked her but a minute ago, she would have said the realization he could have died. But now, after seeing his laissez faire attitude to the severity of the situation, the tears filling her eyes were of anger so strong that if she considered it long, she would embarrass herself. Closing her eyes and taking a long fortifying breath, she then opened her eyes, shot Winn an angry glance, and turned to walk back to the house. She thought he would let her flee until she heard his heavy footfalls behind her.

"Zoe. Zoe. Miss Chase, for the love of God will you stop," he all but shouted.

Zoe stopped, but did not turn around. If she made eye contact, she feared she would either throw herself into the circle of his arms or slap him in the face. Both were possible, and both would cause her more embarrassment than him. "What in the hell is this all about? What did I do?"

Without turning, and thankfully the path was not wide enough for him to step in front of her, she tried to answer. "I was not prepared for the extent of the damage to your carriage. When I saw how mangled it was it made me aware of just how close you came to dying, then you crawled out from under the very thing that put your life in danger, filled with joy because you found your favorite watch."

"It's a good watch," he responded. To that, Zoe squared her shoulders and began trudging back to the house again with new anger flaring.

"Zoe, wait. Stop. I am sorry." His words sounded genuine, making her stop, and this time turn. His face was no longer filled with happiness. Instead, it was serious, as serious as she had seen. "It is obvious you are upset, and I have no right making light of your concern."

"No, you do not," she answered.

Winn stepped as close as would be allowable in public, but it was close enough for a private conversation. "If I were to let every attempt on my life scare me, I would die in my bedchamber alone from fear. I survived. We all survived. That is something to celebrate." Zoe refused to look up at him, for if she didn't stop producing tears, she might drown. He bent her chin up with his thumb and forced her to make eye contact. "The only thing on my mind when I was in that carriage being thrown around like a toy boat in a bath was you. Once the situation calmed, and the beast corralled, I sent Reid to inform you and bring you safely back to the manor. Then when you walked into the study, I knew all would be well."

Words escaped her. If she spoke, words would tumble in such a state that she wouldn't understand the ramifications until she finished. "I am sorry I was angry, but I harbor great concern for anyone who is so close to death and doesn't understand how others could not laugh about their situations. You should be happy you survived, my lord, but I think laughing and making light of such a thing is disrespectful to others who have died but were not ready to do so." Those words, as difficult as they were, came easier than admitting that one day on earth without Winn would be intolerable.

"You are correct. I was a callous ass," he admitted, and she believed him.

"You are forgiven."

"However, there is an update of the crash. It was not a bull sent by a mystical curse to kill me. The poor beast was poisoned. We found a bunch of what was left of the bull's feed. It was hay, but mixed in with the hay was fresh English ivy with the berries still attached. If the poor beast ate enough of those berries, it would have made him delusional. Any farmer in this area would not be so stupid as to mix ivy berries into hay for their livestock."

Stunned, Zoe pieced together what Winn was saying,

"You mean someone did it on purpose, knowing what would happen?"

"We think so, but proving who and proving they were targeting my coach will be near to impossible."

"Then, why are you happy about this news?" Zoe must need more sleep.

Winn broke out his most dazzling smile, catching Zoe by surprise and taking her breath. "Because love, I can fight a murderer. I couldn't fight a curse."

"Oh." Now she understood, but to her mind knowing someone wanted Winn dead and the fact that said person had quite extensive knowledge of where he would be and what he would be doing sent bile to her throat.

"Now, we just wait and be prepared. Reid and I can offer some tasty bait and see who might salivate." He moved passt her with a bounce to his step.

"Wait--What? You will lure a person who wants you dead by allowing them to try and kill you?" She ran up beside him and grabbed his arm. He turned with an expression of utter male superiority.

"It is not as dangerous as that. Knowing the potential danger allows us to be more cautious."

Zoe let out an unladylike snort. "You, Lord Burton, wouldn't know caution if it slapped you in the face. And I daresay Lord Hayhurst has even less concern for the topic as it is not him in danger."

They heard others coming up the path, making plans for an outing to walk to the folly by the stream. Their time for private conversation over, Winn stepped up to Zoe and whispered in her ear, before placing a kiss on her earlobe and walking away. "Let's discuss this tonight. This time I promise to be there."

The hike to the folly did nothing to calm Zoe's mind. She spent half her day pandering to Mr. Smythe as Lord Ruthaford was not back from London yet, and the other half contemplating going to Cyn with his latest plan.

Cyn hated Winn's carelessness. In countless letters, she lamented how fatiguing it was to not know from one minute to the next if her brother would die from the latest stunt or accident. She was so busy with the house party, Zoe did not want to burden her.

At the end of the hike, Zoe needed to lie down to get rid of the headache she created. She would not go to Cyn with this. Winn was a grown man and allowed to make his own decisions. Plus, he would do it anyway, and poor Cyn would have to worry with the knowledge.

Instead, Zoe decided she would, at the very least, attempt to be a neutral observer. She would try to decipher what the two had planned, then attempt to ferret out of the people she had access to who may try to use that knowledge to harm Winn. If he knew her plan, it would not work, so she would have to be as secretive as possible.

As her maid did her hair for dinner, Zoe took the time to contemplate her afternoon with Mr. Smythe. Today, he was an easy fellow to spend time with. He conversed with ease, and to Zoe's surprise, he was not as worried about his own ideas as he was about hers, which was a desirable change. It would take dinner and cards this evening, but she believed she would move him to the top slot on her list. It was not fair for Lord Ruthaford, but he would just have to make strides upon his return.

As expected, Mr. Smythe impressed, but Zoe paid less attention to him and more to decipher Winn's plan. Winn and Hayhurst spent the evening talking and laughing with several of the other guests, both married and not. They paid particular attention to Lord Worth, Lady Sarrafinna's guest, but it was the first time since his arrival that he remained so long after dinner. It had been impossible to hear what they were saying without acting the snoop. Instead, she studied Winn's expressions and his interactions with Hayhurst. Perhaps if she couldn't find out how, she might figure out who.

By the end of the evening, when many guests were finding their beds, Zoe was no closer to figuring out the plan, and it exhausted her. However, as she hurried her maid out to change and head to the lodge, her exhaustion faded, and desire filled the void.

The lodge was ablaze with light on the bottom floor. She wondered at what could be on the second floor, but that thought flew away when she saw Winn in the window, coatless with his cravat hanging on either side of his open shirt.

"Good evening," she said to announce herself. The back door had been unlocked and waiting for her.

"Ah, Miss Chase, it is a pleasure," he said, scooping her into his arms and welcoming her with a heady kiss. "You cannot begin to understand how difficult it is following the thread of a conversation in the parlor when you are in the room."

"I thought you did a smashing job of ignoring me this

evening."

Winn worked his way down her neck to the hollow in her throat, pulling a moan from her. He turned her and leaned her back against the large table. Zoe went willingly, allowing him to lay her out on the table.

"I am glad I could fool you, as that means I also fooled everyone else," he managed, as he continued to work kisses down her neck to the swell of her breast hidden by the over-sized cambric shirt.

It was when Winn rose to open the shirt and get an unimpeded view of her breasts that Zoe heard the sound. "What was that?" she asked with a hissed whisper. The thud came from upstairs in the room above them. She sat up, holding the shirt closed with one hand. "Did you hear that?"

"Tis nothing, I am sure. Perhaps a window is broken, and the breeze knocked something over. We are alone, I assure you."

"Wait, if this is the old original manor,we were sure was haunted as children, perhaps we were correct?" Zoe asked, panic rising in her voice.

"Well, yes, but I have had it renovated."

"You renovated a haunted house?"

Before he could answer another thud followed the first. This time Winn reacted. "What the bloody hell? Something is up there. Stay here," he ordered, and made his way to the stairs. Not wanting to be left alone, Zoe followed, buttoning her shirt on her way.

She wasn't looking up and met the solid wall of his back. He had stopped to listen up the stairs instead of going right up. "I told you to stay there," he hissed.

"Yes, you did," she acknowledged, but said nothing more.

"Stay behind me then." He began to creep up the stairs, one by one. Again, another thunk.

At the top of the stairs, four closed doors met them. To the left was the source of the noise being the room above the main room on the first floor.

Thud.

Winn turned to her and guided her to the top of the stairs and against the farthest door. "Stay here. If I yell, run down the stairs and back to the manor. Do not be brave." He eyed her as she nodded. "Promise me."

"Yes, yes, run to the manor for help." He nodded, then turned back. The thumps were getting closer together and seemed more violent.

Zoe watched as Winn turned the knob and jumped into the room, closing the door behind him. All was quiet for a moment, then the most inhuman sound came from the closed door, followed by Winn.

"You. I thought I evicted you. You dirty little braggart. Come here!"

Zoe relaxed a margin as the noises told her it was a some*thing* instead of a someone. It still could be a ghost, but most likely not a man bent on killing Winn. She listened as more crashes and thuds resonated, followed by oaths and expletives from Winn. Then, when she was sure the fight would crescendo, there was silence. So much so, Zoe started to step for the door, but then it clicked and out came Winn, his cravat askew and his coat torn. In his hands, though, was a box the size of a jewelry chest and perched on Winn's shoulder sat a skeptical feline.

"What in the heavens?"

"It appears our haunting was a mother cat attempting to

settle her brood into a warm nest."

Zoe peered into the box to see six puffs of white and gray fur. She looked up at the matching mother, who's long fur showed her current struggle with life. "Oh, you poor thing." She cooed and reached up, taking the harried cat off Winn's shoulder. The nervous mother leaned until she could see into the box.

"Don't worry, I think they are all here," Winn assured her. "I will come back up with a candle when we get them settled downstairs to make sure that is all."

Zoe smiled at watching such a big, strong lord carrying on a conversation to relieve a mother cat about her young. Winn headed down the stairs with the box of kittens, and before she could take a step, the mother leaped back onto his shoulder. To his credit, Winn never missed a step, just grunted at the extra weight. The cat did a fantastic job of balancing to monitor her precious babies.

Once downstairs, Winn brought the box next to the fireplace, laying a blanket on the floor around the box in case the babies escaped they would have a soft landing. Mama jumped to the floor and ran to the box and nuzzled each ball of fur, then did it again.

"Oh, I think some are missing." Zoe had barely gotten the words out when the cat meowed and raced for the stairs. Winn grabbed one of the tapered candles and followed. Zoe went to the box and, with care, lifted one of the newborn kittens out. She turned it to see its delicate little face. The eyes were still closed. It made low cooing sounds and nuzzled around her hand. "You must be hungry, sweetheart. Mama will return with your brother or sister soon." It was so soft, and it made her heart feel light.

"Here we are. It is a family of eight, not six," Winn announced as he entered the room, cupping another fuzzball. The mama carried yet one more squirming baby in her mouth. Once those two were safely added to the box, Mama jumped in and got comfortable.

They both stood and watched as the contented kittens all mewled and found their spot for feeding as mama cat laid on her side purring, kneading the air with her very large kitty paws.

"Well, it seems the lodge is not haunted after all," Zoe said.

"No, however, a ghost does not require being fed."

"Yes, but you will not have an issue with vermin now that you have a family of mousers. Consider them on your payroll."

"You make a good point. I hope Reid approves."

Zoe got nervous. "What will happen if he doesn't? You won't kill them, will you?"

Winn looked at her as if she had called him a murdering braggart. "Who would kill a cat and her kittens? No, I would tell him to be agreeable or find another place to rusticate."

She felt much better once she saw his reaction to her question. She didn't need his answer.

"What will you name them?" She asked as the heat of his body stepping close to her seeped through her shirt. His breath warmed her neck before his lips covered the spot. "Mmm."

He took a moment to respond. "Why on earth would I bother to name them?"

"Because they will be your pets." He returned to kissing her neck and reached a hand around, sliding it under the opening of her shirt. Her naked breast puckered and reacted to his touch without prompting. She gasped and leaned back into his broad chest.

"I am not interested in pets at the moment. I believe this is where we were interrupted." His hand and his mouth made her heady, and she too was no longer interested in naming pets.

Winn led her backward away from the box of kittens and the table. Instead, he made their way around the stacks of books and sat in a large overstuffed reading chair in the corner where he guided her down on his lap.

She half sat, half laid draped over his right shoulder. He took the time to unbutton her shirt and open it, exposing her breast and shoulder. He took her breast in his hand, teasing it and rolling the pert nipple between his fingers. Zoe watched, heat from her blush and the building desire mingling, fogging her mind.

"Win," was all she could say.

"I love my name on your lips, love." He bent and nipped at the tip of her shoulder before soothing it with a kiss.

Zoe reached up and wound his hair in her hand. She was at his mercy, but she had to move, had to be an active participant. Her nervous energy had her wriggling in his lap.

"Careful love," Winn warned.

"I need--," she didn't know how to put it into words. She needed him. She wanted to see him naked. She wanted to taste him. "You."

That seemed to make sense to Winn because he placed her on her feet and stood to shed his jacket and shirt. Within moments he stood naked from the waist up. She wanted more tonight. The fear from yesterday and the emotions of seeing the carriage this morning made her desperate. Time might not be on her side. Winn could die, or she would have to choose a husband. Either way, their time together was not eternal.

"Take off your pants." The words sounded bold to her ears.

Winn merely smiled, showing his deep dimples and dropped his pants to his knees without question.

Zoe grew up in Rome. She spent time at museums. She knew what a man's body looked like, but to see it in the flesh instead of marble did something to her brain. The skill of forming words or stringing them together escaped her.

Winn laughed and pulled her to him for a kiss, "Now tis your turn love, but I would prefer to do the honors." Without waiting for her to respond, he grabbed the string she used to hold the breeches up and tugged. With the pants no longer tied, they slipped down to her ankles. "I think, love, if you are prone to wearing breeches, we should get you a pair that fit better. I would love to see what you look like in tighter fitting ones, but--" He stood back, taking in her naked form with the cambric shirt holding on by one shoulder and her pants at the floor. "I have to say I prefer this to any ballgown or other pieces of fashion."

Sitting, he yanked her hand, pulling her down with him, his thighs warm on her bottom. She wiggled a bit until she felt his erection rub against her and froze. He didn't seem to notice, being too occupied with suckling one of her breasts and toying with the other. Soon, Zoe was in a haze of desire herself.

He slid his hand down along her side and hip, continuing to give each breast attention. She only barely registered his hand as it slipped between her legs and began a devilishly wonderful exploration. "Lie back, love," he instructed.

In doing so, she opened to him and the sensation. His hand pressed into her, sending waves through her. She reached out and rubbed at his chest in sweeping motions. Then she remembered he, too, was naked. In her desire-muddled brain, she willed her body to move, giving her access to him. She reached down and feathered the head of his erection with her fingers.

"Oh, hell," he groaned and threw his head back.

"Should I stop?" she asked, not sure the proper etiquette.

"I should say yes, but I am a foolish man, so no, you should not stop." She smiled at his humor and settled into the feel of him in her hand. Feeling him made what he was doing to her more exciting, and she liked it. They continued exploring each other's bodies for what seemed an eternity, but just when she was about to come to her release, Winn's other hand grabbed hers. "Stop, love. Stop now," he pleaded, panting. She allowed him to lift her hand and hold it in his. He then wrapped her hand and his arm around her chest and went back to his work. The act of him holding her in his protective embrace drew tears to her eyes, and at that moment, she shattered into the universe.

As she lay in the protection of his body, she floated back to herself, realizing no man on her list could do this for her, because none of them were Winn. She had done what she promised him she would not. She was in love. The sort of love that lives in your bones. She curled her face into his chest to hide her silent tears and absorbed his heat and caring. How she would love one man and marry another was a question for another time.

CHAPTER FIFTEEN

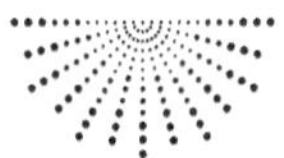

"I will walk you back to the manor then return with some scraps for our underfed mother," Winn talked as they both dressed. The fire had burned down to glowing embers, and the room took on a chill.

"Thank you," was all she could manage. It was necessary that she put on a brave face and not allow Winn the knowledge of her realization. He would cease all interaction with her, and Zoe couldn't bear it.

While Winn banked the fire and extinguished the flames, she bent to the mother cat and her brood. "I will see you lot soon. I promise to bring some delectable morsels for your dinner. You take care of those babies." The momma cat rolled more on her back, nudging the furballs for a belly rub. Zoe obliged, and her heart eased, but only a bit.

"Ready, sweeting?" Winn stood by the door looking for all the world the rake he wanted them to see, but Zoe saw the man he was. Responsible, loving, and scared of his future. So much so, he would not allow himself to consider having one.

She cleared her throat. "Yes." She stepped into the murky darkness. The fog had settled, giving the house and grounds around it an eerie sensation. It brought her back to her childhood, and a time the three of them would make up stories of the old haunted manor. Her memories of this place were vastly improved now.

The walk back was silent, save for Winn's warnings now and then about hazards in the path.

"Mind the stump on the right."

"Winn, I have walked this path in the dark before, alone. I am capable of maneuvering. Thank you for your concern, though."

"I would hate for you to stumble and bruise one of those delicious ankles of yours."

Perhaps she couldn't continue. She forced a mild chuckle, but the tears once freed flowed silently again. Was it wrong she wanted a life with Winn commenting on her ankles, elbows, or whatever part of her body he wished? His easy smile and quick laugh waking her every morning?

As they emerged onto the lawn, the manor stood proud and ghostly itself in the fog. "I shall part ways with you here. I hope to see you tomorrow," he whispered in her ear and bent to place a kiss on the inside of her neck.

Watching him walk to the kitchens, Zoe decided she needed to rethink everything. Tomorrow was another day and an opportunity to determine the direction she would take. Crying about it would solve nothing. She made her way to the servant's door, glancing into a window of the library on her way. Her father sat in a chair by the fire, smoking a cigar with Lord Worth. Her father had arrived. Oh Lord, let's hope he did not call for her upon his arrival.

Her heart, not as broken and withered as she thought, pounded in her chest. If her father had arrived, she would have less time to figure things out. She would need help, and she knew just who to go to. That would be her first stop in the morning. Well, her second. She had missed her father terribly.

After a sleepless night which Zoe had not experienced in some time, she sat at her dressing table, looking at her haggard visage.

"Here, lay your head back and put this over your eyes." The maid handed her a wet, cold washcloth. "The cold will help the puffiness. Ye look like someone who has nay slept for days, miss."

Zoe accepted the cloth and laid her head back, enjoying the coolness on her red, swollen eyes. She wasn't sure if the sleepless nights or the crying was the cause, but was thankful for a solution. "The coolness is very nice, but will it work?"

"Aye, some. Enough so people won't go around asking you if ye slept last night."

"Good."

"Tis must be hard, Miss, to be having to pick from the gentlemen in the house. They all seem like a good catch to me," she said, as she brushed Zoe's hair while it hung over the chair.

"Yes, it is. I never imagined it would be so difficult. How would you choose?" She was curious of someone else's opinion.

"Me?" the maid asked with surprise. "If it were me, I would find the one man who made it hard for me to breathe when he looked at me. I would also choose the man who made me an asset to his life, not a burden. If ye ask me, too many men from any station see a woman as a burden, and we are not. Most o' them would starve if not for their women. They never seem to think o' that when they are complaining, though."

Zoe smiled from under the cloth. "You are correct. I had a list of things, but I am finding the list to be not as helpful. I like your ideas better now that I am in the thick of things." Perhaps choosing a husband was more about how the perfect choice made her feel as opposed to other more logical traits. A vision of Winn last night with his head thrown back, while they-- Clearing her throat, she sat up and hoped she could school her reaction better once out of her room.

"Ach, now ye look much better," the maid said, looking at Zoe's reflection.

"I do. Thank you so much. Do you know if my aunt is awake?"

"Yes, but she is still in her room."

"Wonderful, I will finish dressing and go visit her there." Zoe wanted to see her father, but since he arrived so late, she would assume he would sleep in. No need to wait. The sooner she rallied her champions, the better.

Dressed and refreshed, if not fresh and awake, but at least more rejuvenated than an hour earlier, she made her way down the hall to her aunt's door.

"Come in," her aunt bade from the closed door when she knocked.

"Zoe, come, come. What a surprise this morning. Do you know your father is here?" she asked, munching on a toast point and reading the latest newssheet.

"Yes, I am aware. That is why I am disturbing you."

"Nonsense, you never disturb me and never think you are. What concerns you, love?"

The endearment settled around her like a warm blanket. Zoe was surrounded by people she had not spent time with since she was a child, but they loved and welcomed her just the same. In a chair across from her aunt, she took a breath and began.

"Aunt, I am nervous that my father has arrived expecting to meet the man I have chosen--" She didn't know how to continue.

"And you have not yet decided if one man at the house party is that man?"

"Yes."

"Your father is a wise enough man. I can't see him demanding you make such a hasty choice if you aren't sure. After all, choosing a husband is not the same as buying a new hat."

Smiling at the notion, Zoe pressed on. "If I confide in you about something, can you promise to hold it and not pass it along?"

"Well, my dear, I would hope I can hold a secret at my age. I will not promise, though, if it is something that puts you in danger."

"Oh, nothing like that," Zoe assured her aunt but crossed her fingers behind her, hoping that ruination wasn't the danger she spoke of. "I am leaning toward one gentleman, but I need more time. I am not sure the gentleman's interests are likewise and would not want to put either of us in such a public view if that is the case."

"And it scares you that your father will press the point

and embarrass you, or worse, force you to out the gentleman in question."

"Yes, exactly."

The older woman, who to be truthful, did not look much older than Zoe, put down her teacup, and leaned in to look Zoe in the eye. "How much do you know about your parents' courtship and marriage?"

Zoe wasn't sure why that mattered but loved talking about the love her parents shared. "Mother never went into detail, and father never brought it up, but I got the impression it wasn't a long courtship. It was a love match from the start, and right after the wedding, they left for Rome and father's diplomatic post."

Sitting back, her aunt steepled her fingers. "Your mother told you this?"

"More or less. As I said, Mother never spoke of it much, but when I asked, she would answer my questions. She used to say that how they met had no bearing on how they lived their married lives, so there was no point dwelling in the past."

Zoe watched as her aunt nodded. After a silence, she seemed to come to a decision. "Your father is a wise man. He will not force you into a situation unless you are a willing party, but to set your mind at ease, I will speak with him."

"Thank you," Zoe said, bouncing out of her chair and embracing her aunt for being willing to have such a delicate conversation with her father.

"Make yourself scarce for the morning. I will seek out your father once I finish my toilette and bring him up to snuff. That way, when you see him, it won't be awkward."

"Thank you so much. I will do that," Zoe said, and left her aunt to finish her morning routine.

A walk would do her good, she thought. She went back to her room to grab a shawl, before she breezed through the kitchen to grab some biscuits and sausage for herself, and some kippers for momma cat. She would see how the little family fared through the night.

The path to the hunting cabin was no longer sinister. The sun shone through the trees and gave the area a fairy-like expression. Zoe relished in the forest's silence. She was enjoying her time at the house party, but she needed time alone to recharge her temperament. The quiet broke with the babbling of the stream ahead.

The forest opened to the small walking bridge that connected the entrance to the hunting cabin to the Manor property. Zoe walked onto the bridge and stopped to watch the water bubbling along and disappearing under her feet. It was a happy little scene, and it warmed her heart and filled her with hope. If Winn wasn't in love with her, he was interested. Zoe was taking the chance that he didn't allow himself to care more because of his perceived situation. If Zoe could puzzle that out and he was no longer in any danger, he would be free to love her.

As the brook danced by, she thought back to their first encounter as adults. She remembers her resolute anger that someone would be so careless with their safety and others — the pain of losing her mother at such a young age still a sharp sting. Now, looking at Winn and his antics, she realized it was just the opposite. Winn loved living and intended to live life to the fullest for all the days he had remaining. Be that two days or twenty thousand. Zoe understood now that being safe and not taking chances did not equate to living. She thought about her mother, who would have liked Winn. He would have made her laugh, and her mother loved to laugh. After taking a moment more to consider her mother, Zoe made her way, tripping only once on a board that seemed to be higher than the rest to the lodge. She must pick her feet up more in her half-boots than day slippers.

Zoe went to the back door, pulling the key out of her pocket. She spotted fresh sawdust in a small pile on the ground in front of the door, and to her surprise, at the center bottom of the door, someone had sawed a large chunk from it and then returned it, attaching a hinge. She bent down, pushing on the piece of cutout door that swung in then out until it again came to rest in the spot they cut it from. Winn, or a workman on the property for him, made a little door so the momma cat could get in and out without making a place for the kittens to escape.

Zoe let herself in. The back room was still dark, but the main room had large windows that allowed the sun to brighten and warm the space. In the corner where they left them, the little furry family remained. Now out of the box, the kittens were tugging themselves along by their fat little bellies, making mewling noises as Momma watched on all laid out in a sunbeam.

"Well, hello there," Zoe said as momma cat noticed her.

The long, but very furry cat rose and stretched her sleek body in the sun before stepping over several kittens to greet her.

"I brought you a snack as promised. I hope you like fish."

The cat crouched down in front of the open napkin and began devouring her feast.

"What are you doing?" A deep familiar voice filled the room. Zoe turned to see Winn standing in the doorway, looking as handsome as ever, but his expression was hard.

"I promised momma kitty I would bring her some food, and here I am." She rose, crossing the room with intentions to hug him.

"You shouldn't be here in the daylight," was his reply, stopping her in her tracks.

"Well, that is silly. I am not doing anything untoward. It is more respectable for me to be here in the daytime than at night," she pointed out. She reached for his hand, but he pulled it free.

"No, Zoe, it isn't. Your father is here now. That changes things." His expression didn't soften, but if possible, hardened.

"I, I don't understand. How does my father have anything to do with this?" A panicked feeling rose in her stomach.

"This," he swept his hand in the air to encompass not only the room but everything they had done, "this was a mistake. It was my mistake. You have no fault here. I should have ended this before it advanced."

"Excuse me? I was a willing partner. If you remember, I followed you here that first night," she reminded him. She would not let him dismiss what she was realizing were the best, most significant episodes in her young life. "You did not force me into any such behavior. I went willingly."

"Just the same. It is over." He walked past her, dumped yet more kippers on top of what she left, and walked back to the doorway. "I will leave. Wait a good half hour before you leave. No one will connect us being together alone that way." He took one more look at Zoe, and she could have sworn she saw remorse fill his glazed eyes as he left, closing the door behind him.

Zoe stood in the space for three clicks of the clock and decided. The door opened with ease, but it could have been her anger and frustration as she heaved the massive oak open. Lord Burton could not just walk away from her; he didn't get the choice. They would talk and figure this out.

By the time she got around the house, Winn was on the other side of the bridge and sitting upon his horse.

"Winthrop Burton, you will not dismiss me like I was a tiresome fling." She waited for him to dismount and come back to talk about this. Instead, he stared at her for a moment, then rode off toward the house without a word.

"Well."

Blinking to hold back tears, she refused to greet her father with tear-stained cheeks. Her father tended not to take her tears well. She would be in a carriage heading from the house party quicker than anyone would think possible.

Back in the cabin, she tried to imagine what caused Winn to overreact so. Her father's arrival couldn't be the cause, just a convenient excuse. Something had to have transpired between last night and when he walked in on her.

Perhaps it would take more than just her aunt. She hated to use Cyn against her brother, but if he remains so ridiculous, she will not hesitate. First, however, she would corner him in his den where an angry lion hid. She would do it tonight, her father or no.

An hour later, Zoe made her way up the lawn in the late morning sunshine. Still, no house guests milled about to enjoy the day. Perhaps some were up early and off to the stable, she must be fair and assume, but if they were not, then it was a mark against them. Gentlemen had so much less to encumber their toilet. She felt it showed a lack of industry for them to lag about in their chambers. Her father was always up with the sun and at his desk by six o'clock sharp.

At the thought of her father, her heart leapt, then sank. She couldn't wait to see him. She had missed his smile and quiet strength these past few months. The ship travel had been made more difficult without him to reassure her. She wasn't sure, however, that he would be of great help in the arena of suitor choosing. However skilled he may be, there was no avoiding the reunion. Her aunt, who was not one to rise earlier than ten, had spoken to her father and eased the way by now, she hoped.

The kitchens were bustling, still making some trays for ladies who had just gotten about, almost to punctuate her point.

"Ah, Miss Chase, grab a nice hot biscuit with some jam while you're here. I never let warm biscuits to sit and be idle."

"Thank you. I will." Zoe climbed onto a tall stool at the table where a mound of biscuits sat piled, waiting for plates to be doled out. "Do you know if my father is about yet? He came in so late he might still be sleeping." He wouldn't be, but she thought it better to make conversation.

"He was up with the sun. Just like his daughter," the maid smiled and winked. "I believe he has settled in the library, miss."

"Thank you," Zoe answered through warm flaky biscuit and elderberry jam. As soon as she finished the biscuit, she hopped down, grabbed one more because it was a long time until the next meal, and wandered in the direction of the library.

The library at the Burton Manor was exceptional. As children they would play in the room's corner, because it was like a cave to them. As an adult, she appreciated the shelves lined with first editions. Chiding herself for not spending more time reading since she arrived, she made a note to come and choose a few titles to keep in her room for the duration of her stay.

At the moment, her eyes flew to the man in the large room bent over a pile of papers. Some things never change.

"Papa!" She greeted and headed toward him.

"Zoe, my dear girl!" He bounded from the chair and met her partway, swooping her into a protective hug, swinging her around. "You will not know the relief of laying eyes on you until you have a child of your own. I spent most of my time at sea angry with myself for forcing you to make the trip alone."

"Oh, Papa, I was not alone. I had my maid and Miguel, the man you hired as protection. The voyage went without incident."

"Yes, well, you would say that. Come, I want to hear all about your life since you left."

With her hand in his he led her over to a seating area in a sunnier spot in the room. They sat, but Lord Chase refused to let her hand go. It was then that Zoe realized Rome must have been lonely for him with her mother gone and her on her way to England. She had been so caught up in her own selfish feelings; she did not see the pain he was in.

Zoe reached out and hugged her father again. "I am so glad you are here. We can be a family again."

He hugged her back, but there was something in his embrace that was more distant. "I am certainly glad to be here with you again, but I was hoping your eyes would be on creating a family of your own. Are there any chaps at least in the running? Your aunt tells me you are doing your due diligence, and that I am not to rush you."

"I hope she wasn't too difficult." Zoe didn't want her father to think there were any issues.

"Not at all, I have known your aunt for a very long time, and we understand each other. I want you to be happy, that is foremost. If there are none in this lot that make you feel compelled to put your hat in the ring, then we shall visit every ball, route, and cotillion in London until we do." He leaned in and kissed the top of her head. Immediate comfort washed over her. Why had she been so concerned about her father being here? Of course, he wanted what was best for her, and a husband she could love was the thing.

"There are some superb gentlemen here, but I am uncertain any of them would suit throughout a marriage."

"You will know, my dear, never worry."

"Did you know it was mother?"

"Pardon?"

"Mother, when you met her, when did you know she was the one?" Zoe never asked much of her father about their relationship, but her mother was no longer there to ask. She was curious after Lady Sarrafinna's comments.

"It was a quick sort of thing. We learned about each other

over time. I am not certain when I realized your mother had bewitched me."

Zoe loved how his face softened when he spoke of her mother. His expression was all she needed to know.

"Now, no more talk of suitors. Tell me about your voyage and how you have been getting on in England."

The change of subject was a relief. It would give her the space she needed to decide if Lord Burton was the man she wanted and to convince him in the process. They spent the rest of the morning and much of the afternoon chatting and catching up. When Zoe left to dress for dinner, she was no longer worried about her father's presence.

Dinner was a boisterous affair, the gentlemen telling tales of their fishing expedition that afternoon, and Lord Ruthaford regaling everyone about what was happening in London upon his arrival. Winn presided over the table but added little to the conversation. Zoe wasn't the only one who noticed. Cyn asked him several times what had him in such the doldrums, but he would say something flip, and Cyn would tell him to go to the devil.

To her relief, the gentlemen seemed to see the need to give Zoe some breathing room, with her father now in attendance. It gave her time to observe the men without volleying answers back and forth to pander to them all. She had to admit they all struck appealing figures. None would be considered not good looking, or not refined enough, but it was Winn's dark features and hard edges that drew her. When he smiled, which wasn't tonight, his entire face softened. But in a resting position, the candles played with the shadows bouncing off his hard planes. Could she choose another man at this point?

Her thought stopped when Lady Burton rose and declared the women would proceed to the parlor. Zoe hated this British custom but followed the other ladies out. If Winn left before attending his guests in the salon, she would not know if he retired to his room or if he was going to the lodge. He avoided all contact with her at dinner, clearly his main objective. She planned on pushing the matter, but in a place, she could back him into a corner.

"My brother might well kill me before I can find an adequate suitor," Cyn complained once they were situated in a corner with their sewing in hand.

"Is he upset about something?" Zoe asked, digging.

"How would I know? He just stalks around the manor like I stole his favorite wooden soldier, but won't speak of what got him in such a state," she complained.

Zoe felt the guilt in her chest. She could relieve Cyn's concern because Zoe knew she was the cause of his ill-temper. The ladies spent the better part of an hour chatting and enjoying the warmth from the large fireplace. When the clock chimed the hour, Zoe could sit idle no longer. Winn may have already left for the lodge, and she wouldn't know.

"With all the excitement of father arriving, and the threatening storm, I am afraid I am getting a headache. I think I will turn in."

"Would you like me to have a maid bring you a poultice, dear, for your head?" Lady Burton asked, overhearing.

"No, that won't be necessary. All I require is a good night's sleep, I am certain." Zoe answered. She didn't want anyone to get the idea she was ill, and if her father thought she was sick, he would hover.

Making her way up the stairs, she asked a maid to send

her maid to her room. She undressed as much as she was able alone, then waited for her maid to help her. While she waited, she planned what she would say to him. She would sit in his rooms until the blasted man returned. It might be her ruination if at dawn he has still not entered, and a maid, or God forbid, his valet comes to ready his room for dressing and there she is asleep in a chair after waiting all night. Still, she didn't give a farthing about her reputation at the moment. All she cared about was Winn.

CHAPTER SIXTEEN

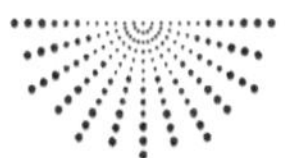

Zoe stood outside the door, listening. Did she knock? He might refuse her entry. Storming in was an option, but if he was with his valet, that could pose even more problems. She said she didn't care about her reputation, but with her future on the other side of a door, her bravado was melting.

The urge to turn and run down the hall and back to the safety of her room made her feet tingle with anticipated movement. She drew in a deep breath. She would rather live as a ruined woman, knowing she did everything to find love, then live as a pious spinster never giving love a chance for fear of retribution.

The drapes tied back around the bed were a sumptuous red velvet that took on a lusciousness with the light from the fire dancing around the room. It was not a large room as a master's bedchamber would go. Not that she had seen many, but she had been in her father's rooms from time to time.

The fire had been lit some time ago and had burned down to a comfortable glow, making the room toasty and inviting. Thankfully it was empty. Zoe noted his greatcoat hung over a chair. Hope flared. Perhaps that was a sign he had not left for the lodge or that the threatening storm was keeping him at the manor.

The bed loomed in her vision, and heat crept through her. She considered the times they had enjoyed each other's company. She walked up to the high bed memories of being cradled in his embrace in the sheets, and her being splayed out on the work table, sending desire shooting to her belly. They would relive that scene here. Then she spied a large overstuffed chair hidden in a corner next to one of the floor-length windows. The massive four-poster bed impeded the light from the fire, casting it in shadows. Another image of them in the chair at the lodge took her breath away.

She made her way to the chair and sat in her nightdress, tucking her feet in to keep out the coolness of the floor. Here is where she would wait. If she was lucky, the shadows might hide her if someone other than his lordship returned to the room before him.

She reached up and pulled the bulky deerskin throw draped over the back. The position of the chair was terrific for hiding. But the heat also did not travel to the far corner of the room. The throw smelled of leather and Winn's shave salve. As her heart tightened in her chest, she snuggled down, drinking in his scent.

A sliver of light streamed across her face, waking Zoe. She must have dozed. What time was it? The stream of light cast when the door swung silently open and only just a gentle click when the door latched closed. Zoe held her breath and tried to disappear into the chair, waiting. Was it a servant come to stoke the fire or the valet to ready his lordship's bed?

The person came into view with their broad, muscled back to her. Winn. She let out a breath, then stopped because he froze in the middle of the room, listening. Her purpose was to let herself be known, but she knew it was Winn. She watched to see if he were getting ready to leave, or if he was settling in.

He first removed his coat, then waistcoat, then discarded everything from the waist up. Her mouth dried up. As he reached down to the placard on his pants, she found her voice.

"Hello," was the only thing she thought of saying. Her mind went blank, looking at Winn's muscular back, with muscles flexing at his every movement.

"Who the hell--" He said, then stopped when he realized it was her.

"Please don't let me stop you." She tried to jest, but the joke fell flat when his eyes blazed with annoyance.

"I told you we were finished at the lodge. This will only be trouble for both of us."

"I don't believe that."

He stared at her for a moment then turned to stir the fire. "I am sorry if you are not capable of understanding--"

"I didn't say I didn't understand. I said I don't believe it." She rose and walked around the bed in her night rail.

"Zoe, you should not be in my room," Winn said as a plea. She could feel his desire coming off him in waves. He was not done with her any more than she with him.

Taking a steadying breath, she stepped up to him and

placed her hand on his bare chest. "We need to discuss this. You and I. You don't get to just decide anymore. We are beyond that."

"It is for the best," he said, looking at her hand on his skin. "We knew it was a dalliance, and with your father here, it is clear we both should have been more responsible."

"I don't believe it is my father's arrival that has caused you to break things off."

He stepped away from her to slip his shirt back over his head. He was determined, she would give him that, but she had hours before fear of being caught. She was more so. "Isn't having your father under the same roof not enough of a deterrent? If he caught us, you know he would force you to marry."

"That is it then? That is your argument for parting ways?"

He turned, and the dead look in his eye told her if not the truth, it was the only truth he will give up. "You knew I had no intention of marrying before we started this. You will do well on the marriage mart Zoe, no need to bag the first fat goose you come by."

The steadying breath Zoe took soothed her anger, only slightly allowing her to stamp down the desire to slap him as hard as possible. Winn was trying to make himself irredeemable to her. If he was an arse, she could walk away. He was not as clever a man as he thought.

"I believe that something has come about concerning whomever it is trying to hurt you. Perhaps they figured us out and are threatening to out our tete-a-tete or to bring harm to me. I am sure of it. My father is not a man to incite fear into a budding suitor, or a current lover."

Winn swept his hands over his face, pushing his hair

back, which had come out of its tie. It hung in thick sheets framing his face when it was loose. It shimmered in the fire-light, making her want to replace his hands with her own, while she kissed him senseless until he forgot this nonsense. Instead, she stood with her arms crossed and what she hoped was an expression letting him know she would not let this go.

"You are wrong about your father. The man is quiet, I'll give him that, but something in his eyes reveals something fierce beneath the surface. He wouldn't show that to you, his beloved daughter," Winn explained, but his shoulders sagged, and he sat with his back to her, looking into the fire. "You're right, though. I got a note, slid under my door. None of the maids saw anything, and I do not recognize the script. He knows, but not in the respect you are suggesting."

Fearful of breaking his current chatty mood, Zoe didn't dare move to him. She stood, arms at her sides, hands fisted. "Then, in what respect was he referring?" she asked, restraining her frustration. She wasn't a child and deserved to know when something affected her.

"He knows I have feelings for you. His note claims his only goal is to take away the chance of having an heir to the title."

"But why? With no heir, the title will go into abeyance. What good is that to anyone?"

"The note hinted at a wrong done by my family, but I have no idea. We Burton's have been dying off for three generations, so I would not know of it." Winn stood then, and went to her, encircling her into the safety of his arms. "I could not forgive myself if something were to happen to you, Zoe. It isn't worth it."

Zoe pulled back from his chest, anger now so raw it would not be held back if she wanted. "I again disagree. Regardless if you want to acknowledge what is between us, I understand it, and I will not let some person take that from me over some slight that happened generations ago. I don't give a fig about my reputation or my safety."

"Zoe--"

"No, you listen to me Winthrop Burton, I love you. Honestly, I think I have loved you since you were ten, so no need to argue with me. And if you do not feel the same, we can figure that out at another time. However, I will not allow some unidentified man or society take from us the right to figure this out between the two of us."

Winn looked down at Zoe. Her color was high in her cheeks, giving her impassioned speech an air of haughtiness. The words 'I love you' hammered into his chest, almost sending him flying forward. For so long, he professed he wanted nothing of the emotion, and God forbid a woman to declare it to him. He hadn't wanted to marry. No point in marrying only to leave behind a widow when the inevitable happened. Then this petite titan storms into his world, and all hell breaks loose. "I will not embroil you in something that has already proven to be fatal at least thrice."

"Well, I am sorry, sir, but you already have." She stepped into his embrace again and raised on her tiptoes to place a kiss on his lips and damn it; he bent so his lips would meet hers. She was warm and soft and smelled of sleep and blankets. things that meant comfort to him.

"Damn," Zoe sat back as he scooped her into his arms and headed for the bed. Before he made the ten steps, she had nuzzled into his neck and was busy tasting and kissing her way around to his chin. "Perhaps it is not the threat from outside my walls I should be as concerned about, but the assault happening in my bedchamber." His voice was pitched low, and did he sigh?

"Perhaps not."

"You minx, did your plan tonight include taking my virtue?" Winn laid her down on the bed and leaned over her. Her mahogany hair shone in the firelight. And since when did he consider the hue of brown of a woman's hair?

He didn't give her time to respond but took her already plump lips and tangled his tongue with hers. A fierce protectiveness swamped him with emotion. Not unlike the rage that surged through him when he read the threat on Zoe. He would burn in hell for a thousand years before he allowed this fool -or more than likely given the time span *fools*- take one more person he loved away. He was also done with pushing those he loved away. It would end tonight.

Pulling back for a moment's breath to clear his head from the desire swirling a veil of need in him, Zoe lay looking up at him, breathing matching his own. "I'm lost to you, Zoe. If you don't want to go anything further, you need to leave. I won't stop you, but I don't believe I will play the voice of reason with any realism. I want you."

Her cheeks reddened still more, but she didn't look away or get missish. "I wouldn't have broken into your room in my nightdress and waited for you if I didn't want the same."

Something in his body shattered, and with no more control than a feral animal, Winn's desire rose to an inferno.

He took her mouth again but worked the buttons of her dress as she slid her hands across his back, leaving goose flesh in her wake. Her touch was amazing, but when her hands slipped below the waistband of his pants, he groaned into her mouth. And when she maneuvered her petite fingers to the buttons, pulling them free and lowering his breeches below his hips to his thighs, his kisses expressed his excitement.

"Damn Zoe, your hands feel so good." He groaned in her ear before nipping her earlobe. "Touch me," he instructed, and she did.

She laid her hand palm up under his cock and took the weight of it as she stroked the length. His entire body shuddered in response. So that he didn't cry out, bringing the whole household staff to his door, he freed her breast from their confines of billowing fabric and bent to suck one pert nipple into his mouth, smothering his outburst.

"Oh, my!" Zoe threw her head back and wriggled underneath him. With more confidence now, she gripped his erection and began a slow, lazy caress.

Winn switched to the other breast and maneuvered the dress below her hips, hooking it with his barefoot to yank it the rest of the way off the bed. He then did the same with his drawers and collapsed next to her so as not to crush her.

"We will be cold if we don't find the covers soon," he pointed out, but her skin was radiating the heat of her desire, and she just continued stroking him. She turned in to him, connecting her body with his from her shoulder to the tip of her dainty toe. Winn lost his grip on what little control he still had and pulled her tight to his body. She fit as if molded for him. Did he know this at ten? When he followed her and his sister around the manor grounds doing whatever crazy stunt he thought would make her smile? He looked down into her face, and he saw that smile again. His heart swelled. He did. He knew at age ten what his blind adult mind forgot. This woman was made for him. All thoughts of danger, threats, and curses faded from his memory, and it was only Zoe.

Rolling, he covered her body so he would not crush her and balanced on one elbow. He used one hand to trace her feminine curves to her hip. A hip that settled into his hand as if molded for it. He followed the natural curve to her buttocks, pulling her body down while running his hand along the back of her thigh, raising her leg to settle it over his back, all the while spreading kisses over her neck, shoulders, and chest. Her sweetness sat on his tongue.

When he was certain she was drunk on her desire by the little mewling sounds she made and how her body writhed under him, he ran his hand down her thigh until the curls of her center brushed his knuckles. Her intake of breath told him she knew. Her hands were everywhere on his body at once, rubbing, exploring, pulling him closer to her. Winn found the folds covering her most private part and slid his finger along it.

"Oh, Winn--" she moaned and broke off.

He found the bud he searched for and rubbed with just the right pressure. Zoe thrust her hips up, and her breath hitched. She was ready for him. He had been ready for her since he first laid eyes on her in the road before he ran her over with the balloon. He had wanted to cut the way off and lay in the road with her soft body on him then. Now, he could barely contain his need.

"Zoe, love, are you still sure? I need you to be certain. I won't be able to stop soon."

"Yes," she moaned, the haze of desire filling her eyes. "Don't stop. Never stop." She continued and closed her eyes again, enjoying his ministrations.

"I am afraid, at some point, I will need food and water, love, but as you wish." He bent and kissed the hollow in her neck.

Winn rose above her, positioned to take her virginity. Her beauty made more so by the desire flushing her cheeks, making her eyelids heavy, captivating him. Her hair was a chestnut riot of curls shining and unkept, covering his pillow. Her scent remained in the air, adding yet another layer. He would never forget this moment. He was sure if he lived to be one hundred, this would be the moment he held most dear of all his memories. Unable to ignore her squirming beneath him any longer, he kissed the tip of her nose and, in one smooth motion, buried himself in her soft heat.

"Oh, Lord. Zoe, you feel--"

She lifted her head with a comical confused look on her face. "I feel what?"

"Amazing," he said as he laid over her, covering her face with kisses. "Perfect." He bent to suckle one breast to distract her from any discomfort. He had never taken a woman's virtue, but he knew there might be pain. "Like you were meant for me and only me."

The last statement landed somewhere in the vicinity of his heart. Zoe was now his. If she decided she wanted him. He pushed the possibility away and allowed the sensations to take him.

She was a natural, and her body met his stroke for stroke and caress for caress. Her hands were everywhere, and the taste of her warm skin made him hungry until he could take it no longer and let his release take him and her over the edge into a haze of desire.

CHAPTER SEVENTEEN

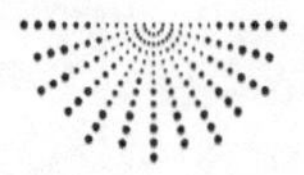

Winn calculated the time to be well passed one in the morning. He should have woken Zoe an hour ago but found it impossible to leave the warm comfort of his bed, with her tucked up beside him. As far as mistakes go, deflowering Zoe Chase was by far one of his most reckless.

In the moonlight, she looked like an angel at rest. Long, thick lashes that were a slight hue lighter than her hair swept down to settle on her cheek, still pink after their lovemaking. Her lips, while not still swollen from his kisses, still plump above her chin. Plumper than a person should be allowed, that was certain.

If the bastard planned to ruin her, Winn would counter that. If he married her in a matter of a few days, with a special license, there would be no scandal. His bigger fear was that Zoe's reputation was not the end goal of whoever wrote that note. And now, Winn had put a more damning bullseye on her. If the fool's goal was the end of the titled line, he would more than certainly want her dead if they thought she was with child.

Winn slid his hand over and covered her stomach with it. Even now, at this moment, his child might be nestled inside Zoe. He couldn't think of a place he would rather spend the next nine months. After giving up having a family, he had always been careful and took precautions against pregnancy. Not with Zoe. Just the idea seemed wrong, and he was sure had the discussion come up earlier, he would have felt the same.

He wanted to wake her and make love to her again, but that was out of the question. For her protection, he could not let it out that he compromised her. Winn would not ask for her hand, while a lunatic threatening her life and his was still at large.

"Zoe," he whispered, rubbing her cheek with his knuckles. "Sweeting, you must wake."

"Mmm." She rolled and snuggled into his chest further. His heart all but burst; this was the woman he loved.

"Love, love, you need to wake, darling. We must get you back to your room before the household rouses for the day."

She blinked up at him, assessing her surroundings. He gave in to the urge, pulling her on top of him, covering her mouth in a long kiss.

"Were you waking me to take me to my room, or ravage me again?" she asked a few minutes later when they both had to stop for air.

"Well, the latter sounds more promising, but I am afraid for the time being stealth is required, so it is back to your room with you."

Winn rose and pulled on his sleeping pants and robe. Zoe slid out of bed and fumbled around the floor until she found her nightdress. It was a sad moment when Winn watched her slip it over her head, covering her lush feminine body from his view. He sighed with a protest.

"Ready?" he asked, extending his hand to her. She stepped next to him and took his hand with both hers.

The hallway was black, with no signs of life. Winn threw up a prayer of thanks that the household did not rise so early. The two of them snuck along the hallway in the family wing, not making a sound. Winn kept Zoe tucked tight behind him, in case he needed to shield her from view. From the view of whom he didn't know. The family wing was set apart from the guest rooms in the manor. There was no reason a guest would be over here by accident. His mother said it was important for the family to have a place to retreat during long house parties, and he now agreed wholeheartedly.

Winn reached her door at the end of the hall and slid the door open without a sound. He slipped in, taking her with him. "Here we are."

"Yes, here we are," she mimicked him. "Thank you for escorting me back to my room. The hallway is dark at night with no candles to light the way."

Winn pulled her into an embrace one last time. This would be the last embrace for a while. "We must not speak of tonight. You are aware, are you not?" he said, looking down into her eyes as sternly as possible.

He saw hurt flair, then a mask of pure ladylike compliance covered it. There was no time now to go into his reasoning. There would be plenty of time for embraces and sleepless nights between them, but that was not now.

"Of course, I understand," she said, and stepped out of the circle of his arms.

"No, I am certain you do not understand, but for now, that is how it needs to be." He pulled her back in and kissed her forehead.

"No, you are correct. This must remain between us," she assured him. "It makes the most sense. Can we still meet at the lodge?" she asked.

He should say no. He needed to say no, but the thought of having no contact with her was unbearable in the dense darkness before dawn. "I'll send you a note about when."

She nodded and stepped back. It was time to end their entertainment. He bowed, and left the room. On Winn's return trip to bed, he formulated a plan. Reid would need to help him. He couldn't do this alone, and his one true friend would be the only person he confided in to make the import of catching this braggart known.

As long as they kept their night a secret and their meetings at the lodge, he could keep her safe until he found the criminal, or criminals, behind his family's so-called curse. He hoped.

The sunbeams stretched across the room and licked the bottom edge of Zoe's bed covers. Sleep had not washed over her after Winn left her standing alone in her room hours ago. She laid down and cuddled into the blankets hugging a pillow, but sleep never came. Instead, a wash of emotions flooded her with no mercy. Elation of what happened, fear of not knowing what happens next, then hurt mixed with a good bit of anger that he wanted to keep it a secret. She understood, of course, she understood. She was an unmarried, unbetrothed female. Logic dictated secrecy. Plus, the threat Winn received about her safety. Logically, it made sense. Still, she wanted to yell it from the rooftops.

Zoe slid from the bed and curled up in the chair next to the window. The day was starting, and it seemed her life was grinding to a halt. There was no doubt in her mind that Winn was the one she needed to marry. Even if she could secure an offer from another, she wouldn't go through with it. It was always Winn. Now, she only needed to convince him of the same, which would be difficult with him trying to keep her at arm's length. It would have to be when they met at the lodge next. She must figure out a way to convince him. There was no other choice.

Several hours later, Zoe descended the stairs and made her way to the breakfast room. There was no place set for Winn, which indicated he had been and gone already. Did sleep elude him as well?

Zoe took her plate and filled it with all her favorites. Amorous adventures must increase one's appetite. At this rate, Zoe would be plump as a prize pig before she dragged Winn down the aisle.

"My dear, good morning," her father greeted her when he entered the room. "I was hoping to run into you this morning. I would love to spend the afternoon with you again, catching up."

"Good morning father, I would like that very much," Zoe agreed. She missed her father, but it also gave her an excuse to avoid the rest of the house party, at least for the foreseeable future.

"Well, I see the kitchen is taking good care of you. They cooked all your favorites today."

Zoe smiled. "Yes, however, I rather think it was more that my favorites are everyone's favorites. I hardly think the kitchen staff has the time to consider what I want to eat."

"True enough," her father agreed. He was a very handsome man. She wondered at that moment if he considered remarrying. It had been a respectable time since her mother passed and he was still considered quite young for an eligible man. She would like to see her father happy again.

They sat eating in silence, each in their own thoughts. After what seemed like an eternity, Lady Sarrafinna breezed in and stopped.

"Good morning," Zoe said, but the awkwardness hung heavy in the room.

After a pause, Sarrafinna took her eyes from Zoe's father and greeted her. "Good morning, dear. I popped in to see how you were faring this morning, but I can see your father has it well in hand. I will bid you a good day." And Sarrafinna disappeared.

Her father let out a breath like he was holding it and went back to eating. Zoe knew she had witnessed something, but no idea what. Her father launched into suggestions for their day, leaving no opening for her to ask.

"Oh, and before I forget, I need to tell you about the townhouse I have acquired in Mayfair for us. You will enjoy it. I am certain."

Zoe gave no thought about where she would go when the house party was over. This was the only home she ever knew in England. It was where she came the few times she visited with her mother. "Really?" she asked, forcing enthusiasm in her voice.

"Yes, and tis only down the street from Burton's townhouse. I thought it would be a comfort to be close to your friends."

The weight settling heavy in her chest vanished. Her father understood her better than anyone. "Papa, thank you for considering that. It does make me more at ease with the prospect of leaving here."

The rest of breakfast was comprised of Zoe listening to her father praise his choice of new homes, and Zoe holding her breath every time a house guest entered the room, hoping and dreading the possibility of Winn walking through the door. How should she react? She assumed she needed to carry on as she always did, but how, after doing what they did, does one do that? Zoe decided most adults would have a vocation in the acting arts if they played it off as if it was just another random Tuesday.

CHAPTER EIGHTEEN

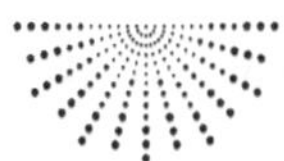

"You know how to correct that noise coming from your stomach?" Reid asked as they rode into the village to follow up on an idea Winn had about how to find the culprit trying to end his life and his line.

"How?" Winn asked, playing along. He would not admit to avoiding breakfast because he was sure it was impossible to school his facial expressions if he ran into Zoe. Going days without eating, if it protected her virtue, was fine. The virtue he destroyed last night in his bed.

"Eating. Sustenance? Sausages and biscuits?"

"You don't say."

Hayhurst just shook his head, but reached into the bag slung over his chest and pulled out an apple and a fresh-baked roll. "That was a snack for later, so now you will be forced to buy me lunch at the Inn."

"Thank you."

"When did you get the idea of asking at the posting inn about recurring visitors?"

"While considering all the different ways this braggart could have been close enough to cause havoc. He would need to stay somewhere, if he wasn't from the area, and we can assume he is not a local because near misses happened in London and at that horse show as well as at home."

"Ah, yes, the horse show. I quite thought perhaps that was the end of you."

"Yet, here I am."

The two chuckled and made their way down the hill into the village of West Oversly. It was a town that Winn knew well. He had grown up here and could tell you how many times the boys in town would get in trouble for sneaking into the dry goods shop and stealing candy. Winn's mother always made sure the shop owner was paid back tenfold for what they took, and Winn never went unpunished. The same shopkeeper and he are now on good terms, and Winn pays for his candy at the counter.

"Where should we begin?" Reid asked.

There were three inns in the village, two as you entered from the south and one west of town. The only one that welcomed the post and all who traveled that way was the Duck and Hound.

"Let's start at the Duck and Hound. If they are coming in with the post, it would make sense they would just stay there."

The inn's main room was quiet now that the breakfast rush was over, and patrons were back in their rooms or moving on to their next destination.

"Lord Burton, Lord Hayhurst, welcome. What can I do

fer ya this morning?" The Innkeeper, a stout, solid man, greeted them at the counter.

"I am hoping you might solve a mystery for us. I am wondering if your records are complete enough that we might see if any patrons match up to dates on a list."

The man beamed like he was introducing his first-born son to them. "My lord, I can assure you my records are spot on, they are. My Ellie makes sure of it, and she is nary wrong, ever," he assured them and bent under the counter to produce a massive leather-bound ledger.

Winn decided his was a happy marriage, as he allowed his wife to always be right. No doubt, Winn will feel that way about Zoe when they have been married for some time. His body heated at the remembrance of how she looked when he left her early this morning in her room. His day would be better spent in bed with her than chasing a bastard like he was.

"How far back does this go?" Winn asked. The book was huge, but being the posting inn, it was busy.

"Two years, my lord. If you want to go further back, I can ask Ellie--"

"No, two years is more than enough, thank you. The first date is ten July last year."

The man turned the massive pages until he found the date halfway down the page. "Here, tis, my lord. Now, we'll need another date to see if any overlap."

"How about fifteen October of that same year?"

The man slid a piece of cloth on the July date and turned to the next date. Then the three men looked down the list and made a note of any names that came up on the same day. There were more than Winn would have thought.

"Many come this way monthly for work or visiting relatives in the country," the innkeeper explained.

"Let us see if the next day narrows the field, third of March of the next year?"

And sure enough, there were only two names that matched the other two dates. One of those names was familiar to Winn and Reid, having also been present at the Sussex horse show at the same time as them. Winn thanked the innkeeper and commended Ellie on her stellar record keeping. He assured the man he would recommend the inn to all of his friends who might pass through.

"What are we going to do now?" Reid asked as they mounted. "I mean, he is currently residing at your home and basking in your sister's exceptional hosting skills."

"We need to be careful," Winn advised. He couldn't throw blame around without more than a few incidents of him being in the same place as Winn. They traveled in the same circles. "I will take you to lunch, and we will discuss how to proceed. I think we will force the issue and catch him in the act. That and the dates we have here would be a strong indicator of proof, I think."

"Very well." The men left the inn yard and headed to their favorite inn for an early meal. This inn was not at all the most popular, but as boys from the area, they were aware of where the best quail pie in all of England was baked daily, and they never gave up an opportunity to eat their fill. Winn also was better off staying away from the house, because watching the other men fawn over Zoe would be difficult. And to see their suspected villain making nice with the very woman he threatened only hours earlier might well send Winn over the edge, and the outcome would look different with him dangling from a noose instead of the actual braggart. No, before he returned to the house party, he needed to find the resolve to keep himself in check for everyone's safety. At least for the moment.

Zoe was exhausted. Her father had kept her moving and chatting all day long. She had talked him out of a horseback ride around three, claiming she needed to call for a bath and take a nap before the entire party met in the salon before dinner.

Now, lounging in a hot tub of water, she considered her father. He would be alone once she married. He was not a man that would do well alone. Perhaps he would find another bride or, at the very least, a companion. She wasn't sure how that would be. She had only ever seen her father dote over her mother but was sure her mother would want him happy.

That made her mind go to Winn and her current predicament. She was confident he was the man she should be with. He was attracted to her, and thanks to their endeavors last night, proved they would suit well in bed. The problem was to pin him down and have him admit it. As long as he was concerned about the note he received, threatening her life, Winn would not budge.

He had been absent all day. The only thing Cyn said about it was that he was off with Lord Hayhurst on a matter. It was not apparent if Cyn knew what that business was or not. She said they were both expected for supper, but not before.

She would attempt nothing while the entire house party was present. Her maid said there was already some discussion among the gentlemen about my preoccupation with Lord Burton. Not that it worried her. She was preoccupied with him, and after what he did to her last night, she was confident that would not end in her lifetime. Life would not change because some men thought it odd. Zoe would wait until after the house was quiet. If he did not summon her to the lodge, she would sneak back into his room and demand he admits his feelings.

Until then, she would enjoy the company of the guests and perhaps inquire about what events to attend once they get to London. She liked the idea of going to London. It was not as overwhelming, knowing she would not be trying to circulate through the marriage mart. No one else might know, but she was off the market.

Once dressed in her favorite emerald green evening dress and hair in a perfect coif, thanks to her Mary, Zoe entered the parlor and found Cyn.

"Good evening, you are fetching in that gown. Wherever did you get it?" Cyn asked as she directed a footman with a tray of lemonade to offer Zoe some. The drink was sweet, but Zoe took it anyway.

"Thank you," she said to the footman. "My mother and I shopped not long before she took ill. This dress came from a dressmaker in Venice. It took so long to be delivered to me in Rome. I was nervous that I might not get it in time before I left. Mother never got to see it on me, but it is by far my favorite gown."

"I am so jealous. We have wonderful modistes here in

England, but just once, I would like to go to a new place and see what ideas they might have," Cyn said wistfully.

"Ladies." Mr. Smythe came up to join their group.

"Good evening, my lord. I trust you are settled back in after your trip. I hope your business went well," Zoe said by way of including him. She was not at all interested in his business and was relieved when he was absent by surprise the other day.

"Oh, very well, indeed. I have been working on a large project, and it is coming to an end."

"Oh, do tell my lord, what are we to look forward to?" Cyn asked.

"I am afraid I cannot speak of it now, but it will be clear soon."

Zoe found that cryptic and off-putting, but the conversation turned to the weather and if they could go for their hike to the folly as planned the next day.

The air in the room changed, and before she saw Winn, he was at her side.

"Good evening," he said to the group, but it washed over her like a silken sheet between lovers. Her breath caught, and her cheeks flamed. Then she looked into his smoky gray eyes and could have melted into the floor.

Zoe bobbed a curtsy and looked away. "Good evening, my lord. I trust your business dealings concluded on a good note."

"They did. I have moved forward quite well on my latest endeavor."

"Ho, what is it now, Burton? Are you attempting to buy a flying apparatus, or perhaps a submarine, for more of your adventures?" Smythe asked with enough mocking to clog his throat with it.

"No, actually, I am not. For my next adventure, I will be closer to home than sailing the depths of the ocean. It is not something that is at the stage of announcement, however."

"You men and your secret dealings. One would think we were all surrounded by espionage and spies," Cyn commented dryly.

"Well, sister, perhaps you are. Perhaps I could not divulge the import of my activities for fear of breaking national security."

"Of course. Tell me, brother, how was the donkey influencing national security?"

Winn threw his head back and laughed. He was happy, genuinely happy, and dare she say, almost carefree. Now, she must talk to him to find out what progress they made today. He made it a point to stand a very respectable distance from her, and she could tell he was attempting not to pay her any extra attention.

Zoe found it difficult to not out-and-out stare at Winn. After last night she only saw what he looked like under his very respectable formal attire. When he turned to greet someone into the group she was aware of what the muscles on his back would feel like as they rippled under her hands.

"Are you well, Miss Chase?" Mr. Smythe asked, which brought all of Winn's attention down on her at once.

"Yes, I--I would like more lemonade though, it is hot in here, don't you think?"

Everyone agreed, but it was on the chilly side near the window they were at. Winn gave her a look, and she gave him a slight shake of her head to fend off his concern.

What would she say? *I am fine, but when I look at you, I am overcome by visions of our lovemaking and would like to throw you down on the settee and have my way with you?* She swallowed the giggle at that image — no need for everyone to think her going crazy by laughing at nothing at all.

"Oh, thank you." She broke her connection with Winn when Mr. Smythe shoved a lemonade in her hand.

"Dinner is ready, my lady," the butler announced to Lady Burton, and that was the end of their little group. Zoe sighed with relief that she would have dinner to compose herself before she confronted Winn. She would need to keep her thoughts better focused, or she would not be getting any declarations from her in words, at least.

CHAPTER NINETEEN

Winn needed air. More specifically, he needed air that was not circulating around Zoe. Never had his body reacted to a woman as it had to her. Since they made love, she was everywhere. In the village, he counted no less than five times he thought he saw her out of the corner of his eye.

It took only a moment's lapse in a conversation for his mind to flashback to her lush naked body below him. He got hard now thinking about her. And tonight at dinner was the worst sort of torture. Unable to walk up and sweep her into his embrace had him frozen in the parlor's doorway when he and Reid entered.

The slightest whiff of the soap she used, lemon and honey with a hint of something herby, perhaps sage, spiraled him. It had assailed his senses last night, and standing next to her tonight, when she would turn or move the surrounding air, he was all but drunk on it. Winn wished the house party was over so he could get her a safe distance from him and concentrate on dealing with the real threat.

The walk to the lodge was not long enough, but Hayhurst didn't seem to be aware of Winn's current state of unease. The coolness of the rain on his face didn't soothe either.

"I'll get the fire going," Winn offered, heading to the woodpile to exert some energy and remain outside longer. Reid continued inside to light the candles.

Finally, after coaxing the stove to a warm blaze and dispatching a whiskey or two, Winn was feeling more himself. He still wanted nothing more than to be wrapped up in the sheets with Zoe, but that was not for the present time.

"The nerve of that braggart tonight. I'm furious on your behalf," Reid complained.

"We do not know for sure if it is him or someone else at the party."

"It makes the most sense. He is the only one we can connect to most of the places where you were in danger by some fool thing. And the ones that we can't place him at were very public, well-attended events, so it is a good possibility he was also there."

Winn opened his mouth to agree, but a noise outside caught his attention.

"What was that?" Winn asked as he moved the very content mother cat from his lap to go to the window.

Before reaching the window, a knock sounded on the back door. Zoe. He should have known she would not let their last conversation go.

"Miss Chase. It is late for you to be strolling this evening," he greeted her but opened the door wide to allow her in. If there was one person he trusted above all else, it was Hayhurst in keeping his secrets.

"Miss Chase," Reid rose to greet her as they both entered the warm cozy living area. "I didn't know Winn was expecting you."

She smiled. "I am certain you know he was not expecting me."

"Please, sit." Winn offered his now vacant chair. She settled in, and before she leaned back, the mother cat resumed her position on Zoe's lap, curling up. The kittens were asleep near the fire on the pile of blankets that was now their bed.

"I was hoping to have a private word with you," Zoe said without holding back.

"Yes, well, that would be my signal to leave." Hayhurst rose and bowed to Zoe. As he passed Winn, he gave him a commiserating smile and a pat on the shoulder. "In the morning then."

Winn waited for the door to click and Reid to pass the window, before taking Zoe in an embrace. One he was itching to create since he left her in her room alone in the wee hours of the morning. Before his lips connected with her sweetness, she was tapping his shoulder and pushing out of his arms. "Hayhurst is back," she said, turning from Winn as the back door opened again.

"The rain is getting relentless out there, I am afraid, but that is not why I returned. You have another visitor," he said with a sardonic bent to his voice.

"Who?" Winn asked.

"I couldn't be sure, but the silhouette looked eerily familiar," Reid said. "I will leave perhaps he might follow, but be warned the two of you are not alone, and may not be a secret from this point on."

Winn nodded, too angry to respond. This was what he was afraid would happen. If the bastard wanted to ruin Zoe's chances, this would be perfect. He didn't want Zoe like this. She deserved a choice.

"I will leave and make sure I run into him. You remain here for an hour then come back to the house. Be careful, it gets deuced slippery on that moss in the rain."

"Wait, aren't we going to talk?" Zoe said, stopping him from moving her away from the window.

"Zoe, we may have been compromised, can't our conversation come at another time?" Winn asked, exasperated. He was attempting to save her virtue here.

"No, I do not think this particular conversation can wait."

"Fine, what do you need to talk to me about that is so important?" He dropped her elbow and crossed his arms in front of him to stop himself from pulling her in for a kiss. Her bottom lip stuck out further from her top one, giving him a delicious destination point for his own.

"Last night..."

"Is that what this is about?"

"Well, yes," she said, annoyance clear in her tone. "That may have not been very serious to you, but I--"

"Shh, someone is outside the building. Come." Winn cut her off and shoved her into the back stairway of the house where the door was. There were no windows, and Winn knew she would be out of sight if the braggart had the nerve to knock on the door. They waited in silence, but nothing.

Since his fears of Zoe being forever ruined because of his

lack of control weren't enough, he had the threat on her life and the fact that they were both in this old lodge together, and that no one other than Reid knew they were here, to add to his distress. It would be a perfect time to solve all his problems, whatever those might be. He could block the door and set the entire place on fire.

"Change of plans. You are leaving now. Through the window on the other side of the house. Come on."

Without giving Zoe a chance to protest, he had her at the window, a large riding cape over her kept for such a purpose. The window protested but opened. A gust of wind and rain greeted them, sending mama cat to the floor to cover her babies as a clap of thunder rattled all the other windows. Zoe jumped and let out a little gasp.

"Sorry to send you out into the weather, but it is the best course of action."

"Says you, the one who will remain dry," she complained, but allowed him to bustle her through the window into the storm.

"I'll check on you when I return to the house," he said. Winn closed the window and headed for the back of the building again. The rain drenched his shirt with a cold, blistering patter. He would make his way around the building and make sure Zoe got across the bridge without slipping. He walked against the wind, which he hadn't considered when deciding on the shortest way around.

He made his way around the house at the front as Zoe was already crossing the bridge. In the forest's darkness, the shadow of his intruder glowed like a lamp. He would wait until Zoe was past him on the trail and pounce.

As Zoe made her way across the bridge, she stopped to look back at the house, but when she turned to step toward the other side of the bridge, she vanished from sight.

"What the--" Winn was on a panicked run before he formed the thought. She fell through the bridge. When he got there, sure enough, there was a considerable gap in the planks. They were removed, and that had been since Reid left, unless he too took the misstep and ended up downstream. First Zoe.

"Zoe! Zoe!" He shouted in the darkness. "Damn it!" He bit out as he backed up a step and took the leap over the gaping hole. Who they were targeting was beside the point; either way, it would kill Winn. He continued to run along the edge of the river calling for Zoe. Did she even know how to swim?

The flash of them as children swimming in the frog pond on the property reminded him that she did at one time.

"Zoe, damn it answer me!" He cried out.

"Winn! Here, I'm here!"

Winn's heart slammed in his chest when her cries over the storm and raging water reached his ears. Another bright lightning bolt lighted the river, and Winn saw Zoe sopping wet, fighting the current to get across the river in his direction. He jumped down from the bank and all waded out to meet her. If his clothes impeded his movements when wet, how was she was doing it in full skirts? Another point positive for keeping this woman in breeches from now on.

"Come on, come on, I've got you. You're safe," he kept saying as he reached out and grabbed her cold, wet hand in his own and tugged her to the bank. He pulled her shaking body into his for his own comfort as much as hers. "I've got you. It's going to be fine."

Once they were both back up on the trail, Winn wasted no time to sweep her into his arms and head straight for the house. With a house full of guests, and a storm raging outside, there would be little hope to get her to her room and avoid what Winn knew was coming. He thought about the priest hole, but the stairs would be too slippery to attempt it. This was not the way he wanted things. In the silence, the quiet sobs of Zoe crying in the already wet collar of his shirt thundered. His waistcoat and jacket were forgotten at the lodge, one more nail in Zoe's coffin.

"You're safe, love. I've got you," he tried to comfort.

She nodded but did not come out of the folds of his shoulder to look at him. The house was ablaze with light. He would attempt to get her into his private study, at least. The parlor would be too public.

When he entered through the kitchen, the cook jumped and gasped at the import of the situation.

"Get Peter, and dry linens and blankets. Also, tea, lots of tea. We'll be in my study."

"Shall I summon her father?"

Winn felt his face harden at the conversation he was about to have. "Yes."

He whisked her down the butler's hallway passt the salon where voices filled the space, then into the side door of his study. He placed her on the couch and closed his main door to keep their privacy. Within moments, the side door opened and the cook along with the butler entered with enough linens and blankets for a shipload of people. Zoe, at the moment, looked as tiny and fragile as he had ever seen anyone. Fear surged at the sight of a fine red line of blood coming from her scalp. She was injured.

"You're hurt," he said, as he knelt by her and tried to find the cause of the red stream in the matted wetness already. Her wet hair hid a long gash along her scalp above her ear. If she had hit more to the left, it might have hit her temple. He grabbed a corner of linen and dabbed it, but even the lightest touch sent her jerking away from him. "We need to stop the bleeding."

She nodded and allowed him to press the cloth on her head. She reached up and wound her hand over his as he held it there. When he looked at her, relief filled her eyes.

"Thank you." The softest of sounds rushed between her lips, but it was enough for Winn to take a breath for the first time since he watched her vanish.

"Peter, you need to send someone to check on Reid. He left the lodge before us and may have done what Zoe did and not see the hole in the bridge. We may still have someone who needs rescuing."

"Yes, my lord." He left by the same side door, as Lord Chase slammed through the main door and froze. Winn began holding his breath again.

"Zoe, my dear, are you hurt?" Lord Chase crossed the room, paying no heed to Winn. His eyes were all for his daughter.

"I am safe, papa. A few bumps are all," she assured him, but he checked her himself.

Then, he turned on Winn. "What in hell were you thinking of having her out on such a night?"

"No papa, Winn didn't--"

The foreseeable future would be challenging for Zoe, and Winn could not allow her to own this. "You are right sir, I should not have. It was all my fault."

When Zoe would have protested, Winn shook his head at her to remain silent, which she did not.

"No, papa, Winn did not have me anywhere. I went out in the rain alone. I was lucky he and Lord Hayhurst were in the area to hear my calls for help."

Lord Chase turned his attention back to his daughter. "What in the devil were you thinking going out in such a storm?"

"I wanted to check on the kittens at the hunting lodge. It worried me they would be cold and hungry in the storm. And it wasn't so bad when I left."

Zoe sat up with help from the cook who busied herself with trying to dry her more. Zoe's was a plausible story that Winn had not considered. It should go a way in dampening the gossips, but the result was still the same.

The butler came back in, followed by Zoe's maid. "Miss, we need to get these cold clothes off you. I have asked that a bath be brought to your room. We'll get you warmed up in no time."

"Thank you, but I would rather not retire until we get word that Lord Hayhurst is safe," she protested, and took over the drying of her body, though her lips were blue and shivering.

Winn looked to the butler. "I sent someone, my lord. We should know soon."

Winn nodded but stood in the middle of his private study at a loss of what to do. Lord Chase took no time to decide his next move. He passed by Winn to get a glass of brandy from the drink tray and brought it back to Zoe, who took it and drank a long draw from the glass.

The door opened, and Cyn entered with her mother. Winn was surprised it took them so long.

"The guests are concerned and beginning to talk. You know that is not a good thing, Winn," Lady Burton announced. "My dear, what happened?" she asked Zoe.

"Well," Zoe's forehead furrowed. "I had been to the lodge and was making my way back. I am not sure if I misstepped in the dark, but I don't think so."

"You did not; there were two planks in the center of the bridge taken out. You stepped right through," Winn said with a hard edge to his voice. The emotion of watching her vanish was still too raw in his chest. "One moment you were there, and the next gone." Winn crossed to pour himself a healthy portion of brandy.

"How did that happen?" Lady Burton barked. Zoe gave Winn a pointed look. She knew well how it happened. The question was, did she get a look at who was standing in the shadows? Not a question to ask her now, and he would not get a moment alone with her, well, until after Lord Chase escorted her down the aisle to him.

"You and I need to speak," Lord Chase said, standing over Zoe with his arms crossed, but it was not his daughter he was talking too.

Winn opened his mouth to speak, but again his mother stepped in. "You do indeed, but if you will allow me, that is a conversation better had when all the parties are much drier and more well-rested, don't you think Lord Chase?"

Winn had not been afforded much opportunity to watch

his mother handle a male of the ton, because his father passed before he had those memories, but she was rather adept at it. Lord Chase was not a duke by several rungs of the Peerage ladder, but he was a man none-the-less and one with sufficient political clout, and he played right into Lady Burton's hand.

"Of course, Lady Burton, you are correct. A night of rest to let the emotions calm would be the better idea." Lord Chase gave in and turned back to paying attention to Zoe.

Winn stood drinking his drink, not sure what to say or do. What he wanted to do was send for a Bishop and a special license, so that when he retired to his bedchamber, he would have a still sopping Zoe tucked up tight against him. Winn set his drink down, not wanting to create a situation where he was not able-bodied enough to go out looking for his friend if they decided that was the case.

He walked away from the small group, now comprising his family and Zoe's father. The cook had gone back to expedite the tea and the hot water for the bath. He looked out on the storm that still raged, but none of its anger had been tangible since he got Zoe into the safe warmth of his study. The lightning flashed, and from the stables came Reid and a groom across the lawn. Winn let out a whoop. "Reid is safe. He is on his way up now."

The small group all began talking at once, the relief lifting the quiet from the room. Zoe stood and announced she would retire but would be down early in the morning to speak with her father and Winn. The men shared a glance stating they would both rather not have Zoe's input in the matter.

"That is a marvelous idea, my dear," Lady Burton stated. "I too would like to sit in."

"Mother, I--" Winn attempted, but was shut down by identical looks on all the female faces in the room. Winn noted Lord Chase had not been so foolish as to comment. He stood in silence.

Before Winn could make his way to Zoe to wish her good night and make sure one last time she was fine, her maid whisked her from the room, using the back stairs to avoid interested house guests, who were no doubt getting an eye full of Hayhurst as he entered from the storm. He walked in, dripping on the expensive carpet. To his mother's credit, she only gave the forming puddle a cursory glance.

"I am happy you are safe, Lord Hayhurst," Cyn opened the greeting. As his closest friend, Winn knew that Reid and Cyn were also close.

"Yes, so am I. It must have been pure luck that I crossed over the bridge ahead of the bridge planks giving way," he explained, giving Winn a pointed look. "Is Miss Chase well? No injuries, I hope, though as fast as that river is running, it is amazing she held onto something. The groom filled me in on our way over. I was almost ready to retire when he pounded on my door."

"Well, thank you for coming, though there is nothing to do tonight. I will have the bridge repaired at first light, so no one else is in danger," Winn said.

"If you don't mind, I will stay for a drink and hope that the storm lets up in the meantime."

"Nonsense. You will stay the night. No reason to dry off only to go back out into such a storm," Lady Burton said. The storm gave over a loud clap of thunder and lightning close enough to rattle the very windows to punctuate her statement.

Hayhurst nodded his assent. The butler put himself to use pouring more drinks for the gentlemen and offering to take their new guest's coat to slow the steady stream of water into the rug.

"Well, Cyn, let us find our beds, shall we. We also need to get our now overly stimulated house guests to find their rooms. This will take a while."

The butler left to make sure the tea service for Zoe got to the correct room, and that left the three men. "I will see you at first light, Lord Burton. It would be best to get this settled before we have assistance."

"Yes, I agree. First light, it will be. We can meet here. We won't have any house guests wandering in on us."

"Very well," Lord Chase answered Winn with a nod. "Tis good you are safe, and thank you for your concern over my daughter. It is good to know she is cared for here."

"Very much, my lord. She is a delight," Winn assured him.

Once Lord Chase had left, Winn threw himself on the settee, now wet from Zoe. He didn't care. He was beyond tired if there was such a thing.

"Meeting? What was that all about?" Reid asked, finding a dry seat next to the fire.

"What do you think?"

"Oh," Reid answered and took another drink. After a long silence, both men in their thoughts. "Do you want to?"

"Yes, I want to. I wouldn't have slept with her if I didn't," Winn snapped, keeping his voice at a whisper. There were still house guests banging around downstairs. "But not this way."

"You romantic," Reid joked.

"No, not romantic. I didn't want to make any inroads to marriage until I had figured out who was trying to harm us, but now Zoe's reputation must come into consideration."

He would admit he wanted Zoe more than anything, but not if she didn't want him. She had said she loved him, but that was before. He could not bear to love Zoe more every day, and never be sure if she loved him back. English marriages were built on arrangement, not love, but if Winn was to do something he swore he never would, he wanted it to be for him and him alone, not what she brought to the title, or what others considered of her character.

"Well, if we are to be up at the crack of dawn, I suggest we find our beds." Hayhurst drained his glass and rose.

"You do not have to be awake so early."

"Oh, do you think I would miss this meeting? I'll perch a chair outside the door if I have to, but I want to witness this. After all, I have been present for all your other near-death experiences; don't close me out now, my friend."

"I am sure mother had someone ready your usual room," Winn said, ignoring the barb.

"Till the morning then." Winn waited for him to leave before falling back against the cushion, cold and wet from Zoe. He hoped she had found her way to a warm bath and wasn't as cold as the water seeping into his back.

His mind darted to Zoe in a warm bath. What would she do if he joined her? Damn. Winn adjusted on the couch to accommodate his growing erection. It would be awkward with her maid in the room. She had been through something traumatic and needed her rest. She didn't need some randy fool, unable to control himself even for her own good.

Throwing back the rest of the whiskey in his glass on the table, he decided bed would be a better option for all, but he tucked a shared bath into his memory for the future.

The rest of the house outside his closed study door had been silent for some time, and Winn deemed it safe to find his way to bed. The staff or his mother were successful at ushering all the guests back to their rooms. The one thing that rubbed was the fact that the very person who almost took Zoe from him tonight was enjoying a solid night's sleep because of his hospitality. That alone deserved a beating once Winn had more proof.

Walking up the hallway in the family wing, he didn't notice Zoe's maid until she spoke up when he was next to her.

"For the love of-- you can't sneak up on a man like that," Winn protested to the young, nervous woman.

"I'm sorry, my lord, I didn't mean to scare you. I was trying to be inconspicuous, as Miss Chase asked."

At those words, his ears perked up. "Zoe, is she well?"

"Oh, yes, my lord. She needs to have a word with you and asked me to wait and tell you as you walked by."

Winn looked at the closed door to her room. Zoe was on the other side of that door. She might well still be in the tub, or she is out of the tub, her skin still warm from the water. Winn shook his head. "Tell her I will be available to her all day tomorrow at which any time she chooses, so long as it is after the meeting with her father."

"Well, my lord, she said you would say that, and she needs to speak to you now."

"Now?" Winn asked, feeling a bubbling of anticipation at seeing her rise in his gut.

She nodded so adamantly, her cap almost slipped off her head, "Now," she repeated.

Winn sucked in a deep breath and squared his shoulders. He would be the man Zoe needed, not the randy green buck he was feeling. He nodded once, and the maid scurried off down the hallway, leaving them alone. That was not good. Winn assumed the maid would remain as a chaperone to protect her mistress's virtue.

The door opened silently, and Winn closed it behind him. The room's fireplace blazed, giving off all its warmth. He felt sweat beaded on his upper lip. It was so warm. He looked around, and the room appeared empty until splashing sounds came from behind the large screen across the room. She was still in the bath.

This was penance for all the stupid acts of bravery he had attempted. God wanted him to suffer, that had to be it.

"Winn, is that you?" Her rich voice carried across the room.

Winn had to clear his throat. "Yes, tis I. Your maid said you needed to speak with me."

"Well, I thought it wise considering your meeting with Father in the morning. We should have our stories straight."

She was scheming. She had not called him into her room to profess her undying love after her near-death experience. Winn didn't realize that was what he hoped until he realized it would not happen. "Yes, good idea. I suggest we go with your story about checking on the cats. It is the most innocent and plausible, and with Hayhurst being in my company, it will be more proper than if we were alone."

"That was what I was thinking," she answered. A large whoosh of water signaling she had risen sent Winn's heart thudding and his cock rising to attention. He could do this with the screen between them. However, once she came around the screen, he wasn't sure he would maintain his composure. He still wanted her damn it, regardless if she considered their relationship nothing more than a dalliance, he still wanted her. "Do you think Lord Hayhurst will go along with that?" she asked, walking around the screen in a thick wool robe tied at her waist with a large piece of linen in her hand, drying her long dark hair, which cascaded around her shoulders in waves.

Again, Winn's mouth went dry, and he had to clear his throat to make it work. "Yes, he will say whatever I wish," he said, walking around to be next to the fire and behind a high back chair for distance. "By the way, I wanted to ask if you saw anyone in the shadows when you were on the bridge? Our visitor disappeared, and I was hoping to know what direction he fled."

"Um," she furrowed her brow. Winn liked that expression on her and wanted to walk up and rub those wrinkles away with his thumb. It was something he would often do if they married. Marriage seemed a forgone conclusion, but perhaps Winn could never gain the better part of that, which was all he wanted. Her love. "No, I didn't see anyone. I was too busy trying to walk through the wind and rain. The last thing I remember before I fell into the river was when I looked back and saw you," she said, stepping up to him before he could find an escape. "Thank you for saving me." She rose on her toes and placed a warm kiss on his cheek. The smell of lemons and chamomile spun around him like a haze.

"You are most welcome. It wouldn't do to have our Miss Chase floating down to the Thames now, would it?" he jested. Best to keep it light. "Well, I think we have our stories in the right, and if I am to rise at dawn to meet with your father, I should get some sleep."

"It sounds like the two of you will duel, rise at dawn with pistols ready," she said in her best manly voice.

"I hope it does not come to that, but how good of a shot is your father?" he asked.

"With a target, deadly. A living moving thing, I am not certain," she answered. "I would suggest keeping moving to be sure." She smiled then and damn his heart; it heated and pounded heavy in his chest. How can something work so hard when it was breaking?

"Good night then. I am glad you are safe." He bowed and made haste to leave the room and get to his own without being seen.

A chill traveled from Zoe's toes to her shoulder. She was cold, but was it still from last night, or was this a new cold that woke her up? She felt around the bed for the pile of blankets her maid insisted she crawl under last night when she returned to make sure she didn't need anything else. The blankets had all found their way to the floor in the night. Zoe leaned over the edge and yanked a heavy quilt back up and over her body. The fire was out now, and she would need to get out from under the one blanket left to rouse the coals and add wood. In a minute. Right now, she was enjoying the warmth of the blanket.

She would be much warmer if Winn were curled up with her, but he was all proper gentleman last night and didn't stay long enough for her to coax more than the chaste kiss she gave him on his cheek. She intended to spend time curled in the safety of his arms, against his chest. Instead she stood still wet, which seemed to be the order of her evening, in the middle of her room to cool her heels.

It was then that she remembered the meeting. Forgetting how cold the room was, she threw the blanket aside and rose to stir the fire, then worked on getting herself dressed. It was imperative to be present at this meeting, but she was not sure why. Once she donned her easiest morning dress and pinned her hair into a high bun, the only thing she knew how to do without her maid's help, she left her room still trying to tug on one of her shoes.

The house seemed dark, but the smell of strong coffee, tea, and hot rolls wafted through the halls, making her stomach protest when she turned away from the breakfast room. It didn't appear that anyone was about yet, so she could settle into a chair in Winn's study and wait, but the doorknob wouldn't budge; locked. She stepped back and considered. Perhaps they keep it locked while having house guests. It is Winn's private study, but from under the door, she saw a stream of light showing the room was occupied. Zoe stepped back up to the door and knocked once. The door opened. Winn stood in the crack.

"Good morning, can I help you?"

She blinked once, but rallied. "Yes, you can let me in."

"I'm sorry, but I cannot do that. This is a meeting between your father and me."

"Yes, it is about me," Zoe pointed out. He just stood there staring at her. "When my father comes down, he will--"

Winn opened the door wider to allow Zoe to see that her

father already sat with his coffee on the settee. Then, without so much as a word, Winn closed the door again, and she heard the lock click. Zoe couldn't believe it. They had shut her out of a meeting designed to decide her future. Tears threatened. Her worst fear was that Winn would be forced to marry her without having said he loved her. She wouldn't stand for this, but before she had time to decide what to do next, the voices in the study rose and remained at shouting level.

Now, added to her humiliation last night, the entire house will wake to the two men in her life arguing, or worse yet, what if her jest the previous night about a duel became a reality? Dueling was illegal, but it still happened on occasion. She rapped on the door, but the added noise would only bring everyone running sooner. Zoe began pacing back and forth, trying to plan, while the men in her life screamed at one another.

"What in the devil is going on in there?" Lady Sarrafinna asked with annoyance as she swept down the stairs with Lady Burton and Zoe's aunt in tow.

"I, I tried to get in, but they wouldn't allow it, and then they started yelling, and won't open the door," Zoe explained, tears now falling at will down her cheeks. Her aunt went to her and drew her into a hug, which was more comforting than Zoe would have thought.

"Oh, for the love of-- Can you open that door?" Lady Sarrafinna asked Lady Burton.

Lady Burton left and entered the parlor, only to return a moment later with a large key ring. "There you go," Lady Burton said, and opened the door wide for Sarrafinna to enter the room- and enter it she did, like the daughter of a Duke.

"What in the bloody hell are you two trying to do? Wake the entire house and make things only worse for poor Zoe?" she snapped. The two men stopped in their arguments with their mouths open in silence, at least for the moment.

Zoe's aunt shuffled her into the room against the wall, and Lady Burton stood like a warrior in the doorway. Zoe wasn't sure if she was trying to block any prying eyes that might appear or to keep anyone from leaving the room until Sarrafinna finished.

"Why don't you two just pull your cocks out and I'll have Lady Burton get a tape measure so we can be finished with this."

She struck the two men dumb, and Zoe's aunt tried miserably to stifle her shocked giggle. Zoe's father was the first to speak.

"Sarrafinna, this does not in any way pertain to you. I will appreciate it if you did not involve yourself."

"I am sure you would, but I made a promise to your wife years ago that no matter what, I would protect her daughter and at the moment I am the only voice she has speaking for her."

Both men then all at once tried to plead their case that they were interested in her best interest.

"Oh, will you both be quiet?" Sarrafinna snapped. From the corner of her eye, Zoe saw movement in the hall. Her fear of it being house guests, however, died quickly when two footmen brushed past in the hall with large trunks heading toward the door.

"Now, Lord Chase, since you are Zoe's father, you go

first." She waved her hand, giving the peer permission to speak his case.

He was red-faced and more than a little frustrated, but he took the chance to express his side. "No matter what the scandal, no child of mine will ever be forced into a marriage not of their choosing. Zoe has options, and I will not see her married off to quiet gossip mongers."

Sarrafinna softened a bit in her stance and her expression. Something passed between her father and the woman that Zoe did not understand. She nodded and turned to Winn. "Your turn."

"The entire household saw me bring Zoe back from the woods last night, alone. She must marry me. That is the only way to protect her reputation. He will promise her a life of solitude and angry words if he does not agree to the marriage."

"Better a life of solitude than a life of unhappiness because someone trapped her into something she never wanted."

"Stop." Sarrafinna put her hand up between the two men to stave off the argument more. "I am certain you both think you are doing what is best for Zoe, but have either of you considered asking Zoe what she would prefer? It is, after all, what she will have to live with for the rest of *her* life, not yours."

Both men looked sheepishly at the women present, all of whom were not hiding their disgust of the manly assumptions being bandied about. Zoe's father turned and walked to Zoe. "I'm sorry, my dear, but I am trying to save you from a life of misery."

Zoe nodded at her father, unable to speak and not sure

what could be said, anyway. Winn cared for her, but her father was correct. If in her naive knowledge of love, she was wrong, and he did not love her, what would that marriage look like? Could she make him love her? Would he resent her for being such a stupid girl and chasing him down last night? Now that he was sure he wasn't cursed, what if there were another woman he would consider marrying over her?

"Zoe," Winn shoved his way past the small group surrounding her and took her hand. "Zoe, you need to listen to me. If the gossip gets as bad as I fear, the life your father is suggesting would be no life at all. You would be ruined. You would never be invited or accepted anywhere. At least if you marry me, you can continue your friendships and entertainments. You won't be shunned. I will not have such a thing happen to you under my roof."

Her heart flew into her chest, anticipating his declaration. Shouldn't there be a declaration other than him not allowing this to happen to her under his watch? She wanted to throw her arms around him in front of all these people, and have him hug her back, but would it be real? A wedding was the last thing Winn needed to be focusing on with a would-be murderer in his house. Perhaps after the threat was dealt with, Winn would have time, but this was not the way to begin her life with Winn. Stepping up to him, Zoe reached out, cupping his cheek in her hand, the warmth of it seeping into her, warming her. His eyes were swimming in emotions she couldn't fathom at the moment. Did she see love there? Who knew?

"Thank you, truly, thank you for such a grand sacrifice, but I cannot accept your suit. It would not be fair."

"But--" She dropped her hand and stepped back into the

circle of her aunt's embrace. He was within his right to point out she may very well be standing there with child, but he wouldn't. If that became a problem, she would have to rethink, but for now, she wouldn't take him without his love.

"You heard her," Lord Chase said, standing to shield her from Winn's view and further protestations. "We are finished here. My daughter and I will head back to London this afternoon if we can get packed."

Winn stood silent. His expression pushed a sob into her throat, which she swallowed. They gave her a choice most young women her age are not, but at some point, Winn would fight for her, hopefully. If not, the scandal would not matter, because Zoe knew she would only marry Winn and no one else.

Her aunt hustled her from the room, where Cyn stood in the hallway, waiting. "I'm coming with you," she declared, pulling Zoe into her embrace.

"You can't, Cyn. You have a whole house full of people to host. I will be fine, I promise."

"Nonsense, mother is still here, and she is more than capable. However, I have an idea that once we leave, it won't be long before the house party breaks up. My fool brother will no doubt be in a rage for days after this, which will not improve the mood of the house."

Zoe knew Winn had other matters to contend with and would not have time to dedicate to being angry about her leaving, but she chose not to voice her opinion on the subject.

"I would enjoy the company if you felt you could come with us, but I am uncertain I will not be much company in return."

Cyn squeezed her once more, before heading them both to the stairs. "I only hope I can salvage from this mess my brother created the happy, smiling friend I once knew."

Zoe gave her what was sure to be a broken smile. It was not yet apparent she would ever enjoy smiling again.

CHAPTER TWENTY

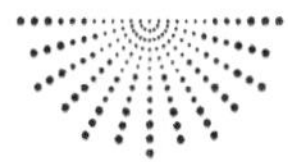

"She's safe now," Reid pointed out the obvious as they sat atop their mounts, looking at the work being done to fix the bridge from last night's attempt on someone's life.

"Yes, she is," Winn agreed, but that didn't make it feel right. He saw the hurt in her eyes when he hadn't fought harder to keep her at the house. If he knew she loved him, he might well have ruined it this morning.

"You no longer have to tread gently in fear of the braggart lashing out at Miss Chase."

"True."

"Isn't that what you wanted?"

Winn turned to look at his friend, who had yet to find the one woman he would be miserable for, for the rest of his life. "Every instinct told me to throw her over my shoulder and run as far from this mess as possible. Seeing her put in that position and having to make that choice was worse than anything a single man might have done to me."

"What did Lord Chase say when you explained the full situation?"

The full situation left out key details, like the fact he had well and truly defiled his daughter and that she could well be carrying his child off to London with her. "He understood my desire to take Zoe out of harm's way. He also agreed she wouldn't go willingly unless pressed. And for the bastard to believe I don't love her or have a chance, she needed to leave by her own accord."

"Well, the sooner we can end this ridiculous nonsense, the sooner you can go mend things with your love."

The last words slammed into Winn's chest. He opened his mouth to protest but then realized he already knew he loved her. His reaction was his old self-preservation tactics. "I hope there is something left to salvage when this is done."

"Me as well. You will be a miserable companion if she does shun you," Reid joked. Winn wished he felt as confident as his friend.

"I can see why you brought me into this mess. You need all the eyes you can get," Lord Sutton said.

"Thank you, Sutton--" Winn turned to the large man sitting on a massive mount on his other side.

"Max. No need for such formalities at this point," Max interrupted.

Winn nodded. There was no need to discuss it. After appraising Sutton of the situation, there wasn't much more that he could know about Winn. Reid suggested pulling him into the fold for extra eyes. The fact Max pulled himself from society put him in a unique unbiased position to give observations.

"What next?" Hayhurst asked, as the men turned and made their way back to the house. Winn hoped he had dallied long enough for Zoe to have already left, fearing he might not contain himself if that was not the case.

When they rounded the drive, four carriages sat waiting, Lord Chase's, Lord Worth's, Lady Sarrafinna's, and one of his own. Lady Burton told him Cyn was picking sides and hieing off to London with Zoe. He didn't blame her. He would rather be tucked up in a carriage with Zoe himself.

The three dismounted and headed into the foyer. Winn hoped he could make it to his study without another ugly scene. Zoe was nowhere when he entered, but his sister was waiting for her shawl to be brought down from her room.

"Sister, I wish you a safe trip to the city," he said, and he meant it.

She leveled him with a stare only an angry sister would bestow on her sibling. "I am not sure yet what you are playing at, but just know if you have dragged my dearest childhood friend into one of your schemes and you keep her heartbroken, I will never allow you to live one more day without making you sorry for your actions."

Reid stepped back a step, not wanting to share in that promise. Max stood firm but had an odd smile on his face. Winn silently cheered Cyn for her loyalty, but little did she know if this did not work out to his advantage, she would not have to utter one more word of it to make him suffer.

"I am handling the situation Cyn, you need to trust me," he assured her.

"See that you do," was all she said, as the maid came

bustling down with her forgotten shawl. "I shall be in residence at Lord Chase's until such time. I will not return home."

Winn gave Cyn a look that should tell her he planned on fixing everything, but since he wasn't sure himself, he doubted Cyn would take him seriously.

"Thank you," was all he said, walking toward the door of his study, but was again waylaid — this time by Lady Sarrafinna.

"Lord Burton, might I have a word?" she asked, walking between him and his study door like she wasn't giving him an option.

"Of course, Lady Sarrafinna." He did not hide the frustration in his voice.

"I am not sure what you and Lord Chase are scheming at, but I will remind you the reputation and the very heart of a young woman that is well-loved is at stake here." Winn opened his mouth to speak but thought better of it when he looked at her expression. Weren't courtesans supposed to be beautiful, likable women, whose demeanor put men at ease? "I believe you love her, and I am certain she loves you. Fix this before it gets out of our control. Here."

She reached into her reticule and handed him a folded piece of paper. "What's this?" he asked, starting to unfold it, but being stopped by her gloved hand over his.

"I believe it will help move your little investigation forward. Send word if you need anything else. I promised to help see Zoe settled and happy, and I will not fail in that."

She swung from him, her skirts raking over his booted feet as she went to embrace Cyn, and according to what he heard, make plans for meeting once they were all settled in London.

Before anyone else could grab him, or before Zoe was put in a situation where she needed to speak to him again to be polite, Winn took his chance and slipped into his study, shut the door, and turned the lock. He had no idea where Max or Reid had stopped in the maylay, but he was sure the men were capable of finding their way to the study. Winn took the paper still gripped in his hand and read it.

Lady Sarrafinna saw much more than anyone gave her credit for, Winn thought. The note had a list of names with instructions to talk to them about Mr. Smythe. It also suggested Winn call his solicitors and search how the two families might be connected.

That last line intrigued him. His original plan was to become a close confidant with a bottle of something imported and strong, but he sat at his desk, penning a note to his solicitor, and made it clear this was to be put on the top of the man's priority list. Once sanded, he pulled the bell pull, hoping he wasn't too late to get his letter on one of the coaches leaving. To his surprise, luck was on his side. It would be handed off to his groom, that would deliver it as soon as they settled Cyn.

Now, where was that bottle?

"My dear, a word please." Lady Burton stood outside the private family parlor at the entrance of the family wing. Zoe's heart sank. After everything else, she hadn't wanted to let anyone down. Her goal had not been to cause a scandal for Lady Burton to contend with.

"Of course, Lady Burton. I wanted to apologize for this whole debacle," Zoe said.

"You apologize? Whatever for? This is in no way your fault, my dear. I am certain there will be somebody to blame, but you will not be that person. Of that, I am certain." She enveloped Zoe in an embrace that Zoe melted into. Lady Burton seemed talented in what to say and when to say it.

"That is very kind," Zoe said as she pulled back before the tears spilled over, "but I am afraid no matter the culprit it will be my last time visiting, and I am just sick that I am leaving in such a melancholy mood."

"Ack, I do not believe that for one moment. My son is a lot of things, but he is not a stupid man--I hope at any rate. You are his perfect match, and I am certain he will come round to give you the declaration you need. The first thing you must learn about men of any age or station; they come to tow much more slowly than one would hope. I have always understood it to be too much pride. Most men seem to have an overabundance of the sin, and it takes a bit to wiggle them free of it."

Zoe smiled despite the pain in her heart, hoping this was true, but aware to what extent she had not been such the perfect epitome of an English bride. Winn had been vocal about never marrying. Perhaps the absence to come could remind Winn of his life choice.

"Dear? I am familiar with that look. All will be as it should in time. You hold that close to your heart. Your aunt and I will remain here with the house party and try to mitigate the story reaching London. Sarrafinna, who was heading back to the city anyway, will handle the situation from there. She has the ear of some of the most powerful men in London." Lady Burton lowered her voice on the last sentence in a conspiratorial way.

"I-I don't know what to say. I am so thankful for all of you to help. I wish Cyn wasn't so persistent in coming with me, but I have to admit I am looking forward to her company."

"We all loved your mother, and we love you just the same. You are already family, my dear. As long as my son steps into position as he needs to, we will settle all. I am so glad you came to us, and I will not allow this foolishness to dampen the reunion." She grabbed Zoe for one more quick hug and then stepped back, clearing her throat.

Oh Lord, if Lady Burton cries, Zoe would not be able to contain the emotions roiling through her. She bobbed a curtsy and headed down the hall before that happened. This was the first time since her mother passed away that she felt genuinely taken care of. Her father had done his best, but there was something about the love of a woman in a motherly role no father could fill. It might take three or four women to take her mother's place. She was glad her mother had chosen so well.

At the foot of the stairs, her maid stood in the hall, holding Zoe's shawl and bandbox, which she would take in the carriage with her. Zoe had learned after the long journey back to England that she needed things to keep her mind busy when traveling. The box carried two books, a journal, and a sketchbook. She doubted that this trip would be the same. Instead of fending off boredom, she would occupy her mind to not go down the long dark path it seemed determined to travel.

The maid handed over a pair of gloves, and as Zoe slipped into them and put on the hat the footman handed her, she looked over to the study door, which was closed. Was he in there? Was he angry? Zoe wasn't sure. He could breathe a sigh of relief for all she knew.

"Are you ready, Miss? The others are outside waiting," the maid asked.

"Oh, yes, I am ready. Off to London, we go. I hope it is a pleasant ride," Zoe said, trying to sound light-hearted and excited for her new life in London. Her voice was flat, even to her ears.

"Aye, miss, you will love London. So much more like the life you are more used to in a city," Mary chatted as they met the others in the drive.

"Zoe, you will ride with me in my carriage if that suits you."

Zoe looked at her father, who nodded and waved her along. "I have work I can do on the ride into the city, and I will spread my papers out better if you ride with Lady Burton. I hope you don't mind." He walked up, kissing her on the forehead. He looked at her with all the love he had and then settled into his carriage, last in the group of carriages. Lord Worth's carriage led the troupe, then Lady Sarrafinna's, where she already sat waiting for them to get moving, one long peacock plume bobbing out the open window. Next was the Burton coach with full livery, glistening in the sun with the gold accents. They would make quite the parade traveling through the village then on to London, she thought, as Cyn was handed in. Before Zoe ducked into the carriage, she took one last look at the front of the house, which she considered her English home away from home since she was a child. In the window to the left of the grand front stairway was Winn, watching her. Not watching the entire group, but staring at her. At the same time, she was buoyed and felt the weight of what she may turn her back on. Again, she forced away the tears.

"I, for one, am glad to leave the house party. It was getting tedious, don't you think?" Cyn asked as they both settled their skirts and made room for their maids who would ride in the coach with them.

"Yes, I guess you are right," Zoe said, hoping she put enough enthusiasm into the statement.

"It is a good day's ride, depending on how the roads fared from the storm last night. I am certain you must be exhausted and suffer from at least a mild headache from your wound." Zoe reached up and touched her head, having forgotten she struck her head on something unforgiving as she rushed along with the water. "I would not at all think you rude if you slept." Cyn patted her leg in reassurance.

"Thank you. I did not sleep well at all, but I am not certain I will sleep here any more than I did last night," Zoe explained.

"I understand, but I am sure the three of us can keep ourselves occupied if you nod off," Cyn assured her.

The carriage jerked forward, causing a surge of panic to course through Zoe. If she left Winn, would he find her? And the tears did what they were threatening all morning. There was no stopping them, and she let them come.

Before she could react, Cyn and her maid had shifted, not

an easy feat in a moving carriage with skirts involved, and Zoe found herself engulfed in Cyn's arms.

"You dear, dear thing. I should shoot my brother for this farce. How dare he break your heart."

Zoe didn't pull away, she leaned in and let the tears wash her face. How can this be happening? She had never been a rebel, wanted no excitement. She remembered back not so long ago, when she ridiculed Winn for what she saw as his lack of respect for his life. Would she ever be allowed the opportunity to have a say in his wild adventures? She hoped so. Between the rocking of the carriage and Cyn's kind whispered words of assurance, the exhaustion got a foothold, and she slept for the entire trip.

CHAPTER TWENTY-ONE

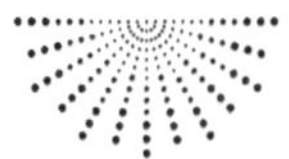

"Damn it, Winn, you got him!" Reid shouted as he also slammed the desk and the missive from the solicitor.

Winn sat back in his chair to take it all in. Lady Sarrafinna had been the one to lead them to the answer. She would never say where she gathered her information, or how she put it together, but if he had the chance to ask her, it would be too good to pass on.

"Winn? Hello?"

"Oh, sorry, I am needing some time to reconcile all of this." Winn ran both his hands through his hair. "I mean, this information implies that three generations of this family were murdered in hopes it would send the title into abeyance. That is a lot to bite off, I'm not ashamed to say."

"You are not wrong," Max admitted, sitting in the chair across the desk from Winn. "How do we find out the truth?

It isn't as if we can ask your father or grandfather if they were murdered."

"No, we can't," Winn sighed. Where these documents brought much to light that Winn didn't know about his own family and title, they also raised more questions than they answered.

"So, assure me I have this correct. Your title was not always yours. Sometime in the 1500s, some Lord Burton did something so terrible that the king stripped him of the title and bestowed it onto your relation," Hayhurst repeated.

"Yes."

"And that sent the once Lord Burton's family into ruin. For all these generations that family, presumably the Mr. Smythes, have been working tirelessly to clean their books of whatever this horrible thing is. Still, the one thing they cannot get back is the title, which your family has held, respectfully and responsibly, for these so many years," Reid finished.

"Correct."

"So, somewhere along the lines, in the last fifty years, someone thought it would help their endeavor if, by some strange happenstance, the current Lords Burton started dying, hoping the line would die, allowing them to petition to get their title back."

"Exactly."

All men sat in silence, doing the math. Unless there was an elemental flaw in the family's makeup in question, Winn didn't see how murder passed down from one generation to the next, but it would appear it was plausible.

In the silence, his thoughts wandered to Zoe. It had been

over a week since he watched her enter the carriage and leave for London. Cyn had not bothered to send him word of how she was faring. He might well mend things with Zoe, but his sister would not make it easy. His nights were filled with dreams of him watching Zoe disappear on the bridge. Waking in a cold sweat, he would realize she had also disappeared in his traveling coach as well.

His only priority was to untangle this ridiculous knot so he could go to her and explain. His mother still required him to attend dinner with the remaining guests, who were now down to only four. They were remaining because their own London homes were not yet ready for the season. He complied to help perpetuate the idea that he and Zoe were not at all involved. He feared it would get back to Zoe. If it did, perhaps it would be too late when he got his life solved.

"What is our next move?" Reid asked.

Winn considered him. Hayhurst had been his friend since Eaton. He had gone along with every scheme Winn came up with, but this was not a well-calculated stunt. Winn had no control over Smythe and how much he wanted to see Winn dead. Tallying the deaths and attempted deaths thus far, it was three dead, Winn's attempted death multiple times, and Zoe's attempted demise at least once. "I will go forward alone. I thank you both for your help, but--"

"Whoa," Reid said as he leaned into the desk from his seat. "You are not closing me out of this now. You forced me to go along with your wild schemes that, in all honesty, should have put you in your grave long before this. I am in this until it is done now. I will either follow you and get in the way or be part and parcel to the plan. You choose."

"Please don't think I am going to go back to a London townhouse that my pregnant wife is in the process of redecorating. I never wanted to leave my lands in the country. This is the first glimmer of a worthwhile endeavor I have had since I agreed to enter society again," Max pointed out.

Winn assumed his friend had already foreseen Winn's desire to protect the ones he cared about and was ready for that. He was surprised that Max was so invested.

"Very well then, but if you get yourselves killed, do not come back and haunt me. I am afraid after thinking I was cursed for most of my life. After this, I will be done with the supernatural."

"I can't say I blame you, now what is our next move?"

"A message went back to my solicitor, giving him our theory now with this new information. I asked if there is any way to delve back into my grandfather's and father's deaths to prove anything there. I am not holding out hope. The best we can wish at this point is for Smythe to come out with the entire truth when trapped, and I don't hold out much hope there either. If, however, we can set up a situation to catch him in the act, then we will end this once and for all." Reid stared in silence at what Winn implied. "What? It is a solid plan."

"Yes, except for the part about needing to catch him in the act. I assume the act you speak of is your death?"

Reid looked to Max, who shrugged. Winn liked a man who let another make his own destiny.

Winn rose from his chair and hitched his hip up on the edge of it, unable to sit idle any longer. "Well, I would hope we can choreograph it so we catch him before that exact point, but yes, that is the basic plan."

"I don't like it."

"Then, you can remain here, as I had originally planned."

"Fine, when do we leave?"

"I have someone monitoring Smythe since he left the house party a day after Zoe. He is to proceed with extreme prejudice on my behalf if he goes near her. We need to see where it would give him a window of time to act, but I found just the place." Winn shuffled some papers on his desk until he found the invitation, then handed it over to Hayhurst to read.

"Lord Buckley's horse auction?"

"Yes, Buckley has quite a massive set of grounds in the heart of London, plenty of places during a horse auction for me to be alone and out of view of witnesses, but it is also set up so I do not need ever actually to be alone."

"This might work, but what will Buckley think if we cause a commotion and upset his auction? It will be a scandal, no matter how this plays out."

"Yes, I worried about that, but this is an instance where Buckley is better off finding out after the fact. Once he understands the facts, he will not be too upset. And, if he is, my stables always need a few more horses, which would also make Cyn happy."

The auction wasn't for another week and a half. Winn wanted to ride to London now and wait there, but he knew he would want to see Zoe, and that would not do. Smythe was not targeting Zoe right now, because it appeared there was no interest between them; he wouldn't risk that. He would have to wait.

The sun's warmth seeped through the large glass pane and into Zoe's dress, heating her. The weather had been mild since they arrived in London, and today was no doubt going to follow suit. Outside, London bustled along in a rhythm only city dwellers understood. The park across the street was filling up with women holding brightly colored parasols to protect their faces from the sun and men on horseback parading through the colored waves, greeting all who passed.

Zoe observed as two carriages pulled up next to the townhouse and four well-appointed women exited and headed for her door. It had been a steady stream of ladies arriving to visit since they were settled. It exhausted Zoe. All she would like was to be left alone so she could lie on her bed, feeling sorry for herself. Oh, and cry. Tears were never far away from her. She saw a stray cat on Bond street yesterday, reminding her of the kittens at the lodge, and she was almost overcome there on the street.

One of the party knocked on the door, and Zoe watched the butler cross the hallway to answer the door.

"Well, you might as well come sit," Cyn said from a chair with her embroidery laid across her lap. "We will go to the park after this visit if you like."

"Thank you, Cyn. I am sorry I have been so melancholy." Zoe crossed to take a seat on the edge of the settee closest to Cyn.

"Nonsense, if I were in your position, I would be curled up in my room, inconsolable, but I believe you are not as dramatic as I am, and I have not found another that drives me to such emotion. That is something you should be grateful for, that you have one such as that."

Cyn was best at pointing out those things in a situation

others would overlook. She was right; she had found someone she loved. Many people in this life are not afforded such luxury. Lady Sarrafinna came to mind. Zoe seemed to be thinking of her quite a lot. She was sure if not for Lady Sarrafinna traversing London and talking about Zoe's accolades, they would not have been visited as much as they had. Some came because they were acquainted with Cyn, but the majority were there to meet Zoe.

It seemed that a great scandal was averted. Invitations to the season's most exclusive events were arriving daily, and when out shopping or strolling in the park, there was any number of people greeting them.

"I have never been one to allow myself to dwell on my sadness. After experiencing my mother deteriorate, I swore that as long as I could do for myself, then I had no reason to complain about life. Still, I agree in this particular situation, wallowing is something I must fight."

"Miss Chase, you have visitors," the butler intoned with a degree of importance. It made Zoe want to giggle every time. She was coming to like the elderly man, but he was serious.

"Thank you, Franklin."

"The ladies Danforth and Miss Hovington." He bowed and let the ladies enter. All four bustled in with good mornings all around. Cyn knew them, as she had all the visitors, and made the introductions. Zoe couldn't help but stare a bit at the two younger Danforths. She had never spent much time with twins, and it was almost unsettling how similar they were. Thankfully, their mother didn't seem to subscribe to the idea that her twin daughters had to dress alike, and Zoe thought that a good thing.

"It is kind of you to call on us. Do you live in London

year-round, or are you here for the season?" Zoe asked. She asked all the guests. It was easier than trying to find new topics to start with. And as people most liked to talk about themselves, she could listen with one ear and allow her mind to wander to what Winn might be doing.

"We live in the city and only go to our country home when the city gets too hot late in the summer," Lady Danforth answered.

"And I am here for the season. I do not care for the constant motion of the city. I think it bad for the digestion," Lady Hovington explained.

"I love coming to the city, but I do so love our home in the country. I miss it about halfway through the season every year," Cyn commented.

"And you, my dear? Do you prefer the city or the country?" Lady Danforth asked, trying to pull Zoe into the mix.

"I am afraid I haven't yet spent enough time in London to tell. I was raised between Rome and Florence, which are two large cities, but when I would come to England, we would stay with the Burtons, and I do consider that home as much as Cyn. My answer will have to be reserved for after this season."

"A true Diplomat's daughter," Lady Hovington proclaimed, and everyone laughed.

"Tell me, have you been to the latest play at Vauxhall gardens?" Lady Danforth asked.

"It is truly magical. It will be a sensation; I am certain," one twin added, with real passion.

"We have not ventured to the gardens yet. Lord Chase could not take the time to accompany us."

"Oh, that's right. Well, when your brother arrives, see that he takes you to his box," Lady Danforth asserted, but then gave Zoe a disconcerting gaze, like she was hoping just speaking of Winn would cause her to burst into tears.

"Thank you. I love the theater. If I have time, I would love to attend. This season will be my come out since I was abroad and then with my mother's illness. This is the first season I will participate in. Are you coming out as well, or perhaps you came out last season?"

She turned her attention to the twins, who were younger than her, but close to the age they would be to come out into society.

"We are coming out as well," they said together, both pleased to be acknowledged.

"That is wonderful news. There were only two other ladies close to my age at the house party. I hope we can become better acquainted. It will make the whirl of the season much more enjoyable when you can anticipate seeing people you are familiar with in the crowd."

Both girls beamed, and so started a long conversation about which events would be considered the events to attend, and the times at those events when a woman of marriageable age should arrive for the best chance to interact with a potential suitor.

By the time the group left, Zoe was drained, but also enthused that there would be two friends in the crowds they encountered. Looking for a man to marry made her feel sick. She didn't want anyone other than Winn. If she had to attend the season and play pretty to every man she encountered, it might do her in.

"Very well, time for fresh air and some exercise." Cyn walked up behind her in the hallway.

"Oh, I'm not sure I am up for it, but thank you."

"Oh no, you don't. We can walk in a less populated section of the park, but you need fresh air. Well, as fresh as one can find in London at any rate. Here." Cyn handed her gloves and a parasol that matched her gown's trim, a light green.

"Fine, but just a short one. I would like to lie down this afternoon." There was no point in arguing with Cyn. Zoe would expend more energy than she had. The day was warm, and Cyn was correct. As soon as they stepped out of the door, the warmth and the gentle breeze made Zoe feel better.

They walked in silence across the street, acknowledging those they passed as they went. At the pond, a path trailed down to the less populated section of the park. Zoe moved back the parasol to let the sun warm her face. She turned it up to the sky and eased at the warmth on her skin. Perhaps all would work itself out.

"Well, I-- I just might kill him in broad daylight for the whole of the Ton to witness," she heard Cyn growl.

Zoe turned to see who Cyn was talking about, and coming up the lane on horseback with Lord Hayhurst was Winn. Her heart slammed into her chest, taking the breath from her lungs. Her instinct was to run to him and throw her arms around him, but the expression on his face was not one of mutual affection. His expression was anything but joy at seeing his sister and her walking.

"Brother, I had not been told you would be arriving," Cyn said as they all came to a stop in the path.

"Tis good to see you as well, sister. I hope all goes well," Winn answered.

"Good day, Miss Chase, ignore them," Hayhurst said with a warm smile. At least he was, if not happy to see her, polite would be the proper term.

"Good day, Lord Hayhurst. I am doing well, thank you."

"We have only but just arrived, and I had not had time to make you aware of our arrival," Winn explained.

"But, you had time to take a ride in the park?" Cyn asked with full sarcasm.

"We needed to stretch our legs. I was planning on calling on you later today after I unpacked and knew better my schedule," Winn turned from Cyn and greeted Zoe. "Miss Chase, I hope your trip from our manor was not too taxing on you. Have you settled in well?"

Zoe itched in her dress. Any fool could see through their polite conversation. Winn wanted to be anywhere but here with her. She straightened her back and took a breath. "I have settled in well. My father chose a most suitable home, and so close to the park and shopping. I believe I will be happy calling this home." She would not fall apart, not in front of Winn and all the eyes that she now felt staring at her.

The facade she had been living with crumbled. None of those visiting cared to know her. They were looking for a scrap of gossip to bring to their next call. If she broke now, the scandal would no longer be held at bay, and all the work her aunt, Lady Burton, and Lady Sarrafinna had done would be for naught.

"It has been nice speaking with you. I hope we run into each other again this season. Cyn, Mr. Smythe is over by the fountain. I will walk over and say hello while you finish reconnecting with your brother."

She curtsied and turned her back on the group. She would hold herself together because her heart might well be broken and just taking up space in her body, but her pride was alive and well.

CHAPTER TWENTY-TWO

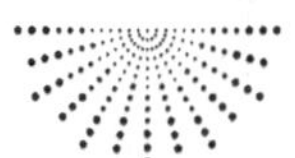

Winn watched as Zoe walked away from them, her hips swaying, distracting him. And the fact she would talk to Smythe hurt like a stab to the heart. His horse sensed his body tense and flicked his mane and sidestepped in agitation.

Reid shot him a warning glance. It had been the plan to be seen in the park at the busy hour today to let everyone know he was in town. They had not taken into account that Zoe and Cyn would most likely be there as well. It was imperative not to let prying eyes know he was happy to see Zoe. Happy didn't explain the jolt he felt when he laid eyes on her walking up the path. It was like giving a dying man a drink of water, and he wanted more- so much more.

He had not prepared himself for Zoe's disinterest. She looked uncomfortable at their meeting, but he had hoped when they ran into each other that there would be a spark in her eye or some type of movement or comment to give him hope, but there was none. Her eyes were empty of the liveliness that once lived there. Did he do that to her? Did his attempt to protect her kill the spark in her? He couldn't live with himself if that were true. He did not want to see her happy with another man, but if she no longer cared for him, he would learn to live with it. If, however, he turned her from love altogether, that would be most painful.

"Is Zoe truly doing well?" Winn asked his sister, who had abandoned talking to him when she realized he was no longer listening and turned to talk to Reid about the reason they were in town- the auction. She turned back to him with a look his sister rarely bestowed on him, but to suitors who can't take a polite passing and push their advantage.

"No, she is not doing well. I had to all but shove her out the door today to force her to take some air. If I had not accompanied her, she would remain in her chamber in a miserable state," she spat.

Winn hated the idea of Zoe hurting so, but perhaps there was a chance. Maybe she still had feelings for him and was just playing a good game for lookie-loos.

"I hope that is not a smile playing at your lips," Cyn said in a tone that was anything but loving. "If you are feeling manly because a woman suffers when you set her aside like she was nothing more than a plaything, I may be inclined to--"

"Cyn, you know your brother better than that. It was never his intention to hurt her, in fact, quite the opposite." Reid came to his defense because Winn was beyond words. He was just buoyed that perhaps she still cared for him.

Cyn hmphed, but seemed mollified for the moment. "If you are going to the horse auction, I will send some information to you about a mare I am interested in. I was afraid I would be left to send the head groom at the London house to bid for me, but now you can do that."

"What? Oh, well, I am not sure if I will get the chance to bid," Winn said dismissively, and didn't realize his error until his sister's eyes narrowed on him.

"Just what scheme are you up to now? Zoe cannot handle seeing you back to your old brainless self in the tabloids."

"Don't worry, Cyn. We will see that you get that mare. No worries."

"See that you do," Cyn said, only giving Reid a passing glance. "Take care brother, Lord Hayhurst." She turned to join Zoe, who was talking with the group surrounding Smythe.

Winn watched for a bit longer, but once Zoe reached out and laid her gloved hand on his arm, he couldn't stand there any longer. "Come on. We've done what we set out to do. I don't feel very social any longer."

Winn turned and left by the eastern gate where they entered. It allowed him to turn and not go past the small group. He wasn't sure he would hold himself from grabbing Zoe by the parasol and riding off with her. Hayhurst followed but didn't bother talking. Their next stop would be White's to announce their presence further and their intended plans while in the city. By the time they returned to Winn's London residence, he retired to take a nap.

Hours later, Winn woke and made his way down to the parlor, not feeling any better. Reid had used his time to create a replica of Buckley's estate, including all the grounds and outbuildings. Max had arrived with news of help that neither of them had connections to.

"Well, I am glad to see if this Earldom seat doesn't work out for you, there is always a future in miniatures," Winn drolled as he crossed to the drink cart and filled a healthy portion of whatever was in the first decanter he grabbed.

"I just thought that one of us should be productive. Are you rested, or should I ask Victor to bring some smelling salts?"

"No, I am fine, just as I was before I napped."

"Obviously," Reid agreed.

"So, what are your thoughts now that you see what we have to work with?" Winn asked, moving on. No need to discuss his mental wellbeing; they both knew it was a tenuous situation.

"It is hard to say because we don't know Smythe well enough to predict how he may go about dispatching you. He may try to finish the deed before the day of the auction. If that is the case, it will be blind luck for us to stop it."

"Always the optimist," Winn commented. "There is not very much to entice us to leave the townhouse between now and the auction. It would be plausible that we might be at White's or ride in the park. We can make provisions for watchers in the park, and I am certain as long as we remain together in White's, I would be safe."

"One would think."

Winn raised his glass to his suspicious friend and took a long drink while he studied the elaborate model on his gaming table. "What about here, behind the barn?" He pointed to a secluded spot behind the main barn, but it was boxed off by two other buildings, giving a degree of privacy. "I could wander through the barn and come out here and appear lost."

"That isn't bad, and your groom is situated here," Max pointed at the hayloft, which was an open section at the back of the barn. "Lord Hayhurst will lurk in the shadows as well." He plucked a small red piece of paper stuck through with a pin and pinned it on that area. "Where are other locations that would make it easy to kill someone then slip away?"

They continued to mark off three other locations that they would make sure were well guarded. The idea was to create a situation where Winn got him talking before he took aim, and to have someone, preferable Buckley, within earshot as a witness, then take him into custody. Max reached out to someone connected to the Bow street runners, and one would stop by to be brought up to speed.

"What happens if this doesn't go as planned? Any consideration on that point at all?" Reid asked, lounging in a chair.

"I am meeting with my solicitor tomorrow to talk about my grandfather and father's murders, and I will draft up paperwork to see that Zoe is taken care of if she is carrying my child."

"What about talking to Zoe?"

Winn made his way to the matching chair, filling his glass first. "I am not sure she will even receive me. I could pen a letter and send it over the morning we leave for the auction."

His lifelong friend stared at him. "A letter?"

"Yes, if she won't see me, it is my only option."

Max tsked, like an old schoolmarm.

"Do you love this woman? Have you even admitted the fact to yourself?"

"I-- yes. What, though, if she doesn't love me?"

"Impossible. I am witness to how she looks at you when you aren't paying attention. However, if you play the ass, she is a strong enough person to walk away, and I would bet a letter sent by a footman is the surest way to do that."

"Giselle would never allow such a thing to happen in our relationship. I tend to agree with Hayhurst," Max agreed.

"You are probably right. I cannot risk being seen calling on Zoe. I don't want anyone to conclude we are once again interested in each other. Right now, after the meeting in the park, it is clear at least that Zoe has no interest in me. We need to keep the attention and interest on me, not her."

"True," Reid agreed.

"What if I called the night before the auction? Perhaps I can find another way to get in and surprise her in her room. That way, I can get in and out without being seen."

"That could work, if she or her father don't hear you, or hear her screams and dispatch you before Smythe has a chance to," Reid pointed out. "What if I call on your sister the day before and let them know you need to speak with Zoe, but it needs to be secret, and you will explain when you are here. That way, at least you will know if she wants to see you or not."

"What about when I am meeting with my solicitor? I won't be alone then and I will wait for you to join me at his office. No one would think anything of you not accompanying me to my solicitor, and you are just visiting a family friend."

"Perfect."

"Good, I believe dinner is about to be announced, and then the bow street runner should be here not long after that." Winn heard the footfalls of the footman announcing the meal. Winn was satisfied, considering how much they were unsure of. They had every possibility covered. He was more nervous about talking with Zoe than he was about meeting his attempted murderer face to face. The next few days would be the most trying of his, he decided.

The next day, Winn sat in his solicitor's private parlor, waiting for Hayhurst to arrive. Something unsettled Winn. The rather spacious, well-appointed room made Winn feel closed in. He made a mental note he would need to send his solicitor a bonus at the end of the year because the man was none too happy to be awakened before dawn this morning to attend to Winn.

Last night when Reid found his bed, Winn tried to fall asleep but spent most of the night pondering his future. A future, until recently, was not a luxury afforded him. He considered everything, from ideas for the estates he had, to helping his sister get settled. He imagined racing around the yard, chasing puppies with a hoard of little brown-haired, gray-eyed children. Then there was Zoe. Despite his renewed zest for growing old, he wasn't sure she would take him back, not that he had made any declarations before all this.

"My lord, your friend has arrived," the house servant entered his thoughts.

"Thank you."

"Would you like me to collect your things?"

"Yes, please, I will meet you in the hall entry," Winn instructed. He rose and took up the bundle of papers that he was there to make sure were in order. He had always kept his affairs well in order and up to date, because when you have a curse chasing you, your death is a constant partner. These papers were to add Zoe into his benefactors.

If hell came tomorrow, he needed a reassurance that if she was carrying his child she and the baby would be taken care of. He assumed he would feel more remorse having false papers stating they had married by special license, but he felt no such guilt. To him, she was already his wife. Papers were just that- paper. That way, she was free to remarry with no fear of scandal. Inside his coat pocket was the special license he hoped to use in the next few days if all played out in their favor — no need to wait to start the rest of his life.

"Here you are, my lord." The servant handed over his hat and gloves. Reid stood on the stoop, ready to knock.

"There you are," Hayhurst said. His expression was unreadable to Winn, and that unsettled him.

"Well?"

"Let us get heading home, and I will explain on the way."

The two got settled on the bench on the high phaeton. Winn loved the vehicle but had not bought one of his own, citing it as a waste of money that would be better served to take care of his sister and mother if he died, but now, perhaps he would look into one for himself. His companion steered the matched bays onto the street, maneuvering through the pedestrians and other coaches.

Once they were in a more open thoroughfare, Winn couldn't wait. "Well? Will she see me?"

Reid looked over at him with a grin. "Yes. At first she was reluctant, and your sister who is, by the way, squarely in Miss Chase's corner thought you should have your ears boxed for such a suggestion."

"That doesn't surprise me." Cyn was loyal to him only as

far as her sense of right and wrong stretched. At that point, he would be on his own.

"I explained you needed to speak with her before the auction tomorrow. She tried to press me for more, but I told her that was not my story to tell."

"Good. Thank you."

He nodded. "You will need to find the back entrance through the small garden fence. Since the house is across from the park, it makes more sense, if you still want to keep your interest hidden. She said it would be unlocked."

"Perfect. Now that everything is set with my solicitor, we can move forward. Have you heard from the bow street runner?"

"Yes." Hayhurst maneuvered the phaeton into place in front of Winn's townhouse, and threw the reins to a waiting groom. "He is all set, but still a bit skeptical. It would help if we had more proof than what we do."

Winn understood. He wished they had more, too. "Well, as far as my father's death and my grandfather's, there was no question my grandfather slipped on the unfastened rug falling down the stairs." They entered the house and proceeded to the parlor. "It may have been murder, but it also made perfect sense that it was a tragic accident. My father's accident was a bit more suspicious. There was some question about foul play, but it never progressed from mere speculation. So, aside from a full confession, those murders will go unavenged."

"I am certain your relatives would be happy as long as you put an end to this before it ends your family line," Reid pointed out.

"Of that, I am certain." Winn crossed the room and hit a

latch on the side of the fireplace. A small door popped open. "Did you see that?"

"Yes, I did, damned inventive."

"I am putting the duplicate papers from today's meeting with my solicitor in here, just in case. If something does not go right tomorrow, and by chance the papers my solicitor have are destroyed, please see that these papers get to my mother and sister, and Zoe."

"But is he that smart to consider your final requests?"

"I am banking on him not being that smart, but after two deaths and at least several attempts on my life and an attempt on Zoe's, I don't want to make assumptions."

"Agreed."

"We should go to White's this evening and talk about our plans at the auction. The more public, the better."

"Very well, will we go together or in separate vehicles?"

"Together, I will go down the street and hail a hack to take me to Zoe's."

"Do you think it wise to travel the streets alone? Considering--" He didn't finish his statement.

"Good point. I can ask the majordomo when we arrive to procure a hack for me then."

"Better idea, I think. Now, I want to go over this again, to make sure we understand where everyone will be. Is Lord Buckley still unaware of all this?"

Winn walked over to the makeshift stable area at Lord Buckley's estate. "Yes, he still has not been appraised. The fewer who know, the better."

Reid didn't agree with him on that front, but with less than twenty-four hours, it was not an issue anymore. He allowed Reid to take them through all the places Smythe might strike, and options for countermeasures, as many times as his friend wanted. It would all be over tomorrow. There was a chance he would not have someone to celebrate with, but it was a good sign that Zoe agreed to see him. He wanted nothing more than to have a future with her. Until he ran her over in the road when she arrived for the house party, he was content with never marrying and never having children.

The idea he had ever allowed something as foolish as a curse to take away his future angered him. Regardless of how this ended, he owed his newfound life and future to her. He could never repay that.

After what Winn considered an ample amount of prepping time, he excused himself and called for a bath. He wanted to be at his best tonight. If this would be the last time Zoe saw him, he wanted it to be memorable.

CHAPTER TWENTY-THREE

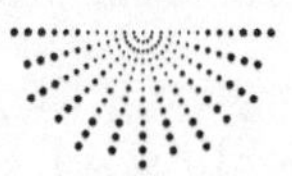

The clock struck the hour at ten o'clock and Zoe jumped. After Lord Hayhurst called and said Winn needed to talk with her, she had been a basket case. She considered it a good sign that he wanted to speak, but the fact he didn't want to be seen coming or leaving her father's house bothered her. He thought he was protecting her, no doubt. If the bridge plank was meant for her, she understood. The problem was that her brain never stopped at the practical reasoning. All afternoon, she spun stories of him coming to tell her he had a secret wife that no one knew about because she was some poor farmer's daughter, and they had an entire parcel of children and were exceedingly happy.

This bothered her so much, she brought it up to Cyn. "My brother? A secret wife with a dozen children?" She burst out laughing, and Zoe heard her snort.

"Well, it is possible he is in love with someone else," Zoe shot back.

"Oh, but my dear, it isn't. Winn has been adamant for most of his life that he would not marry or have children. He never as much as flirts with a marriageable woman. Plenty of married women and a few widows if I recall, but none with expectations of him beyond bedroom play."

"Cyn!" Zoe said, not wanting that much information.

"Oh, yes sorry," she said, but Zoe calmed in her words. "I am just demonstrating that no matter what story you make up sitting there waiting, there isn't one where he is in love with another that will be remotely close to the truth. The fool loves you."

Zoe sighed and slumped into a chair next to Cyn and her embroidery. "Very well, I will defer this to you."

"Thank you."

"But, whatever could be so important that he needs to speak with me in such a secretive way?"

"As you said before, if he thinks you are in danger, I am surprised he is chancing it at all. He is a protective male, that is for sure. What I wouldn't give to be present, but I understand you two deserve some privacy."

"I promise to come to your room as soon as he leaves to fill you in," Zoe assured her. Cyn had commented right after Hayhurst left that she thought whatever was afoot was dangerous, and she worried about her brother.

After dinner, both ladies retired early. Since her father was at White's and would not be home for hours, she hoped Winn would arrive before that. It could be problematic if her father caught him in the house.

After the servants retired, Zoe snuck downstairs and

unlatched the back door, then made her way back to her bedroom, leaving the door ajar. Now, at ten o'clock, she thought perhaps he had changed his mind. At half passt, she stood to blow out her candle, but then she heard footsteps on the front stair. The front stairs? He intended to come in the back, didn't he?

Before she could go to the door, it swung open and there stood Winn dressed as if he had been to a ball or some other entertainment. Her heart broke a little more.

"Did you come up the front stairs?" she asked, looking around him to the hallway.

"No, the back like you requested. Why?" He turned to peek behind himself.

"I just thought-- Never mind. It was my imagination. Come in." She stepped back and let him enter. She didn't know the servants well enough yet to know if they would tell her father.

Winn entered and stood with his coat still on and his hat in his hands.

"Please take your coat off and set your things on the table, unless this will not be a long visit." She tried to keep the emotion from her voice, but she sounded flat to her ears.

Winn took off his coat and put his things down and walked up to her. Without asking, he pulled her into a long embrace. "I am sorry, I should have asked, but I am happy to see you and see that your head is well healed from the fall." He let her go and stepped back.

She didn't hug him back. She wanted to, but she might not let go. She remained, but let him move across the room. "What is it you needed to speak to me about?"

He was silent for a time. Zoe was about to ask him again,

but he turned with tears in his eyes. "I wanted to apologize. I needed to. You did not deserve any of this."

"Could you be specific about what any of this is, because I am not sure I know."

Winn swung his arms wide. "All of this mess. All you wanted to do was find a husband, not get pulled into such a melodrama that almost got you killed." His expression made her heart ache for him, but she had suspected her father and Winn had more at play that morning than she realized, and was sick of being played the puppet.

"Now, which part of this whole thing are you calling your own fault?" She walked up to him with her finger pointed at his chest. "The part where I followed you into the woods and to your private hunting lodge dressed in man's clothes? Was that your fault?" She jabbed him and walked him backward as she spoke. "Or perhaps it was when you suggested we partake in a dalliance, and I agreed with no forcing or arm turning? Or, maybe it was that the night of the accident, when I decided to hunt you out once again to talk with you, without your knowledge. Hmm."

He was now backed against the wall with a look of confusion on his face. "I would also like to point out that frequently you made it clear you were not interested in marrying, not to mention that you were not even aware until recently that someone might be trying to kill you."

"I-- well, still you are now embroiled in all this, and I take responsibility," he managed.

"Oh, I am holding you responsible, but what I am holding you responsible for is your clear lack of ability to consider my thoughts."

"My what?" His look of confusion made her smile a bit.

"You and my father staged a situation where I was not given any of the power whatsoever. If it hadn't been for Lady Sarrafinna calling you to task for your loathsome behavior, I am certain the situation would have gotten worse."

The look he gave her told her he was about to argue. "Don't. Do not bother to plead your case. You and father knew I would not leave unless you led me to believe it, my only recourse. You never allowed me to work with you when trying to ferret out who wanted to harm you and your family." She put up a hand. "It means nothing to me that you claim you were protecting me. If we are ever to sort this out and become affianced, then you need to understand that I will agree to nothing more than a partnership, where we work as a team with no subverting if the situation is a bit messy. I won't have it."

She turned her back to walk away from him and to not look at his face in case he truly did not share her affections. That is when the heat from his broad chest came behind her and his arms wrapped around her. "Does that mean I haven't made such a mess of things that you will give me a chance to make it right?" he whispered in her ear, sending chills down her body.

"I only say that if that is what you would like. If you are no longer interested in pursuing something more official, I think that you should go now," she said, with sadness in her voice but hope in her heart.

"I love you, damn it. I don't know when it happened, but I am certain you were dressed in those damnable breeches when it did."

Zoe swung around in his arms and wrapped her arms around his neck. "I hoped that's what you would say." Then, before she could take a breath, he took her lips into a kiss meant to devour her, and she opened to him for his tasting pleasure.

After several minutes, they pulled apart, panting and heated. Zoe had to sit on the edge of the bed to stabilize herself.

"Now that we have that sorted, I need to discuss tomorrow with you. I will also point out that we made these plans before I just promised to make you a partner. There are too many things and people involved to change things."

"And?"

Just as Winn opened his mouth to speak, a large crash sounded, and a man wielding a large blade slammed through her door and with all speed launched at Zoe, still sitting on the bed. Before she could think to move, Winn threw her out of the way and into a chair and small writing table. Zoe yelped and turned to see Winn and a strange man grappling with each other on the bed.

In a moment's notice, Cyn was in the doorway with a shocked expression on her face. When she made eye contact with Zoe, the two met in the middle of the room.

"Get out of here," Winn yelled at them, while still fighting with the assailant. "Get Reid. Now!"

Cyn ran from the room, but Zoe would not leave. This man had been after her. That was the noise in the hallway. If she were asleep instead of up waiting for Winn, who's to say the outcome? Before she was aware of the danger, the attacker would have won. All at once, vulnerability washed over her as she watched the man she loved fight for her safety. Zoe reached behind her and found the ash shovel for the fire-place. It wasn't heavy enough to kill him, she hoped, but it would slow him down. She walked around the bed, positioning herself behind the man in dark clothes. She wished she didn't miss and strike Winn, but she took a deep breath, closed her eyes, and let the shovel swing until the resonance of the empty shovel hitting something hard reached her ears.

When she opened her eyes, the assailant was on the bed unconscious, and Winn stood by the bed holding the blade.

"Who the hell is that?" Zoe asked as Winn broke out in loud laughter.

By the time Zoe had set all the servants' minds at ease and sent them back to bed to remain until morning, and Winn had the bugger tied up in the chair Zoe was thrown in to, Lord Hayhurst came running up the stairs with Cyn close behind.

"What in bloody hell happened?" he asked, panting, staring at the scene in front of him.

"That man broke into my room and tried to kill me. While Winn kept him busy, I struck him with the ash shovel."

Reid looked at Winn, then back at Zoe. "That is what happened," Winn corroborated her story.

"Well, who is he?" Cyn broke in.

"When he comes round, we shall ask him. Zoe is curiously adept with a shovel," Winn admitted.

Cyn shook her head and left the room only to come back a moment later.

"Here you go, miss." A maid bustled in with fear still stark on her face, but holding a tin of smelling salts. "This should wake him up if he can wake." She looked in horror at the large bump forming on the side of his head.

"Thank you," Winn said and took the tin, opening it and

holding it under his nose. As expected, within a few moments he was coughing and sputtering to an awake state. Once he looked around and saw his predicament, he silenced. "Who are you, and why were you in Miss Chase's rooms with a knife?"

At first, it appeared he wouldn't talk, but then Zoe lifted the shovel. "Perhaps another nap will have you waking much more willing to speak the next time."

"No, no damn it. Don't hit me again. I'm Cheeky. That's what me friends call me, anyway."

"Well, don't stop talking now," Zoe coaxed.

"I was here, 'cause a bloke paid me t' come and kill the girl."

"Who?" Winn asked.

"Don' know."

"Why?" Zoe asked, unsettled that someone did, in fact, want her dead.

"Said she might'n be with child, and that wouldn't do," Cheeky answered.

Zoe's face heated. Not that she hadn't thought about it herself, but such a blunt statement put to the room in such a vocal way unsettled her.

Winn leaned in close so that Cheeky couldn't miss his question or his determination to get an answer. "Who? I will only ask one more time."

"Some Lordly fellow, spoke very proper."

"Name," Winn demanded.

The man looked around the room, then sighed. "Smythe, Lord Smythe."

"Mister," All four of them said at the same time.

"Did he pay you all upfront?" Reid asked from behind Zoe.

"Half, then I am to meet him in the morning with proof, and he would give me the rest."

"Did he say anything else of his plans?" Winn asked, hoping now that the fool was talking, he wouldn't stop.

"Said she was the last loose end, and that he would finish with his problem tomorrow and be free of the entire ugly business. Whatever that meant."

"Cyn, be a dear and see if one of the staff can go fetch a bow street runner."

She nodded and left the room. Zoe stood in shock. Smythe wanted her dead. Well, not her, as much as her potential offspring. She eased her hand to cover her stomach. Then her mind caught up to the conversation. "What is happening tomorrow?" She turned to Winn.

"That was what I was about to tell you. Tomorrow there is a trap set for the bastard. As of tomorrow night, I will be free of it all. And now that we have someone to vouch for his plans, there is proof, not just speculation."

"Hey, wait, Just a--I never said I was a witness," Cheeky complained.

"You are now, Cheeky. You got caught," Hayhurst pointed out the obvious. The man just slumped in the chair in defeat. "Does that mean I won't get the other half of my money?"

"Afraid so," Reid answered with laughter in his voice.

"I don't like this. I don't like any of this," Zoe said, as she put the pieces together. If they had a trap set for tomorrow, that meant Winn was the bait.

"I do not disagree with you," Hayhurst agreed with a haggard tone in his voice.

Winn crossed the room, and took the shovel from her hand, setting it on the floor and taking her into his arms. "I know it is dangerous, but I promise it will be the last dangerous stunt I pull. We need this to end if we are to start our lives with no worry. It is as well planned as possible. Lord Hayhurst has seen to our safety at every turn."

Zoe looked to the man, who nodded while keeping an eye on their captive.

"I love you, and now that I know you still love me, I promise I will be here tomorrow evening with a special license in hand. Once Cyn gets back and hears of the plans, she will gather my mother, your aunt, and half of the Ton in the parlor to be waiting on us when we return."

Zoe didn't know what to say, or think, or even what part of what he said to grab on to. "You could die," was the only thing she could say.

"I hope I will not. I have the woman that I love to dote on for at least the next fifty-odd years."

Before Zoe could respond, Cyn came back into the room with a rather harried man, looking as confused as Cheeky. Winn kissed Zoe on the forehead and went to discuss things with the bow street runner and Reid.

"What in the hell is going on?" Cyn asked, coming next to her.

"I think I am getting married tomorrow if Winn isn't killed baiting in Smythe to kill him."

Cyn stood silent for a long moment. Zoe decided she was trying to choose how she needed to react. "Well, then I guess we need to send the coach back for my mother and your aunt. We should also be downstairs when your father arrives. He will be perplexed, I am sure."

And just like that, Cyn bustled Zoe from the room, leaving Winn and the others to deal with her assailant, and she to plan a wedding with a special license. Would she ever be bored once she was a Burton?

Morning rose, but Winn had been waiting on it for what seemed like an eternity. After having explained to the bow street runner what was going on, and making him agree to put Cheeky somewhere isolated, Winn crossed to the parlor where Lord Chase had many questions, but top on his list was why some man attempted to attack his daughter in her bedchamber, and how Winn was in said bedchamber when the attack occurred.

After much explaining, and a promise from both him and Zoe there would be a decision soon, Winn and Reid were allowed to leave. Winn still had the impression Lord Chase wouldn't have pressed for the nuptials if that was not his daughter's wish.

Winn went to his study upon arriving home instead of bothering to exhaust himself, pretending he would sleep. Sleep would not come to him until tomorrow, perhaps. If he were lucky, the next time he found himself in a bed, it would not be to sleep, it would be to make Zoe Chase his own.

The day was clear, with much sun it looked like. He made his way to the bell pull to rouse the staff and get a bath drawn. A bathe, then a fortifying meal before allowing Reid to go over the plan yet again seemed the best order of things. Winn was certain few people in his circle slept much at all, either.

The bath helped him feel more like himself, and when he entered the breakfast room, he managed a smile at Hayhurst's scowl.

"You seem very chipper for a man that may die today."

"You are not looking at this the right way, my friend," Winn assured him as he piled his plate high with all his favorites. "Today is the start of my new life. Today will solve all my problems."

"It might kill you," Reid pointed out.

"True, but then again, I wouldn't have any further problems."

Hayhurst nodded his head in agreement.

"If, however, this goes more to plan, I will marry Miss Zoe Chase before the clock rings midnight."

He looked at Winn with a vicious grin. "And that is not creating a whole new set of problems?"

"Yes, but I am hoping most of those problems can be settled in a much more enjoyable manner."

Reid shook his head and chuckled. Both men then put their attention to eating their breakfast.

"My lord, there is a visitor for you." The drone of the butler interrupted the silence.

"Who is it?" Winn asked.

"The gentleman who attended you the other evening."

"Ah, send him in here," Winn instructed. "Can you set another plate?" he then asked the footman by the buffet.

"Why is it we had to find the only bow street runner that doesn't trust to give out his name?" Reid asked.

"I do not care if he prefers to be called Clementine, as long as he does his job well."

"Good morning." He entered before Reid recovered

enough to comment, but he managed to stop laughing to greet the man.

"Good morning, please come, eat. Do you prefer coffee or tea?"

"Tea, if it is strong."

Winn signaled to the footman to get the man some tea. Winn waited for him to pile his plate high, to the point of it almost toppling onto the carpet.

"I spoke with the runner that came to your call last night. You have little of a boring life, don't you?"

"I am looking forward to boredom, I admit. Are we all set for today?"

He nodded while shoveling eggs and ham into his mouth. He talked around the mouthful. "Yes, I am going from here, to make sure my men are in place. What time will you be arriving on-site?"

"We will leave once we are finished here," Winn said. "I want to give him as much opportunity as possible."

"Good enough. I will work the stables. When I spoke with Buckley, I explained there were horse thefts at a similar event, and we are hoping to protect his stable. He was very interested in protecting his interests."

"Very well, I will try to find you to give you a sign when I make my way to the back area."

The man nodded again, as he spooned the last bites of his feast and drained his tea in one gulp. They said goodbye to the man and sat in silence once again. The silence continued in the coach. Winn knew his friend worried for his safety, and he didn't disagree. His life was teetering on the edge. His future laid in front of him, and it was sweet, but it was a fragile thing ruined in a moment.

Winn cleared his throat. He could not go down that dark path. More dangerous adventures than this occurred with no ramifications, and while he didn't always come out on top, he had survived. He would survive today, for Zoe.

"And, here we are," Winn stated the obvious to help Reid come to life as the carriage fell into line with the numerous others waiting to unload their passengers.

"It appears so."

"Are you still bidding on that mare for Cyn?"

"What? Oh, yes, I told her I would. I may just take Buckley aside and offer to buy her outright."

"How much is that going to cost me?"

"I have no idea. I was under the understanding that Cyn was paying me."

"Oh, well, even better then," Winn answered with a big smile, hoping to lighten the mood.

By the time they alighted from the carriage, Reid appeared a bit more relaxed, and Winn was feeling more confident. The crush was even larger than Winn had expected. He knew some of the best horseflesh in England would be on the market today, but this was a larger group than even that.

They gave each other looks saying more than words could, and Winn watched his closest friend disappear into the crowd.

Surveying the crowd, Smythe was nowhere to be seen, but it was early yet. Winn wandered around and checked out the horses. The day was warming up. As he went, he greeted many people he had not seen since last season.

"Burton! How are you?" A voice from behind him.

"Ah, Finch, how are you?" Winn greeted the man. Finch

attended Eaton the same time as he. Winn always felt terrible for Finch. He was a good enough lad, but his birdlike features! Winn had to admit that his nose was a bit much, but still, he didn't deserve the ribbing he got. "What are you up to these days?"

"Well, I am in town for the season. Mother has a list of eligible brides for me to consider," he said with zeal.

"Good for you, any you are leaning toward?"

"I have not laid eyes on a one, to be honest. I am certain once the social whirl picks up, I will be wed before the last ball."

"Well, congratulations in advance if I do not see you."

"Are you considering that one?" Finch asked, pointing to the Arabian passing the stall.

"Oh, that one? No. He seems a bit too excitable. I prefer a better temperament in a mount," Winn explained. He caught sight of Hayhurst coming toward him. "It was wonderful to talk, but Hayhurst appears to be looking for me."

"Of course." He tipped his hat and bowed.

Reid nodded in the direction of the barn, then turned and walked in the other direction. Winn glanced, overseeing Smythe for only a moment before he ducked into the stables.

"Here we go," Winn said to himself, walking in a straight line to the entrance of the barn. It was dark inside, and his eyes would need time to adjust. He wanted this over, but knew haste would not play in their favor. He took a deep breath, squared his shoulders, and sauntered into the large horse barn with as much ease as he could muster.

Once inside, it was teaming with auction patrons peering over stalls and talking with stable hands about the specimens on display. To the far left, he saw Reid and Lord Buckley standing by a stall, with an almost white mare. Once again Cyn had picked well, he thought. Max had yet to show himself but assured them he would.

Winn walked to the right, making sure those in his direct area saw him.

"That is a good choice, Burton. Would suit you well in the country," a man commented next to him, as he looked at a dapple gelding.

"I am not sure I could mount it without a ladder," Winn commented about the massive size of the horse. Winn was confident the beast was capable of moving a house if needed.

The man laughed. "You might be right, but he comes from a good line."

"Thank you. I'll keep him in mind," Winn said, and moved along. In front of him, he caught sight of Smythe exiting the barn and making a left turn around the corner.

"May I have your attention!" A booming voice came from where Winn had entered the stable. "The auction will begin in ten minutes. Please take your last looks, and all make your way to the large paddock area."

Now was Winn's chance to find himself alone. As he made his way to the end of the long barn, he spotted their bow street runner in the open space behind the barn raking. The man glanced up and nodded once to acknowledge Winn was getting into position. Winn's goal was to get Smythe to talk about the history of his hatred for him and to confess to the other crimes, which Winn knew could not have been perpetrated by himself.

He turned the corner without care and was brought up short by Smythe holding a pistol aimed at Winn.

"Smythe, what in the hell are you doing with a gun out

here? You'll scare the horses." He threw his arms up and pasted a look of alarm on his face. "What was it, a mouse? I hate those miserable things myself."

Smythe smiled a dirty little smile. "Some would think a mouse, yes, but it has blinded others for years seeing a peer of the realm, instead of the title thief he is."

"What in hell are you talking about?" Winn asked, happy at how easy he was to get talking.

"Your family stole my family's title and plunged us into ruin. It has taken generations for us to gain back a modicum of respectability."

"I hate to break it to your man, but I was not alive for such things. I am not yet even thirty."

"And, thank you for the idea of the curse. It is a very handy way for our family to pass off the deaths of the men in yours. It has also been a blessing that your family is not adept at making male heirs. One a generation has kept things clean."

Winn put his hands down. The beady-eyed man standing in front of him was not a threat; Winn was becoming more and more certain Smythe didn't have it in him to spill blood by his own hand. He was more the type to hire it out like he had last night. Winn wondered if he realized Zoe was safe.

"I am glad our family could be of such service to yours. Doesn't that constitute an act of good faith on your behalf?"

"No," he said like a petulant schoolboy. "We must strip your family of the title, so that I may petition to have it returned to me."

Winn nodded like he understood now. He saw from behind him a shadow stretch across the side of the barn.

Winn could not decipher if it was friend or foe and figured he would ask forgiveness if it was a friend after the fact.

"I hope you are aware Miss Chase may well be with child at this moment. A healthy, strong heir." If he weren't watching for it, he would have missed it, but Smythe, with his free hand, made a slight stopping motion, and the shadow froze.

"Have you not heard the sad news?" Smythe said with a contorted smile crossing his face. "I fear Miss Chase was the victim of a horrible crime last night in her own home. It appears while her father was out at his club, an assailant broke into their home and stabbed her. Tragic loss."

"Oh, you must be talking about Cheeky," Winn said without missing a beat. His heart, however, all but stopped at the joy on Smythe's face to be the one to share the news of Zoe's death. He would get this man if he had to die doing it. "He is a very talkative fellow, once pressed. And I am afraid your version of events are a bit inaccurate, for in reality, Miss Chase beat the bastard over the head with an ash shovel, knocking him unconscious."

Smythe blanched, and Winn felt triumph course through him.

"What, no witty retort Smythe? The fact my heir could be safe and protected as I stand before you seems to unsettle you," Winn pushed.

The shadow moved, and with lightning reflexes, Winn spun and landed his elbow squarely across the nose of a burly street urchin, from the smell coming from his clothes. Blood sprayed the air as the crunch of the delicate bones comprising the nose rang out.

There was, however, the matter of a pistol still pointing

in his direction, and as he was dealing with the first assailant, Winn missed the other one, standing behind him. Before he could recover, that next brute grabbed him around the neck and shoulders and turned, dragging Winn along to the opening of the barn.

Smythe followed, stepping over the prone man with the broken nose, never taking his blazing eyes off Winn.

"I will say you were a challenge, but with your wild ways, it made my plans for killing you so much easier. Sometimes you almost did it for me. This time, however, I will not assume you will do something stupid to die. My friend here will make sure of it. It will look like either a suicide over the death of your lover, which will be taken care of as soon as I leave here, or some might decide you were trying some fantastical stunt, and this one finally got the better of you."

As Smythe rambled on, the huge man flopping Winn around like a rag doll wrapped a large rope around his neck. Winn saw they threw it around the hay hook at the top of the barn. He had demanded his men wait until it was apparent he was being killed, but perhaps they were cutting it a bit closer than Winn would like. As Winn was plotting to save himself, the cavalry appeared.

"That's enough. We have all heard enough, haven't we?" Reid said as he walked out of the barn with his pistol in hand and Lord Buckley- but along with Lord Buckley, the entire group attending the auction. Well done, Reid.

"Yes, more than enough to bring to the magistrate. This, along with Cheeky's knowledge, and these two brutes, it should be a neat case," their friend from the bow street runners said.

For Smythe's reaction, he stood, pistol in hand, still

aiming in Winn's direction, with his mouth gaped open. He worked it open and closed, but no words came forth.

Hayhurst stepped toward him to take the pistol, and that movement put him into action. "Stop! Don't come near me. I will shoot him! I swear it!"

"Now, Smythe, this is over. Be a good lad and--" Buckley tried to reason.

"No! I promised my father on his death bed that I would finish what he started. He knew this was the only way; he made me promise."

Winn undid the rope around his neck and stepped away from the large man, now being handled by several stable hands, or possibly more bow street runners; he wasn't sure at this point.

"Smythe, do not do something more stupid and continue your father's legacy of murder. If I am correct, you have not yet killed anyone. There is still a chance to redeem yourself," Winn coaxed.

Smythe stood looking at the pistol, then at the huge crowd of men from every respectable family in the Ton and its outliers.

"Smythe no, there are other options here, don't--" but before Winn could finish his statement, Smythe put the pistol to his head and ended the entire ordeal in one pull of the trigger.

The deafening silence allowed the entire group to hear the echo of the shot ricochet off the surrounding buildings. Winn had no words. He would never have thought it would end this way, but it made sense. His entire worth was rolled up in his family's reputation, and he was not leaving here with any of that intact since the whole of the Ton would know about this before the dinner hour.

"Are you all right?" Reid came up behind him and put a hand on his shoulder. Lord Sutton followed to add to the well wishes.

Winn looked at them, then back at the body on the ground. Buckley called for a tarp, and two stable hands appeared, covering Smythe's body, hiding it from their eyes. After that, the surreal bubble they all seemed enveloped in faded away, and the noise of life seeped back in. Even so, Winn stood frozen.

"I think this calls for brandy for us all, come to the house. We will fortify then head back to the auction," Lord Buckley announced. There was a collective sigh of agreement as they turned and headed toward the house away from the awful scene. "You did good, lad. You represented your family and the title that your family earned very well today," Buckley said next to Winn. He didn't wait for Winn to answer before he turned and followed his auction goers to his house.

Their bow street runner came over. "We are done here. There is no reason for you to stay. We will make sure the body gets to the morgue. If I need anything else, I will be in touch."

"Thank you," Winn managed. For the first time, he turned and looked the man in the eye. "Thank you for all you have done, you helped save my family."

"Lord Burton, if you hadn't been so determined to solve this, he would have killed you. You saved your family," the bow street runner assured him.

"Come, we need a drink, but something stronger than

watered-down brandy." Reid took him by the elbow and directed him to the carriage on the front of the house.

"It's over," Winn said in a ragged, tired voice.

"That it is," Hayhurst agreed. Winn was aware his friend had not taken his eyes off him since they got in the carriage.

The vehicle rolled to a stop in front of White's. "Come, you need drink and food."

"But-" Winn tried to protest.

"You, my friend, are pale as a sheet and not steady on your feet. Food first, your love after."

He followed and sat while Reid plied him with a second large breakfast and whiskey. The food helped. Winn had gotten shaky and chilled.

"Better?"

"Much, thank you. I don't know what got into me."

"Um, we watched a man take his own life, you would be broken inside if it didn't affect you. However, you are now a free man, and you have your entire life ahead of you."

"I do, you are right," Winn agreed.

"How does that feel?"

"I'm not sure. I know that our next stop must be to see Zoe. Shall we?" Winn asked, standing and downing the last of the whiskey.

"After you."

Now it felt like he was heading to his destiny. This might well end up being the most dangerous stunt in his entire life, but the anticipation of having Zoe as his own for the rest of his life was well worth the inherent danger.

When Winn entered the parlor, both Zoe and Cyn flung themselves into his arms in relief. Sitting waiting not so patiently was his mother and Zoe's aunt.

"Tis about time. I suppose you stopped off at White's celebrating," his mother snapped.

"Actually, Ma`me, I made him stop to eat some food and collect his thoughts. Things did not go as we had planned."

"Well, what does that mean?" she snapped. Winn had heard little since he laid hands on Zoe. Cyn had backed away to call for drinks all around, and Winn had taken Zoe into his arms and clung like a drowning man.

"It means, mother," Winn explained, never taking his eyes from Zoe, "that Smythe took his own life instead of living the remainder as a ruined man."

Shocked gasps sounded from all.

"So, this means you are free. No more danger and close calls." Zoe said, looking up at him.

He smiled. She didn't know how scared he was at the prospect of living a long life. He had never assumed he would have one. "Only one more dangerous act, then I am finished. It seems I finally fell off a cliff of my own making. I love you, Zoe Chase, and cannot live my probable long extended life without you by my side."

"Well, that is good, because they called me to perform a wedding," the Bishop intoned as he entered the room. "Shall we?" he asked, wasting no time.

"What do you say, love, fall with me?"

EPILOGUE

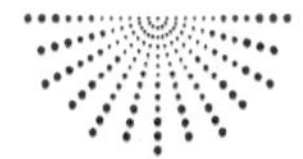

Seven months later

"Oh, where has he gone off to?" Zoe asked no one. She wiggled and jostled her way to the edge of the settee and hoisted herself up off the piece of furniture. Perhaps she should endeavor to remain standing for the next several weeks. She walked to the bell pull, then the window.

"There you are. Mother and I were searching for you," Cyn said, sweeping into the room, carrying three of the now much larger and very mischievous kittens who were relocated to the main house once Zoe took up residence as the Lady of the manor. "Mother, I found her," Cyn called over her shoulder.

"I wish you found me a few moments earlier. Winn was

gone when I woke up from my nap. There is nothing good about being stuck," Zoe complained.

"Ah, there you are, my dear. We must discuss the menu for the house party. The guests are coming in less than a week." Zoe's mother-in-law bustled into the room with sheets of papers and a fresh ink bottle in her hands.

Zoe was so happy. The love she felt every day from people who knew her since childhood filled her heart. It was not something she imagined when she was sent from Rome back to England to find a husband.

"Please, I will take the chair," Zoe said as the women made to get comfortable.

"Whatever for dear, that chair is deuced uncomfortable," Lady Burton pointed out.

"Yes, mother, but with Zoe's large stomach, she has difficulty getting off the settee," Cyn said with laughter in her voice.

"Of course, sorry, my dear. I remember those days. And by the looks of you, we might welcome more than one new love into the fold."

"I hope not," Zoe said as she settled into the chair and winced at the creaking it made as she did so. "I am not sure I am ready to welcome one into the world."

"Zoe? Zoe, where have you gotten off to?" Winn called from the hallway.

"In here, where you left me. Did you think I ran away?" she laughed.

Winn entered the room and crossed to her, placing a warm, promising kiss on her lips.

"You were asleep, but then mother carried into the hall and figured you had woken and left."

"What are you up to now, brother?" Cyn asked with skepticism.

"Nothing... really."

"Now you listen here, Lord Burton. We have a house party in one week, and I need constant help. I can no longer bend over to pick anything up without fear of falling over like an overripe peach. It is harder by the day to even rise from a sitting position with a fulcrum for leverage. Do not get yourself hurt," Zoe demanded.

"Mother, do you think this house party wise? With Zoe so full with child, shouldn't she be resting?"

His mother waved his concern away. "If it were a social event perhaps, but these are the people who are closest to us. Zoe will not be overtaxed, and in fact, they will dote on her, her father, and many friends and family."

"Has my father sent word then?" Zoe asked with hope. It had been at least three weeks since she received the last letter from her father. He told her he was taking on a job for the government that tied back to his work abroad, but that was the last of it. She tried not to worry. Her father was not the most disciplined letter writer, but she was all he had. She hated now that she was married he was alone.

"No, my dear, not yet," Lady Burton answered in a somber tone, "but if anything untoward had happened, we would have been notified. Perhaps, Winn, you should inquire after it?"

"Of course, Reid is heading into London this week. I will ask him to call on your father and see," Winn assured everyone. He had not left the estate since news of her pregnancy.

"Now, brother, what are you up to?" Cyn prodded again.

"I have something to show you, wait here," he said, and

jumped up, leaving the room like an excited child. Zoe knew her life would never prove tiresome. Even once her children were grown and living their own lives, she knew Winn would keep her busy.

"Bring it in here, please," he said in the hallway. Winn entered the room with two footmen following, carrying something big draped with a sheet. "I hope you like it," he said with boyish enthusiasm.

The footmen set the large object in front of the women, and it seemed to sway. The footmen left the room, and Winn pulled the sheet back. In front of her was the most beautiful wooden cradle she had ever seen. Ornately carved animals danced around the top edge, and each spindle carved to resemble a twisted ribbon.

"Oh my," Zoe said on a gasp, putting her hand to her swollen stomach. "It is the most beautiful thing I have ever seen. Who carved it?"

"I did," he said, pride radiating from him.

"I didn't know you knew how to carve wood?"

"I didn't. The carver in the village is teaching me. That is where I disappear every day," he explained. "I can't take full credit. If you look closely, you can tell my work from the work of the carver who had to do the more intricate pieces."

Zoe threw herself out of the chair and wrapped her arms around her husband's neck. "Well, that is good. Cyn and I had a bet going that you were making a new hot-air balloon."

"A bet? It isn't ladylike to gamble," he pointed out.

"Oh, don't worry, we weren't gambling with money," Cyn assured him.

"What then were you using to gamble with?" Winn asked.

"If I won," Cyn explained, "I would go the season without having to play pretty to all the poppycocks this year."

"And if I won, she would accept at least three of said poppycocks to consider seriously."

"Now, that is a bet I can get behind. Tell me, who bet that I was making a hot air balloon?"

Both women looked at each other but said nothing.

"Well, fine--"

"Oh," Zoe said out of the blue and put her hand on her side.

Winn paled. "What? What is the matter?" He put his hand over hers.

"The baby kicked. He must want me to eat. I swear sometimes I think I will bruise from his antics."

She patted Winn's arm, but the color was not quick to come back on his face. It had been almost eight months since they wed, but they both understood she may have been with child before that.

I never knew you had such a talent. I am very impressed," his mother chimed in after inspecting the piece of furniture. "But we must conquer this menu."

"Yes, I am sorry, where are we at?" Zoe sat back down, only to be kicked again by her offspring.

"Winn, go the kitchens and request a tray brought up with food and tea, do be a dear," his mother commanded.

"Yes, mother." He kissed Zoe on her head before leaving the room.

"My dear, I am seeing a side to my son that I have not seen in many years. You brought him back to life. Thank you for that."

"Well, thank you, but I think one cannot underscore the end of the curse as to some of his lightheartedness."

"True, I still think about Smythe from time to time. To think we welcomed him into our home, and he enjoyed our hospitality. Horrid, just horrid."

"Yes, but after getting a letter from the remainder of the Smythe's assuring Winn they were not aware of the plot Smythe and his father had, and that the Burton's would never need to worry about their safety again, I feel confident it is over."

After a few minutes, they brought a large tray into the room, and Zoe took no time in choosing those bits that seemed the tastiest. Everything would be perfect once the baby was here and she got word from her father. She thought about her mother often these days and how her mother made sure Zoe would be taken care of and protected even after she was gone.

And perhaps if not for the curse, Winn would have fallen for another long before Zoe made it back. A small part of her wanted to thank Smythe for keeping Winn's fall at bay until she was there to catch him.

Find out if Lord Harwich and Lady Sarrafinna find their happy ending.

Courtesan's Wicked Desire
Chapter One

"You should be out frolicking in the park with all the others. It is a marvelous day outside."

Lady Sarrafinna Lennox glanced up from the rather modest ledger on her desk. The same ledger she continued to pour her attention into since she received a response to her request of an accounting of her funds from her solicitor.

"Lang, I told you I would go with you later to meet up with Reginald, but these numbers must make sense first. Please, if you want to enjoy the day, don't let me stop you."

One of her dearest friends, Mr. Cedric Langley—Lang to his intimates—was a gem. Loyal to a fault, in his eyes Sarrafinna never misstepped a day in her life. However, he was not a man of leisure, instead one of action. He needed to be in constant motion, so lounging while she poured over her accounts was stifling for the flamboyant man.

"Nonsense, I am at your disposal, I simply do not understand what could be so pressing that you must complete it this instant."

"Lang, you sound like a petulant child. Why don't you call for tea?"

"Did someone say tea?"

Finna looked up as Madame Cantrell, her mentor and

now a companion of sorts, swept into the parlor. Since her retirement, Madame Cantrell had been in residence going on five years.

"Yes, I'm ringing for it now. Should we have sandwiches or cakes?" Lang asked the group but answered for himself. "Cakes it is." He pulled the bell, went back and flopped with one leg draped over the arm of the settee where he sat all morning.

"What are you doing, dear?" Madame Contrell asked as she peered over the front of the masculine desk.

"I am trying to work out how I am still short," Finna explained, exasperated. She couldn't understand it. Her calculations were not off, but she didn't have the amount she set as her goal.

"Where do you stand, my dear? Often you are over dramatic about your impending crisis," Madame Contrell offered, sinking into the stuffed chair next to Lang to wait for tea.

"I stand at being short to make the last of the tuition payments and not enough to keep the household afloat, even after I sell the townhouse." Again, she looked at the letter, then back at the ledger. This meant she would have to meet with Mr. Gilbert Knottingword, Esq., her solicitor. She was developing a headache. "I very well may need to take on one last client to come up to snuff before getting out." The thought deflated what had promised to be such a lovely day.

Her plan as she dressed for her day, was that after breakfast she would go over the letter and confirm she, in fact, had enough money in her accounts to cover her retirement and still leave her comfortably wealthy, at which point she and

Lang were to meet Reginald in the park for a stroll. It all sounded lovely, but now...

"Excuse me, mi lady," Golding, her butler, said and stepped into the room with the post on a platter. "The post arrived. Where would you like it? It looks like some fancy entertainments for sure," he added, his Cheapside accent slipping in as it often did.

"Thank you, Golding, please set it on the tea table."

"Right, right. Here you go, I will be back with the tea in a few." He turned and left them again.

"You really need to work with him on his diction, Finna. It is bad enough that when you have a dinner party, I must put gentleman's purses back in their overcoats, but when he sounds like where he is from, well your guests will wonder," Madame Contrell complained.

Finna bent back to the ledger and proceeded to add up the last four years of expenses, which would mimic what she assessed would be the same as her next four.

"I know. I have been busy. Perhaps you could work with him?" she suggested.

"Oh, I am no teacher. I learned my own manners by observation and determination. And the tutelage I received would not be in an atmosphere that Golding would approve, I am certain."

"Who is Mr. Dylan Birch? Are you keeping secrets, my dear?" Lang plucked an envelope with a bright blue wax seal from the pile of letters and invitations on the salver and dangled it in front of Madame Contrell.

"That name is familiar, why?"

Sarrafinna moved from the desk, her money issue pushed to the periphery. What did Mr. Birch have for business with her? They were acquaintances from her only season, but not much more. Over the years, he called on her to ask pointed questions about people she held company with. Unsure what his title in the government was, she had the distinct impression it was not what his job actually entailed.

"Mr. Birch is an acquaintance of another life and time. I can't fathom what he might want."

She sat just as Golding entered with the tea. While her friends settled themselves with tea and cook's famous ginger and cardamom cakes, Finna turned the contents of the letter over in her mind. The letter had no official seals to show it anything but a friendly correspondence. The note itself told another story.

"Well, what does Mr. Birch have to say?" Lang asked around a full bite of cake, with no concern that Finna wouldn't share the letter's contents.

"He needs to meet with me. He says he may need my assistance in a matter, and that I would be handsomely rewarded for my trouble."

"There, you see. You worried about nothing. Perhaps you will not have to take on another client. But would it be so intolerable if you had to?" Madame Contrell asked, sipping her tea.

"The newest group of Lords set upon the Ton are exhausting at best, and tiresome at worst," Finna explained. "I am much too mature to desire to tolerate their ill manners and assumptions of freedoms based on their peerage, and their manhood. When a courtesan feels defeated in her efforts before she begins, it is time to get out. I have nothing to offer these young bucks."

"Oh, but a nice older gentleman who is only wishing for

companionship would do, wouldn't it? What was the last one's name?"

"You know full well what his name was, and I am quite finished with prattling around on the arm of an elderly gentleman too hard of hearing to talk with."

Lang reached over and patted her on the hand. "You deserve your retirement, love. You groomed some of the Ton's most powerful men into what they are today. For king and country and all that." He waved a hand in the air to punctuate his statement.

Lang's concern and kind words warmed her heart. She did deserve her retirement. It was time for her to settle into the shadows and disappear. It had been a long road. Not one she would have chosen otherwise, but long just the same and her parents were not young anymore. With every day that passed it was a day closer to her brother gaining the dukedom from father. Once that happened, she was certain he would officially disown her, unlike her father who refused to publicly cast her out. She would prefer to be ensconced in the country and out of society when that happened. She knew better than any public ruination and humiliation were best done behind closed doors and not on a ballroom floor.

ABOUT THE AUTHOR

Author of 7 Historical romances, including the Improper Wives for Proper Lords series, Clair Brett lives in NH with her ever emptying nest which includes her children when they visit, two cats, one willful dog, and a mean Pitbull mix, that will lick you to death and run into her kennel when you speak loudly, and an ever harassed husband who takes it all in stride. A lover of all things Regency, Clair, was hooked when she first read Jane Austen. She is a firm believer that a reader finds a piece of who they are or learns something about the world with every book they read. She wants her readers to be empowered and to have a refreshed belief in the goodness of people and the power of love after reading her work

Contact Clair

Website: www.clairbrett.com

Facebook: http://facebook.com/AuthorClairBrett
Twitter: http://twitter.com/clairbrett
Goodreads: https://www.goodreads.com/clairbrett
Pinterest: www.pinterest.com/clairbrett

Join Clair's Newsletter
https://www.clairbrett.com/newsletter-sign-up

ALSO AVAILABLE BY CLAIR BRETT

Improper Wives for Proper Lords Series

Dealing with the Viscount

An Heiress by Midnight

Marked for Love

Courtesan's Wicked Desire

Enduring Legacy Series Book

Visions of Pleasure

Once Upon A Twelfth Night-HTRS-Anthology

Ruination of a Rouge

www.ingramcontent.com/pod-product-compliance
Lightning Source LLC
Chambersburg PA
CBHW020903200626
46814CB00001BA/145

* 9 7 8 1 7 3 5 2 9 0 6 2 1 *